A Crack in Everything

A Susan Callisto Mystery

Angela Gerst

Poisoned Pen Press

Copyright © 2011 by Angela Gerst

First Edition 2011

10 9 8 7 6 5 4 3 2 1

Library of Congress Catalog Card Number: 2011926955

ISBN: 9781590589441   Hardcover
       9781590589465   Trade Paperback

Poisoned Pen Press
6962 E. First Ave., Ste. 103
Scottsdale, AZ 85251
www.poisonedpenpress.com
info@poisonedpenpress.com

Printed in the United States of America

For my mother Mary who walked in beauty every day of her life,
And for my husband Robert who remembers her.

Acknowledgments

My fellow scribblers, Michael Scott, Mary Mitchell, Sherry Nadworny, and Alice Holstein, read and appraised every word of this novel, sometimes twice. A thousand thanks Mary, Mike, Sherry and Alice for your ruthless wit and precision editing, for your luminous insights and savvy critiques, for your fellowship. Without my daughter's close reading, at least one plot thread would have dangled (and one casserole been lost); thank you Morgan, and for your invaluable literary advice. Thanks also to Helen Simpson, Michelle Karol, Harry Chalmiers, and Susan Cohen who read and commented on early drafts of the novel. My gratitude to the many people who kindly provided useful information about biotechnology, the state police, business financing, and popular culture, among them George Corey, Jordan Kraus, Pamela Fall Rautenberg, Robert Elliot Gerst, and Dr. Angeline Mastri who first suggested the microtome blade as lethal weapon. Any errors are mine alone. To my son Andrew, thank you for your confidence in me and for your forbearance. A special thanks to Barbara Peters, Robert Rosenwald, and Annette Rogers, who shook the book and made it better. No one offered finer tea, coffee, and encouragement than Lucy Mastri, Amy Weiss, and Sandy Aylor. Sylvia and Leon, I miss you more than I can say.

There is a crack in everything
That's how the light gets in.
                    —Leonard Cohen

Chapter One

Good Girls Go To Heaven

I was churning out voter surveys when he ambled in, tall, fifty-ish, with a head of thick brown hair going gray. If he knocked, I missed it. Maybe I should've felt threatened, all alone so late in the day, but campaign season was heating up, and all I felt was tired. "Can I help you?" I said.

"Susan Callisto?" His smooth baritone seemed to imply that by Susan he meant something sly.

"That's right. And you are?"

"Charles Renfrow. Chaz, when I'm not signing something." His clothes were a racy mix: heirloom sports jacket, Armani jeans over hard thighs, burnished old boat shoes on his naked feet. He carried a glove-leather portfolio, and his eyes were as blue and bold as taw marbles. Not that I noticed.

We shook hands over the ormolu clock that always says midnight but adds a bit of splendor to my disorderly desk, and he...or was it me?...hung on for one of those heartbeats too long. Maybe, I thought, he dressed like a nouveau-Yankee to compensate for that crooked front tooth and the too-confident eyes which had already surveyed my warehouse establishment and were now scrutinizing my tee shirt-with-a-message, *Good Girls Go To Heaven.*

He bit back a smile. "Thought you'd be older."

Left-handed compliment; I let it pass. Going on thirty, five years out of law school, with two years of victory in the political arena, I figured I was old enough for whatever Chaz Renfrow had in mind. With some ostentation, I glanced at my watch.

"I know it's late," he said, "but I'll only take half an hour of your time." He commandeered the visitor's chair with an affable assurance that got my dander up.

"Sorry. I've got a six o'clock meeting in Newton." I leafed through my calendar. "The only time I can spare is tomorrow afternoon between two and two-thirty."

"Won't work. I have to decide this evening whether to run for mayor of Telford."

Mayor? My candidates chased low-level office, nothing grander than alderman. I should have been pleased by the upgrade. Instead, for no reason that I could articulate, I felt manipulated. "Filing deadline's Friday. Got your papers in order?"

"Not yet, but I only need five hundred signatures."

"Better make that six hundred. More."

He searched through his portfolio and settled a sheaf of papers on my desk. "Not according to the regs."

"You need a margin for error."

My nameplate caught his eye, and he stroked the engraved letters, lingering over the sinuous 'S' of Susan. "I need you."

From neck to cheekbones, I could feel the blush. I covered it by letting my hair fall over my face while I loaded voter surveys into my hobo bag and stifled my anger. This alpha man was damn well going to learn to take no for an answer. "Mr. Renfrow, I can't help you. I'm too busy, and you're too late."

Dusty afternoon light slanted through the high arched windows that overlook Moody Street. Three stories down, a horn blared, cutting through the rumble of rush hour traffic and the hum of my floor fans. I was about to fling my bag over my shoulder, when Renfrow pinched the bridge of his nose and slipped his papers back into his portfolio.

"If I decide to run, I *will* have a place on the ballot. Beyond that, I can't predict. That's where you would come in." He spoke almost wistfully now, which might have been a ploy, though he sounded sincere. "You're a lawyer, isn't that so?"

"Do you need a lawyer?"

"I own a biotechnology company. The mayor is trying to chase us out of Telford. If I don't run against him, I'll take him to court."

I circled the office, closing windows, turning off fans. Near the rent-a-receptionist's desk I paused to switch off a lamp, and from there I veered toward the door. "Sounds like a long story. Let's talk tomorrow."

"Why not tonight, after your other business? Wait, I'll give you a retainer. You can always return it if you decide you can't help me. Minus your consultation fee, of course. Ten thousand? Just to hold my place?"

Words like "sorry" and "no way" died in my throat.

"Twenty?"

"Mr. Renfrow!"

He took out his checkbook. "Let's make it twenty thousand."

Before I could tell him I don't charge for the first consult, he'd signed the check, and then the sight of four zeros hitched to that two froze my tongue. Twenty thousand was way too much money for my vanilla advice. Of course, if he wanted tutti-frutti lawyering too…

He moved closer, the check dangling from his fingers. "Take it. Deposit it. The money will help you think. And please call me Chaz."

I pondered my knotty situation, flip-flopping like a political hack. A debt-ridden Californian, I lived alone in the tight heart of New England, a life that lacked the simplicity only money, or love, can deliver. Love, I flipped, wasn't numbers on a check. But money, I flopped, certainly was. "Um, Chaz, my policy—"

"Ms. Callisto, Susan, I'm drowning in deadlines."

His words broke through my dither, and I averted my eyes from the check, tripping over the plant table on my way out the door. "Why didn't you come to me weeks ago?"

"I only just made up my mind." He kept to an easy pace as I charged down the hall, his long strides putting him slightly in the lead. "You said it yourself. I've got four days to file my papers. I need to discuss things with you tonight. Have dinner with me. Even campaign doctors need to eat."

Our arms touched, and I drew myself in. The man unsettled me: his money, his irony. Or maybe it was something much simpler. Something I tried not to think about since Detective Lieutenant Michael Benedict stopped coming around.

Inside the freight elevator, I caught a whiff of Renfrow's aftershave, old-fashioned bay rum. Michael had used it once in awhile, and I liked the scent, cozy with an edge, like Michael himself. My eyes closed, the elevator descended, and my loneliness retreated for the length of the ride. Renfrow didn't intrude on my silence; he seemed to shift his demeanor effortlessly, a useful trait in a politician.

On the ground floor, we passed the harpsichord factory, closed, and Boris' Bakery, still exuding cinnamony, chocolaty aromas. I hadn't eaten all day unless coffee counts, and for once the smells stirred my never-robust appetite. The exit door opened on a steamy twilight and locked behind us with such a definitive click I wished it were Friday when I'd be off to the Cape for a weekend with friends.

As we closed in on my twenty-year old Beemer, the little engine that usually couldn't, Renfrow's aftershave bombarded me with reassurances. Or were they pheromones?

"What about it?" he said. "There's an all-night diner on Milk Street."

Would it kill me to listen? I could modify my policy on first consults and let him pay me a few bucks to tell him not to run. "Not dinner. Coffee, at Freddie's Donuts." The neighborhood pit stop was just visible at the end of the block. "Eight-thirty."

"I'll be there with bells on. Although you should know," he hung onto my car door while I eased inside, "I am much more convincing over dinner than doughnuts."

"All the more reason for Freddie's." I rolled down the window and, like a trout rising to a fly, I snagged the check he was holding out to me. Just to hold his place.

US Trust reared up on my left. Twenty thousand dollars would lop a chunk off debt I'd incurred going solo, with a cushion left over for a few paltry extras, like rent. In a matter of seconds, I could slip Renfrow's check into the ATM machine and come away moored in safe harbors. On the other hand...the bank whizzed past...I'm the erstwhile Boston real estate specialist who traded buttoned-up security at Fairchild, Volpe, Weiss & McGrath for jeans and sandals in Waltham. Truth is, I have more problems around authority than I do around money. Freedom really matters to me. And "boss" was writ awfully large across Chaz Renfrow's psyche.

Halfway to Newton, I pulled over and examined the check: *Charles L. Renfrow, NovoGenTech, 850 Industry Road, Telford, MA.* My maps told me Telford was closer to Worcester than Waltham. Renfrow had wandered out of his orbit. With twenty thousand to spend on advice, why had he come to a smalltime political consultant tucked away in a rehabbed warehouse off the gritty side of Moody Street? Why, in other words, me?

One thing political consultants do is call in their chits. I dug out my cellphone and scrolled for Beauford Smith, a savvy operative based near Worcester. During the last state senate race I'd done him a favor, and when his dark horse won, gentleman Beau had graciously shared the credit with me. Our paths hadn't crossed since, but Beau claimed to know everybody. After two rings, an automaton gave me a new number which led to Beau's voice mail. I spoke a brief message, reminding him of my existence, and asking about Charles Renfrow. "Even scuttlebutt would be helpful," I said.

Along with my cell, which I'd neglected to charge last night, I left him my office number, linked to Deirdre Wilcot, whose answering service gave my low-rent establishment an aura of size and stability and a kind of earthy-crunchy class. Then I reviewed the five figures on Renfrow's check. Why the hell not me?

Roddie Baird's big stone fake French farmhouse loomed over the circular driveway, crowded with upscale cars. I parked behind an Escalade and waited out the afterburn that always convulsed my BMW in muggy weather. Like my office building, the Beemer had been rehabbed by Mimi, my sister, who'd passed it on to me. And rehab, I was learning, does not mean restore; the second law of thermodynamics, or something.

A woman in a white halter dress left the house and walked briskly toward a Mazda sedan. Chin length hair hid her face, but even from where I sat, I recognized Roddie's wife. Lauren Baird looked thirty but was actually forty-three, which I knew because blabbermouth Roddie, proud of her good looks, had told me. And she *was* pretty if you like skinny blondes who dress carefully and don't have much to say.

Snotty me. But I'm just as hard on myself, a skinny brunette who dresses indifferently and will rattle on. Lauren manipulated the Mazda in that economical way I can never manage, and in seconds, she'd pulled out of a tight space and was gone.

After a last shudder rocked my car, I walked to the house and tapped the half-open door which swung back on a large central hall. In true fake farmhouse style, the entire ground floor was open to view: spacious living and dining rooms, country kitchen off in the distance. Behind the only closed door lay the den where, six weeks ago, Roddie and I had outlined plans for his alderman's race, and Lauren made it clear that the campaign shouldn't expect much from her.

"Hello! Anybody home?"

A teddy bear of a man in chinos and sneakers bounded out of the den, his face etched with smile lines. "Susan! Punctual to a fault."

"I'm twelve minutes late."

He pointed at my shirt. "Good girls go to heaven? Where'd you get *that*?"

"Won it at a feminist raffle." Actually, it was a farewell gift from my old law firm, along with a Tiffany dragonfly charm. The charm brought my campaigns luck, and the tee shirt tided me over on late laundry days. What more could I ask, if not severance pay? "Check out the back." I swung around so he could read the rest of Mae West's sage observations: *Bad Girls Go Everywhere.*

He grinned the loopy little grin that made it hard to believe my genial candidate was an canny businessman with investments ranging from swimming pool filtration systems to apricot orchards. "Bet you don't get out much, am I right?"

"Just far enough to sample the voters." I passed him one of my surveys, which he slipped into his pocket.

"I'll look it over with Lauren when she gets home. Her foodie group called an emergency meeting. Somebody had a vegan attack." A big ham-eating grin overpowered his face, and he nudged my arm. "Come on. Let's go share your wisdom with Finance."

Outside the den, Roddie hesitated, his expression suddenly somber, but after a moment his mood swung back, and he threw open the door. "Hey, everybody, meet Susan Callisto. She guarantees victory, or my money back."

"Got that in writing?" I said, and Roddie winked at me.

I shook hands with three local businessmen and John Snow, who managed Roddie's passive investments. From a vine patterned sofa, retired judge Odette Brenner, all raspberry lipstick and brassy red hair, flashed me an uncertain smile. "They want me to head the committee," she said.

"Go for it. You'll have all the fun." From a carafe on Roddie's desk, I helped myself to coffee, then gravitated toward a rattan chair with rockers like mastodon tusks.

"But won't I have to raise the most money?"

"Not necessarily. You could be taskmaster. Slave driver. Set the goals and let the gentlemen here meet them."

"Oooo, slave driver," she crooned, and there was a little nervous laughter from the gentlemen.

I glanced at my watch. Six fifteen. Plenty of time to scatter every crumb of my political wisdom: Raise money. The rest, as they say, is commentary. "The campaign will need fifteen thousand dollars. More if you can't get enough volunteers."

With a few nudges from me, Odette and the men brainstormed about who would contact which potential donor, and how to pitch. Lists were drawn up. Notes were taken. I passed around telephone questionnaires, and they cross-examined me for a while. Snow promised to have his web-designer son put up a page to solicit donations, and at seven fifty-two, I said a quick goodnight and broke for the door.

Roddie hurried after me. "Wait up. I'll walk you to your car."

Just outside the den, I almost fell over a bundle on the floor. At the sight of me, the bundle scrunched up its eyes. "I want my mommy," it sobbed.

Roddie pushed past me and picked up his little girl. "Delia, why aren't you in bed?"

"'Cause nobody tucked me in." Tears rolled down her cheeks, and she stuck her thumb in her mouth. The other hand clutched a pink blanket, tiny fingers working up and down the silky border.

"Where are Sam and Josh?"

The thumb popped out, moist and shriveled. "In the playroom, and they won't let me stay." Her voice rose to a wail. "When's Mommy coming home?"

"Gotta go, Roddie!" I rushed across the hall, putting distance between Delia and me before she leaned over and drooled on me. "Call me about the survey."

Hefting his daughter, Roddie caught up with me under the portico. "I'll stop by your office tomorrow. It's not only the survey. I, uh, I need a favor."

I wondered if Roddie was getting cold feet. A fifth candidate had recently come out of nowhere, which meant extra work and a primary. "Is everything all right?"

"Sure. It's just…stuff."

Delia snuggled against Roddie's shoulder, and I could see her relax in his arms. "Can I have a cookie, Daddy?"

"'Leven zillion cookies," Roddie said, and gave her an Eskimo kiss.

She wrapped her arms around his neck and pressed her cheek against his.

What a campaign picture that would make, I thought, framing it in my mind. Worth at least a hundred votes.

By eight twenty-two I'd parked in my Waltham lot, smoothed my hair, and smeared on lip-gloss. I mistrusted Chaz Renfrow but evidently I wanted to look good when we met again. This was brain stem stuff. I never try to analyze it.

I jaywalked, wading toward Freddie's Donuts through traffic that never winds down in this part of town. From a ragtop Jeep, music poured into the street, something as sultry and elemental as hot fudge. My spirits jagged up, and I stepped to the beat.

Freddie's door opened on a crowd of chowder and doughnut freaks, and one searching glance told me Chaz hadn't arrived. I sat at the counter and nibbled the edges of an éclair that had no flavor, unless grease is a flavor. Three cups of coffee later, I checked my cell and found the battery had died. Freddie loaned me hers, and I called my service, but Deirdre was busy tonight; I had to leave *her* a message. Outside, my spine fused to the building, I waited near the entrance until nine fifteen.

Annoyed at myself for short-shrifting Roddie and, I had to admit, disappointed, I walked back to my car. I'd been right to mistrust Chaz Renfrow. Not only had he stood me up, his outlandish check was still in my hobo bag. Twenty thousand dollars. Now what was I supposed to do about that?

In the parking lot I changed my mind about heading home and went up to my office, where I reviewed documents for tomorrow's early morning session with an ornery client and his landlord. Then I tried Deirdre again.

She picked up on the first ring. "Susan, I tried to call you but your cell phone's off. Beauford Smith left you a message." Her voice was luscious with warning. "Keep away from Charles Renfrow."

"Oh, for heaven's sake, why?" The Beauford I remembered swung between paranoia and euphoria with every twitch of a poll.

"Because he's a hypocrite and a bloodsucker."

A hard-driving businessman, in other words. I sighed. "Anything else?"

"Renfrow…your friend laughed when he said it, but he called Renfrow an evil man."

My great-grandfather, born near Genoa, buried near Mendocino, would have warded off evil with a forked thrust of fingers. My own contemporary digits tapped the desk, but a decidedly noncontemporary chill scuttled briefly along my spine. "I better try Beauford again."

"Don't bother. He was at some airport, changing planes. Wants you to meet him tomorrow morning, ten-thirty at Memorial hockey rink, so he can talk to you face-to-face."

"Hockey? In July?"

"He's coaching a summer league kids' team. It's the only way he can see you before he leaves for Brussels. Promise you'll meet him, Susan. I have a bad feeling about this."

Her worry allayed mine, the way sharing a burden lightens the load. "Deir, I appreciate your concern, I really do. I don't suppose the sinister Mr. Renfrow tried to reach me?"

"No one else called."

After we hung up I scoured the Web for Renfrow and NovoGenTech, but found nothing of interest except a photo of Chaz on NGT's bare-bones webpage. There was a scanty list of his credentials, those of a few key employees, and three NGT phone numbers. But no private email address and no way to reach Chaz after hours. Dialing information got me nothing for Charles L. Renfrow anywhere in the state.

◇◇◇

Cicadas, and my own gloomy thoughts, masked the sound of footsteps until way too late. A hand fell on my shoulder. I swung around, my key pointed like a gun.

"Chaz!" I dropped my arm. "What are you doing in my driveway? How did you find me? My address isn't listed."

"I…I ran a credit check on you last week."

"You did what!" This kind of snooping riled me, especially as my credit was wobblier than a congressman's knees.

"I always look before I leap. Don't be angry. Aren't you planning to investigate me?"

"That's different. You came to me. On the spur of the moment, apparently."

"It was a sudden decision, but I had you in mind all along."

"Why me?" A kind of atavistic shame made me blush. I had trusted a stranger. Among Mediterranean types this was like putting ketchup on your spaghetti. "I've got a very small practice, Mr. Renfrow. You can afford one of the big boys. I don't know what your game is, but count me out." I opened my bag and rooted around for his check.

"Susan, wait. You've never lost an election. I want your success."

Almost flattered, I hesitated. Renfrow wanted my success, not quite the same as wanting to win. A figure of speech, but the nuance seemed like a warning. Beauford jumped to mind: Bloodsucker. I held out the check.

"You didn't deposit it?"

"Luckily, no. I'm sure it would've cost me a bounce fee."

"Susan…Susie…"

"It's Susan, and if you don't take back your check, I'll tear it up. How could you leave me hanging at Freddie's Donuts and no way to call you? You don't even have an unlisted number."

"Please. Let me…apologize. Explain." The word seemed to relax him, explanations perhaps flowing more easily than apologies from Chaz Renfrow's lips. "My home phone is in my housekeeper's name. I'll give it to you, and my cell phone number."

"A little late for that. Why didn't you at least call my service?"

"I ran into trouble. Since I had to wait for you, I decided to look at property in the old Navy Yard, in case NGT is forced out of Telford. The broker insisted on taking me to Cutters Island in Boston harbor. His launch lost power on the way back. Cost me an hour."

"And the dog ate your homework."

"I don't have a dog." His eyes stared unblinking into mine, and I was tempted to tell him hypnosis wouldn't work any better than lies.

"As soon as we docked, I called your office from my car, but no one answered so I came directly here. Have a little mercy, Susan." His grin was jokey, self-deprecating, and somehow, gently enticing.

I shook my head. "I'm just too busy to help you, Chaz. I can give you a few names. Beauford Smith does good work." I watched for a reaction.

"I know Smith, and I'm not interested." He looked put out, mildly annoyed, as if Beauford were a fly too small for swatting.

I shrugged. "Suit yourself."

"You're still angry. Couldn't we start again? Won't you be generous?"

This was masterful: an appeal to my better nature, the worst kind of flattery.

The money helped.

I relented. "Well, I'm sorry you couldn't reach me."

"And I'm sorry if you thought I'd forgotten you. Look, we've already lost too much time. I'm going to suggest something wild. Let's drive to Telford. We can talk on the way. If you're going to help me, you'll need to get a sense of NGT and the town."

"Can't do it. I'm dead on my feet." But even as I spoke I knew that, between the evening's coffee consumption and my chronic insomnia, sleep was not in the cards tonight.

"Traffic's light this time of night. Forty minutes each way, thirty if I push. We'll take a quick tour of NGT, and forget the town. I'll have you home by one." Chaz looked less polished than he had in my office. The jacket had vanished, his hair was windblown. His face was all planes and shadows in the moonlight. A soft humid breeze, the cicadas, his crooked front tooth, all goaded me.

Still clutching my key, and the check, I followed him to his car, a little white number I'd noticed in my Waltham lot but had missed on the crowded Brookline street where I live. He told me it was an old SAAB Sonett that he drove once in awhile to shake the rust out. "They only built five with a back seat. It's a semi-classic, like your Bimmer wants to be."

"Beemer."

"Beemer's the motorcycle."

"I never heard that."

"You came late to the party. Check Bimmer online. I used to drive a 2002 back when they were rare. Not expensive, mind you. Just rare."

You say tomayto…I say Beemer.

On our way to the Pike we stopped at my bank, and with Chaz standing by, I deposited his check. The ATM machine swallowed it whole, with an eerie metallic hum that sent shivers down my spine. Did those shivers mean, as my romantic half-Irish grandmother would say, that a banshee was howling over my grave?

Nope, my own pragmatic little inner voice replied. It meant that I'd accepted money from a man I didn't quite trust and was already, viscerally, regretting it.

Chapter Two

Never Say Die

NovoGenTech occupied eighteen thousand square feet of glossy industrial park, but Chaz's office was drearier than mine. There were metal shelves, a metal desk, two dark windows, and so many cinderblocks I figured the architect got his start in Albanian fallout shelters. Even the sofa was made of metal and petrified plastic. It chilled my behind, and I shifted discreetly.

"We're on the brink of creating, and cloning, a gene that prolongs life. What popular science writers call an immortality gene." Chaz was slouched casually next to me, but his voice had a sharpness more authentic than his smiles. In easy English, he explained that his ex-wife Johanna had identified an enzyme associated with longevity. Now her lab was developing a drug to slow, if not stop, the aging process. "The irony is NGT could collapse before we finish our work."

He told me how he and Johanna had founded the company a dozen years ago and moved to Telford after they outgrew their Chestnut Hill College labs. "Grow or die, then and now," he said. "We need to upgrade our facility, but last year a few NIMBYs screamed about unnatural life forms and Telford denied us a permit. Then the idiot mayor tried to revoke our current license."

Chaz left the sofa and took blueprints off a shelf. "NGT is as safe as houses, not to mention an economic bonanza for Telford."

He snapped the papers across his desk, and showed me new wings, filtration systems, an underground parking garage. "Our investors are threatening to pull the plug, Susan. My back's against the wall. Either I resubmit these plans, or I get out of town."

"If you resubmit, you'll have to take on the mayor."

"I knew you'd understand." His smile made me feel like a kindergarten superstar. "If I defeat him, well, remember how Clint Eastwood became mayor of Carmel? They wouldn't let him expand his restaurant, so he fought back. He won the election, *and* he got to expand. That's my goal."

Chaz reassembled the blueprints in that painstaking way fanatics fold roadmaps. "If I run, the campaign will work as a forum for biotechnology. But if I lose I'll sue Mayor Talbot Tremain personally. I will not be driven out by a sleazy windbag who'd trample his grandmother for a vote."

Chaz's grim face made me think of Nino Biondi, client and friend, who'd been stonewalling his landlord on my time since the end of May. Was there something about me that attracted obstinate men?

The water cooler burped.

"See why I need you?" Chaz filled two of those paper cones that always remind me of party hats. "You're a savvy campaign counselor, and you're a lawyer." He passed me a hat and sipped from the other. "Running for mayor personalizes my fight with Telford, and NGT's counsel won't handle my personal lawsuit."

"Conflict of interest," I said. "They've got to look out for NGT."

"I am NGT." Water glinted on his crooked front tooth. "For now, let's cover all bases and say I and my company will both be your clients. If you'll have us. I've heard nothing but good things about you, Susan."

"Who from? I've been wondering."

"Political Notes. That brief about you and your Ashcroft candidate. When I asked around, your name came up, and… truthfully?" His voice grew less assured, his smile tinged with melancholy. "It was an instinctual thing."

How could I fault him? I often flew by the seat of my pants.

"What do you say? Should I stand and fight?" His eyes were magnets, and I was suddenly glad for the brass in me. "I can't do it without you."

There were nuts and bolts matters he hadn't considered, I said. Yes, the nominating petition was a hurdle, but the next steps were harder: "You'll need strong endorsements. A fund raising drive. A campaign manager."

"My son Glenn's taking next semester off from Dartmouth. He's only nineteen, but he's a little bit brilliant, in his way. He'll manage my campaign." Chaz crumpled his paper cone. "I can get endorsements when the time comes, and money won't be a problem."

His confidence was as exhilarating as my new bank balance. "Okay. Miracles happen. You have four days to file. If you get the signatures, I'll advise your campaign."

We shook on it, Chaz pumping my hand as if he'd bagged a great victory. But my offer had been prudently qualified. If Chaz collected five hundred valid signatures by Friday, I'd know everything that mattered about him and his chances.

"One thing, Susan. For the time being, don't mention my plans to anyone. I want to take hizzoner by storm."

"Stealth candidate, are you?" His calculation made me smile. Rookies often thought the element of surprise would disarm their opponents. "By Friday afternoon your secret will be public record."

Our tour began in the employee lounge, a simple space near Chaz's office, where we helped ourselves to crackers and bouillon from a machine. "This is *not* the dinner I owe you for coming all the way out here tonight."

"All you owe me is a certified nominating petition."

"That too." The dim light softened his eyes, changing their color from marble blue to chameleon gray.

Outside Lab 45 we heard the soft clop of feminine shoes.

"Who is it?" Chaz called.

"Me." A baby voice preceded the clopper. "I saw lights." A woman about my age flowed around the corner in a cloud of

Jasmine Musk. Her black hair rippled to her shoulders from tiny plastic clips. With every step, an evening bag the size of a lipstick swung on spaghetti straps, brushing her hip.

Chaz kept his eyes on my face. "Susan, this is my assistant, Torie Moran."

Four-inch wedge sandals lifted her close to my height, five and a half feet on a good day. Her slim body was illuminated like a medieval manuscript in a gold and white dress dripping fringe. Fake, or possibly real, diamond earrings dangled from her multi-pierced lobes.

"Hi." I brushed a speck of lint off my tee shirt. Torie didn't acknowledge my greeting.

Still looking at me, Chaz addressed her: "This is Susan Callisto. She's an attorney helping with NGT's expansion."

In a manner of speaking, I thought, remembering Chaz's lust for secrecy.

Torie flicked a glance at my shoulder, then moved in on her boss, touching his biceps with one finger. Images of the witch gauging Hansel's flesh darted through my frivolous, probably envious, mind. "I saw your car," she wisped.

Chaz shifted his arm, and she tottered. She stepped on my foot, accidentally, I think, and now I picked up eighty-proof vapors Jasmine had masked.

"Johanna's party was un-fucking-believable. Forty-five candles. Almost burned the house down." She giggled and leaned toward Chaz. "Bart Bievsky was all over her tonight. Johanna still likes it, in case you didn't know." Inch by inch, she invaded Chaz's zone. Her voice whispered booze. "Poor Glenn."

His face blank, Chaz turned to me: "We store old equipment in Lab 45." He opened the door and switched on a light. "Have a look around. I'll just walk Torie to her car."

He didn't actually shove me into the room.

I wandered in a circle, glancing at a floor drain, crude metal shelves. The discards looked grimly domestic: dented funnels, a weird pasta scraper on a tapered handle, blue vinaigrette bottles. There was even a battered microwave oven. Most of a window ledge was smothered in Persian violets, a massive green and purple dome that put a little soul into the bleak room. Compared to this brawny specimen my office plants were the naked and the dead. Ignoring my spooky reflection in the pane, I walked over and poked among the roots, stirring up the erotic smell of dirt. Immortality my foot. Someday we'd all be plant food.

At a sink at the end of a counter I rinsed my hands, then returned to the corridor: Susan waits while Chaz dallies, a familiar posture tonight. When I finally heard his approach I moved toward the sound, and we met at the corner.

"I am sorry." He clacked his keys against his palm. "We'll have to take Torie back to the party. She's too…disoriented to drive. I'll give you the tour another time."

I swallowed my annoyance. Twenty thousand dollars entitled Chaz to a little of my patience, after all. "You've got your hands full. I'll take a cab home."

"From Telford? Don't be silly. Johanna lives just up the road."

On our way to Chaz's car, we passed a silver Jaguar straddling two spaces. "That's Torie's car?" I tried not to squeak my surprise.

"It is." Chaz moved quickly ahead to the Sonett where Torie was ensconced in my place, her head lolling. I squeezed behind the driver's seat, my knees digging into my chin.

No one spoke until we pulled into a driveway that continued for hundreds of feet to Johanna's house, lit up like a film set. All the windows were open, and laughter floated out.

"I thought you were taking me home." Torie's voice was a sleepy whine that faded as she floundered out of the car.

"Someone else can have that pleasure."

I watched them walk past a line of cars, Torie listing toward Chaz who adjusted his step to her drift. As they climbed the porch steps, she stumbled, black hair and white fringe mixing and flying.

Back in a minute, Chaz had told me, but after Torie's critique of Johanna, I was eager for a look at the woman. And I was damn tired of waiting. Elbow by knee, I crawled out of the Sonett and followed in their wake. Like Torie, I tripped on the porch, proving that even a sober annoyed person can miss a loose board. After I dusted my knees, I stationed myself on the wraparound railing. Through the tall front windows, I could see people standing about, drinks in hand, but no sign of Chaz or Torie or the lusty Johanna.

"Hey!" A voice boomed through the screen. "You on the porch. Come on in!"

"No, no." I slipped off the railing. "I'm waiting for someone."

A balding head popped out. "Why'n't you wait inside? Have a drink." He hooked a thumb around a red suspender printed with what looked like a rooster design.

"Bart!" someone shouted behind him. "Can you take Torie home? She won't go with anyone else."

Bart pulled in his head, and the screen door snapped shut.

So that was Bart Bievsky. He didn't look like a letch, but then, I didn't look like a lawyer. I checked my watch. Chaz's minute was fast becoming ten. I strolled around to the dusky side porch, a better place to spy without being spied.

"Who're you?" The low boyish voice came from a basket chair buried in shadows under a cranked open window.

"Susan. Who're you?"

"Glenn."

"Glenn. Your dad mentioned you."

"You're a friend of my dad?"

"I'm a consultant."

"What'd he say about me?"

In the dim light Chaz's nineteen-year-old son looked barely sixteen and seemed to lack the confidence needed to manage a campaign. Before I could answer his oddly eager question, light flooded the porch, and the side door creaked open.

"There you are, Susan." Chaz moved past Glenn and rested his hand on my shoulder until I took a small step away.

"Hi, Dad." As he rose from his chair, Glenn's smile faltered. In spite of the heat he wore a CSI-type jacket, and in the bright overhead light I saw that his dark hair hung over his ears. "Want a piece of Mom's birthday cake?"

"Not tonight. Susan's been very patient. I'm taking her home."

"Brookline," I explained as we headed for the steps.

"Brookline?" Without warning, Glenn erupted into song: "*So faahr away.*" His light voice actually warbled, and I wondered if, like Torie, he'd gone a drink too far or ingested some mind-bending substance. He flopped back into his chair. "See you tomorrow, Dad."

Where the porch angled left, Chaz paused. "On time, please." His tone told me who would be micromanaging the campaign and, if I felt a twinge of pity for Glenn, I was also relieved. Glenn could manage the paper clips. Chaz would provide the confidence.

Halfway to the car, I heard a shriek that frizzed my hair. Torie had materialized on the porch, waving both white-fringed arms. "Hellooo," she shouted, as if she'd finally remembered her manners. Her mouth was a red dot in the distance. "Helloooo." She put me in mind of a sea gull.

◇◇◇

We were on the open road. Through hazy glass, I could see the three-quarter moon floating on a band of dirty clouds. "Secretaries must make big bucks at NGT," I said, thinking about lustrous Jaguars and boxy old Beemers.

"When she's sober, which is always, at work," Chaz stared straight ahead, "Torie is a skilled administrator with a strong science background. She's highly paid and worth every penny."

Well. That'll learn me to make snide remarks to a man about his beautiful assistant, even if he is pissed off at her. I gave my bag an ironic pat. Like Torie, I was perhaps being overpaid, and by the same man.

In the Sonett's high beams, a farm stand and stalks of field corn flashed in and out of view. "By tomorrow night," Chaz said, in a lighter voice, "I'll be halfway home. In fact, I'll take you to dinner to celebrate the first three hundred signatures."

Dinner again. The man was obsessed with food. He downshifted, and the engine whined pitifully.

"I ought to check my calendar before committing."

"Your desk calendar?" He threw me a smart-alecky grin. "The one with all the blank spaces?"

I bit the smile off my own lips. "All right. I'll have dinner with you, on condition we make it a working session."

"Whatever you say. When it comes to my campaign, you're the boss." There was a certain lack of conviction in his voice, I thought. But if he passed the first hurdle, Chaz Renfrow was going to learn that he could count on me.

"Where should we eat? I love Italian cooking." His drawl was voluptuous, and for the first time in months I took an interest in…nutrition. "Slow, fresh, all the joy that goes into it. Know any place like that? Outside the North End, I mean?"

I wondered if he was fishing for a home-cooked meal, under the delusion that all Italians cook like angels. Tavola Rustica sprang to mind, but I wasn't sure I wanted to bring Chaz there. Nino might tease, or urge me to eat. Or mention Michael. "Let me sleep on it," I said, as casually as if I weren't plagued by insomnia.

◇◇◇

Just after one, Chaz walked me to the front porch of the two-family Victorian I share with a pair of Harvard B. School professors who'd picked it up at a bank auction. I locked the door behind me and ran up the stairs. From my front window, I caught a glimpse of the Sonett pulling away, and an intricate feeling, a tissue of discontent, regret, relief, came near to smothering me.

Or maybe I was hungry. Crackers don't count, and I hadn't bothered about food today.

"How can a daughter of mine be such a picky eater?" my mother, a gifted cook, used to lament, but even as a child I suspected she was talking about love. I went to the kitchen and opened the fridge. Way in the back with all the really weird stuff, I found two clementines left from a box Michael had brought me in March. Under shriveled skin the fruit was as fragrant and juicy as the day he'd carried up the little crate labeled *darling clementines* and called me his darling. I ate them, pretending the last sweet slices were his kisses. Of course, everybody knows what happened to Clementine.

Tired but, as usual, wide awake, I moved slowly to my bedroom. My kind of insomnia is rooted in reluctance to let go of the day, to lose consciousness, to give in. While I slipped out of my clothes, my unease over Beauford's message and Chaz's retainer began to mount, nothing a mindless soak in a hot tub wouldn't rid me of. Tomorrow was soon enough to fret. I'm a world-class avoider. Even when I sleep I try not to dream.

In the bathroom I put three fat candles on the edge of the sink, and lit them with Michael's old Zippo. The mirror doubled the light, painting my face with fire. Shadows flickered on the tile, and my heart stirred, as if Michael had guided my hand. I wished I could step back to April: "Don't go to Tucson," I'd whine. "I'm jealous."

Instead, I'd urged him to take a short leave and help out the ex-girlfriend who had shattered her tibia or her fibula, something Latin and important, when she fell off her horse. "I guess Nancy needs you," was all I'd said. Noble me. But I hadn't been able to speak words I knew Michael wanted to hear, words about love. Words he had never spoken to me. "You first" was the game we had played, and lost. Truth was, I missed Michael, terribly. But love was a fire, not this dull ache; love had perished three years ago, along with Gil. I'd have married Gil, if Gil had asked me.

I filled my clawfoot tub, dropping in ginseng sachet, bath pearls, blue and green salts, oat powder, everything in my cupboard but lemon-fresh Joy and extra-virgin olive oil. Portable radio tuned to Sinatra, I steeped myself in the scented waters. Leaning back, I tried to remember Michael's face that day at Logan airport, but all I saw was his hand gripping the bag I'd helped him pack, and his dark hair, long at the neck the way I liked it. Because all I could see was Michael walking away from me.

A newscaster invaded my alpha state, and I emerged from my bath, snuffed the candles and crawled into bed with a book. Gil Roth was dead. Michael Benedict was out of my life. And there was nothing I could do about any of it.

Chapter Three

Body Check

"Good morning!" I chirped to the two men standing outside my office. Nino Biondi and Peter Lombard were ignoring each other, but given the insults and threats that had ended last week's talks on Lombard's turf, even sullen silence looked promising.

Inside, I left them in the bookcase-walled conference area with copies of the latest, positively last, final, lease buy-out, my nimblest weaving of terms they'd both insisted on. For maybe forty-five seconds, I left them alone while I filled the coffee machine. Over the gurgle, I heard chairs scraping, raised voices. Something crashed.

"Nino! Peter!" I rushed back, too late to see who had shoved first, though odds favored Nino. Even at seventy-three, and dressed in hot flannels, he moved faster than his flabby landlord.

"Stop!" I plunged between the two men, but Nino pushed me away. He grabbed Lombard's tie, one of those rep cloth jobbies. Lombard swatted weakly at Nino's hand.

"Dammit!" I yelled. "Break it up!"

Nino dropped into a chair and closed his eyes. "*Villiaco*," he muttered.

"Susan?" Belly against the table, Lombard lined up his stripes. "Tell your lunatic client he takes the deal, or I see him in court."

Nino's eyes snapped open, blue as match tips. "Go ahead and sue. I got me the best lawyer in town. She'll fix you." He patted my hand. "She'll fix you good."

This was not the kind of talk I wanted to hear from a client who paid me a tenth of the going rate for my legal services, even if he was an old friend. "Let's think things through, Nino," I said, holding the draft like a plate of hors d'oeuvres nobody wanted.

"Nothing to think about. I'm not trading my lease. Cambridge don't interest me."

"Tell it to the judge." Lombard stalked out, an unlighted cigar wedged between his oddly elegant fingers.

As soon as the door closed, I moved in on my client. "Listen to me," I said. "The man wants his building back, and you're the holdout. You've already breached your lease six ways from Portofino. If he sues, you lose."

"Watch how you talk!" Nino chopped the table with the edge of his hand. "I'm the one you're supposed to stand up for."

"That's what I'm doing. Lombard's in a hurry. He made you a fabulous offer. Run with it."

A sigh escaped Nino, who was not given to sighs. "I'm too old to run, Susie." A strand of dyed black hair spilled across his forehead. "Pretty soon, I'll be too old to breathe."

"Don't say that." It shook me, hearing such words from my half-stand-in grandpa. In my mind, Nino Biondi was one of those stocky, energetic types who go on forever. "Don't even think it."

◇◇◇

"*Puck!*"

A cannonball slammed into the Plexiglas, followed by clumps of scuffling helmets and sticks. "*Get the puck out!*"

The man in the stands was yelling at the blue team, I realized, not me.

"*Use your body!*"

My own body was shaking so hard it sent shock waves through my teeth. I hadn't thought to dress warmly this morning. The wrinkled but clean cotton vest I'd found on my closet floor hardly covered my shoulders and chest. I circled the rink. A roar from the crowd told me someone had scored. "Beauford!" I had to shout over hollow thunder. "Beau!"

His hair, formerly ponytailed, was now buzzcut, and when he turned, I saw that his signature ear stud had gone with the pony tail. "Hey, Susan. I didn't see you come in." His smile was way too lazy for such a cold place. "Geez, how long's it been?" Keeping one eye on the game, he hugged me. "Let's use the athletic office."

I followed him out of the rink into a room crammed with shin guards, shirts, socks, everything leaning stiffly against lockers. The reek sent me scurrying out to the fruit machine, where I bought an orange, for its pungent perfume.

At a desk in a partitioned off corner, Beauford sat toying with what looked like two strainers and a gigantic eggshell, possibly a broken helmet. I plopped onto a bench and breathed though my mouth. "So why the scary message? Deirdre's tearing up the Yellow Pages looking for exorcists."

"It's not a joke, Susan." A silence fell, so prolonged I wondered if locker room stench had stunned Beauford, too. "Keep away from Charles Renfrow."

"Too late." I peeled the orange and offered him a slice, which he cradled in his palm. I bit into a juicy wedge of my own. "I've already taken his money."

"Give it back. The man is malignant."

"Come on." It's hard to feel scared with your mouth full of orange. "Are you saying he's crooked?"

"I'm saying he's venomous. Keep away from that…pit viper."

My God, southern WASP Beau sounded like a suspicious Italian, I thought, ignoring the tiny part of me that was listening hard. "Beau, is this something personal between you and Renfrow?"

"I'll get to that. Why did he come to you, if I may ask?"

"Does it matter? I'm having dinner with him tonight. Please tell me in plain English why I shouldn't."

"The man is a killer. Plain enough?" As a political consultant of long standing, Beauford used hype reflexively. "That's the good news."

"Oh, really?" I licked a trail of juice off my fingers. "Who's he killed?"

"You know he owns a biotech company?"

I nodded. "NovoGenTech. His lease expires in January. He'd like to renew it and expand on site. The mayor wants to run him out of town."

"The mayor's got it right." Beauford crushed his orange slice, then wiped his hands on his pants. He made a sound like a chuckling sigh. "Susan, if there's justice on this planet, Renfrow's going to fall into the toils of the EPA. NGT's a secret polluter, with a cancer zone just up the road."

"How come the media haven't jumped on the story?"

"They will. Telford's Biohazards Committee started investigating six months ago. Renfrow tries to buy everybody, but this time the truth will come out." Beauford turned the helmet over and brought it close to his face. "Could be soon."

"How do you know so much about NGT?"

"Grapevine." He found a screwdriver in the desk, and began attaching straps. It was finicky work and the helmet skidded away. "Dammit!" The screwdriver slipped though his fingers. "Look, a little girl in the zone died of myeloma last March. Myeloma! That's what old people get. As far as I'm concerned, Renfrow killed her."

"But it takes years for pollution to do its dirty work."

"It's been years. When Biohazards gets off its duff, the EPA will drag Renfrow through the courts, and he knows it. Is that why he hired you? Don't be cagy. I can keep a confidence."

"You couldn't be more wrong. Renfrow wants a campaign consultant, not defense counsel, and anyway I do real estate law. When I must."

A few bolts thunked on the floor. Beauford opened his mouth and shut it. Finally he managed to stutter, "You're telling me that corrupt bastard is running for office?"

I didn't answer which was answer enough. "So what's your bad news?"

The bolts had vanished under the desk, and he took a long time finding them. "You're right," he said when he came up for air. "It is personal." His neck flushed, and I remembered Chaz's almost contemptuous dismissal of him last night. "I hired myself out to him."

"Then why are you so astounded that he wants to be mayor?"

"Because Charles Renfrow doesn't know a voting booth from a Sani-Kan. The Senator's race was my last campaign. When Renfrow hired me, I was a full-time facilitator."

I couldn't help laughing. "Is that as shady as it sounds?"

"Sounds like political consultant." He threw down the bolts. "I advocated for clients in front of boards and commissions. I know small town ropes and how to untangle them."

"What exactly did you do for Renfrow?"

"Last year he wanted to conduct research not allowed under his permit."

"Wanted to upgrade his facility, he told me."

"He would call it that. His proposed research is hazardous… with a capital H. When I brought his petition before the town, I stressed all the built-in precautions: sterilization, HEPA filters. Sealed chambers. Air locks. Yada, yada. I even lobbied the mayor. This was before I knew about the polluting or I wouldn't have touched Renfrow's business."

Virtue comes easy after the fact, but I gave Beauford the benefit of the doubt. "So what happened?"

"The selectmen turned him down. Never mind all my efforts, Renfrow blamed me. He's a vindictive son-of-a-bitch. Badmouthed me all over the county. I don't know how he did it, but most of my old clients dropped me, and new ones stopped coming. He even spread rumors about my solvency, and my bank foreclosed."

"Why would the bank listen to rumors?"

Beau's face flamed into his scalp. "I…I'd missed a couple of mortgage payments. I'd done that before and always made it up, but this time they cut me no slack. After I lost my house, my other creditors took turns whacking me." He attached the bolts to the straps, little buttons slid through slits, and the strainers became a face guard. The straps clipped together, and the helmet was ready for another bashing.

"I've moved to Boston, learned a new set of ropes. These days I even lobby abroad, trade commissions, Euro agencies. I fly out again this evening, Brussels and Rome. I'll be gone for three weeks." He patted his jacket and handed me a business card.

"Newbury International Associates. Sounds impressive."

"For now NIA is just another name for me and my living room." His smile matched his slow sad drawl. "I'm in the Back Bay now. Nice old brownstone."

I gathered my orange peels, and got up to leave.

"What are you going to do about our talk?"

"I don't know. Check around. Ask Chaz some questions."

"He lies." Beauford pointed his screwdriver at my knee. "What happened to me could happen to you.

"I'm judgment proof, Beau."

Back at the office, I checked in with kindhearted Deirdre, my universal antidote. There'd been a couple of work-a-day real estate calls, she told me, and one from Roddie Baird. "He'll stop by around six unless you tell him otherwise. And Mr. Biondi called. Said you should come to Tavola for dinner tonight."

"No way, Deir." This morning's debacle still rankled. Once more around the merry-go-lease, and I'd wash my hands of Nino's buy-out. "I'm booked." Unless Beauford's story turned out to be unvarnished truth, in which case Chaz Renfrow was history.

"You ought to get back to him. He sounded really angry about something. Ah Susan," she sighed. "Mr. Biondi needs healing."

"Don't we all."

Hesitantly, Deirdre asked if I'd met with Beauford. It wasn't her way to pry, so I knew her worry hadn't damped down overnight.

"He's been spooked by rumors." Like every seasoned political consultant, I told her, Beau had learned to run scared. "That's not a bad thing. Your fear infects your candidate who then runs scared too, and fast, all the way home. Trouble is, Beau's addicted to fear and can't break the habit." I hung up, not sure who I was trying to convince.

I dealt with my e-mail, then pulled out some real estate files and immediately put them away, unable to focus even on boilerplate. Unless Chaz reassured me about children and cancer, the twenty grand was smoke and ashes. I dialed NGT, but he wasn't available.

While I waited for his call back, I had two cups of dark roast Colombian and triaged my debts. A check in full to GreenClean Laundry left enough for minimum payments to MasterCard and Visa. A crumb toward utilities. Nothing for rent. Luckily, eviction proceedings took months, by which time I might be solvent. I tucked the checks into envelopes, all but GreenClean, which I would hand-deliver when I collected my threads. Patched up for the moment, I spun my chair to the window and basked in a hot sunbeam.

Just after noon, I hit redial, and this time an affable Chaz took my call. "Sorry I didn't get back to you," he said. "I'm running on two cylinders. Literally." A big lazy yawn drifted like a cloud along the phone line. "After I dropped you off, the Sonett collapsed. Staties had to send a tow. I spent half the night on the turnpike."

"How did you get home?"

"Yanked poor Glenn out of bed." He yawned again. "What's up?"

"We need to talk. I've heard rumors that could derail your campaign."

"What rumors?" He laughed. "Mutant zucchini rampaging through Telford?"

"Pollution," I said. "The EPA. I'll tell you what I heard when I get to your office."

"It's crazy here. My assistant didn't show up, the temp is a nitwit. Let's talk now."

"I need to sit down with you." And study your face.

"Can't it wait till tonight?"

"Chaz, I won't have dinner with you unless I'm sure I can go on with the campaign."

He didn't miss a beat. "The retainer is yours, Susan, all of it, even if I drop out."

"This is not about money."

"Are you quitting on me?"

"I'm wavering. I've just met with Beauford Smith."

Silence. Then he said, "Come now, and I'll steal a few minutes."

On my way out, I caught sight of my death row plants. Later guys.

◇◇◇

After my car finished bucking, I locked up and trudged across the lot under the blazing sun. Straight ahead, the NGT building shimmered like a two-story mirage. A Lexus SUV was berthed in Chaz's space today, but Torie's Jaguar hadn't moved since last night. The efficient and highly paid Ms. Moran must have a doozy of a hangover.

Up close and in daylight her Jag wasn't all that spiffy. Rust nibbled the panels, and there was a puddle of oil under the chassis near the right rear wheel. But even pockmarked, the Jaguar was a beautiful machine, long and sleek. Sensuous in an obvious way, and when did men ever mind obvious? I peered inside. Ditz had left her keys in the ignition.

I drifted around the car, letting my fingertips graze the enamel. At the trunk, I noticed a strand of yarn dangling over the bumper. I touched it.

Not yarn.

Way ahead of my conscious self, the hidden parts barked orders: Open the trunk! Check that puddle!

I stooped over the oil, though I knew it wasn't oil, and touched something viscous, almost dry, like the skin over your pudding. I stood and rubbed my stained finger on the trunk, which lifted slightly. Another thread of fringe spilled out, and Jasmine Musk, and a strand of long black hair.

Chapter Four

Rope

Two uniformed officers arrived and fully opened the trunk. Torie's body lay on its side, doubled over at the waist. A bare foot stuck up between two wrists. Broken doll. Scribble of red. That's all I allowed myself to see, though I couldn't evade the chill that wracked me until the paramedics came and someone brought me tea.

The locals called in the state police, Telford being unused to murder. Twenty minutes later the Jaguar was surrounded by a medical examiner and crime unit personnel. Curious NGT workers milled around, and by the time Lieutenant Michael Benedict arrived, the parking lot had the air of a country fair struck by lightning.

When I saw him drive up, I tried to vanish among a knot of NGT staff that included an ashen-faced Chaz and a dark-haired woman, Johanna, someone said. Surrounded by sweating bodies, knowing full well that I wouldn't be allowed to hide, I watched Michael confer with Telford police, then make his way toward me.

"Hello, Susan." His casual voice zeroed in on my already weak knees. "See you for a minute?" There was no warmth in his tone. The office, not the man, was speaking to me.

I edged away from the others, torn by the slightly lopsided way he stood on those mile-long legs, by the familiar, tear-shaped scar on his cheekbone. The mustache was new. I clutched my elbows in a self-protective hug. "Hello, Michael," I said, and my voice held the same indifference as his.

His gray eyes skipped off mine. "You found the body?"

"I found the blood. Telford police found the body."

"Always the literalist." He looked right at me now.

"Lieutenant Benedict?" An impatient voice intruded on our stiff reunion. Michael turned, and I stepped back into the crowd. "I'm Johanna Lang."

Chaz's ex was as ripe as plums, and Michael scrutinized her with more interest than even a murder investigation warranted, it seemed to me.

"When can we go back inside?" A few strands of Johanna's dark brown hair fell across her forehead, and she fixed them to the top of her head with her rimless glasses. "It must be ninety-five degrees out here." She spoke with a soft surliness that brought our little group to attention.

"We all need to get out of the heat, Lieutenant." Chaz came up behind me, and Johanna shied away from him as if he were an unreliable dog.

By two-thirty, most of NGT's employees had left, but key personnel and witnesses were still making statements. When my turn came, it was Sergeant Paul Tyre who interviewed me. The dislike between us had sprung up fully-grown the first time Michael introduced us, and it remained as murky and constant as lust. In an office near the employee lounge, I crossed my legs and jiggled my foot, quietly fuming that Michael had, again, abandoned me.

Tyre dropped a note pad the desk and turned on his recorder. "Okay, Suze. You met Victoria Moran, when?"

"Last night, first and only time."

He massaged his temples, fingertips pulling loose skin across his cheekbones and up into eyebrows as bristly and frayed as old toothbrushes. "What can you tell me about her?"

"She'd just come from Johanna Lang's birthday party. She stopped in because it was late and she saw lights."

"What were you doing at NGT after hours?"

"Consulting with my client."

"Where did you go afterward?"

"We took Torie back to the party, then Mr. Renfrow drove me home. We left around midnight and were together until a little after one."

"Ten after? Twenty after?"

"Ten," I said, and Tyre let go of my alibi. He darted from topic to topic, firing questions, barely waiting for answers. He asked who drove Torie home, how drunk she was, if I'd seen her leave. Other questions about the party, Johanna, Bart Bievsky. Most of the time I stared blankly and said I didn't know.

"Was Moran carrying a purse?"

"A little fringed evening bag."

He showed me a group photo of Chaz, Torie, and others at what looked like a Christmas party. "What a hottie, this Victoria Moran. Was she having an affair with Renfrow?"

"She was his assistant. That's all I know."

"What about you? What do you do for Renfrow?"

"Not relevant, Paul."

"I decide what's relevant. Answer the question."

He'd been baiting me on and off for half an hour, and I'd had enough. "What I do for Mr. Renfrow is none of your business! Any more questions, talk to my lawyer."

"Easy, easy, Suze. You always had a short fuse." He tried again, switching gears, the bully backing down. "What made you examine the Jag?"

"Something seemed wrong. It was an instinctual thing."

"Instinctual." His eyebrows said it was a toss up between my truthfulness and my sanity. "And then you smeared your bloody finger…on the car?"

I shrugged.

"You left prints. Your meddling tainted evidence we're gonna need to build our case against the killer."

My meddling. The killer. I wasn't a suspect this time. He probably thought I ought to shout my relief. For Tyre the whole world was a criminal enterprise.

"Who knows how much damage you did?" He turned off his recorder. "All right, you can go."

I made it as far as the door.

"Hold on," he said. "One more thing."

Tyre had always liked Columbo, the dumb, sly, smart, oldies television cop. Was I supposed to be lured into a confidence by a shut down recorder?

"Did you have a look through the glove box? Instinctually, I mean?"

"No, Paul. I did not."

"Did you see a cell phone in or around the Jag?"

"No."

"Any idea who'd want to kill her?"

"No."

Even Tyre's sighs were aggressive. "We'll be in touch. On your way out, send in the zit-faced receptionist, willya?"

"It's rosacea."

He flung down his pen. "I don't care what her name is, just send her in."

They were in the employee lounge, at a rickety table littered with magazines. After the receptionist left, I slid into her chair across from Chaz. "How are you?" I asked, as if I couldn't tell from his pale face and swollen eyes.

"Been waiting for you." His voice buzzed with incipient flu. "I hope you're all right. Finding Torie…"

"I'm okay. You're the one ought to go home and get some rest."

"Not while Lieutenant Benedict is in the building."

Hearing Michael's name, his presence at NGT, felt as surreal as Torie's murder. I hadn't seen him in months. After his Tucson rescue mission, he'd stopped calling me. Just like that. Ex-girlfriend, ex-wife, indigestion, I hadn't chased after reasons.

After Gil died, grief had numbed me, and I'd learned how to stiffen my spine and move on. But since Michael left, numbness was fast becoming indifference, and from there, I knew, it was an easy slide to despair. Only work kept me going.

From the kitchen nook a compressor thumped, startling Chaz who reared back. "I keep expecting Torie to walk in with a report," he said. "Or a brainstorm. Always thinking up ways to boost the bottom line. She was totally dedicated to NGT."

His words sounded like a shareholder's eulogy and, as eulogies will, they rang false.

"Who would want to kill her?"

"Not a soul. Everyone liked her."

More eulogizing. Last night, even Torie's appreciative boss had been pissed off at her.

"About Beauford Smith," Chaz said. "I'll clear up everything over dinner. We're still on, I hope."

"Tonight? I couldn't. Let's wait a few days. You'll get sick if you don't take care of yourself."

"I can't afford to wait." His eyes slewed left, as if he suspected his haste was tacky under the circumstances. "I've got to jump back into the fray."

"I'm not sure you should."

"Christ! You're supposed to be a fighter! What's spooking you now? Afraid murder could derail my campaign?"

My own words. Thrown back at me, they sounded cowardly, even crass. But true, for all that.

"Sorry." He reached for my hand. "I'm being unfair. You came here because Beauford Smith's got a grudge against me. At least give me ten minutes to defend myself."

He only needed five, for a story that mirrored Beau's, with that reverse perspective mirrors give. Beauford Smith was an opportunist, Chaz told me. Worse, he was a liar who sold out NGT to his buddy the mayor. A coward who hid behind bankruptcy. "In a nutshell, Smith cost me millions in lost opportunities. I'm the one ought to be holding a grudge." While Chaz talked, he churned his thumb along the back of my hand, and when I tried to pull away, he clung.

"What about the pollution? Myeloma. Children dying."

"More lies. The little girl who died last year had a rare congenital form of the disease. I don't suppose Smith mentioned that. NGT generates minute amounts of toxic waste, which we dispose of lawfully. Biohazards makes unannounced inspections. They've never found a problem."

Footsteps sounded outside the door, and Glenn shambled into the lounge. As if I'd been caught canoodling with his dad, I yanked back my hand in a flurry of falling magazines. Glenn retrieved them, stacking them neatly on his father's side of the table.

"You're *still* here?" Chaz said.

"Just want to grab me a Coke." On his way to the cooler, Glenn sketched a little wave in my direction. "Anyone else?"

"I'll have one," I said, to soften Chaz's annoyance.

Glenn gave me the soda with a shy courtliness that made me think of country boys and Fourth of July picnics. "Want some ice?"

"Glenn. Make it snappy." Chaz's irritation seemed tinged with uneasiness or embarrassment. Not on my account, I hoped. "Susan and I are in the middle of a private business conversation."

"Sorry. Didn't mean to butt in."

He left, chugging his Coke, and from the doorway, Chaz stared after him for a long moment before stepping back into the room. "Have I put your mind at rest?" he said. "Are you still with me?"

"Get on the ballot, and we'll take it from there."

"Dinner tomorrow, then? Working session? I promise I'll bring along three hundred signatures, and get the rest by five o'clock Friday."

With the filing deadline now three days away, I knew Chaz was right to push, but his relentless ambition was fast uncovering the limits of mine. I could only hope my pessimism wouldn't go viral.

We left together, Chaz guiding me toward the exit. Down the hall a door opened, and Michael stepped out, followed by Glenn and Bart Bievsky in his silly red suspenders. My elbow burned under Chaz's grip, but if Michael noticed me or my elbow he had eyes in his chin. "Got a minute?" he said to Chaz, ignoring my presence the way snooty dames in old movies ignored Groucho Marx.

I walked on, not looking back, not wanting to give Michael even that much satisfaction if he was watching.

"See you tomorrow night," Chaz called after me. "I'll pick you up at seven."

Outside, the sky had gone to chalk.

A few miles from NGT, my car began to shiver and buck, an old habit I thought I'd cured with the last tune-up. I rolled into a gas station, and while the attendant checked the oil and coolant, I phoned Beauford. Although I knew he was on his way to Europe, I left a message. "I'm sticking with Renfrow, but you and I really need to talk." And for the moment, those words put my conflicting emotions to rest, as if I'd transferred a burden.

Fluids replenished, the Beemer crept back to my office, where I found Roddie in the parking lot standing next to his van. I was ten minutes late, not bad considering all I'd been through today. Inside, Roddie insisted on taking the stairs, dragging a duffle behind him, wheezing all the way. "I'm going mountain climbing in Colorado, flying out tonight. Should've started training years ago." On the top floor landing he unzipped the duffle and, with a sweetly self-satisfied air, pulled out a coil of fluorescent orange twine. "*Tahdah!*"

"Clothesline for the legally blind?"

"You really don't get out much, do you. This is premier mountaineer's rope. I found a little backwater company with space age fibers and no interest in promoting their product, so I invested a few bucks. Acid colors were my idea. Here, I brought some for you. You could use it to tie campaign signs to your car, or macramé plant holders or something."

"Thanks, but I'm not artistic, and clamps work better for signs."

"Whatever," he said, a little hurt, I thought. Gripping a knotted end, he whipsawed the rope, which streaked like orange lightning down the stairwell. As I watched him, I imagined the wild child living just under the skin of the clear-eyed man, and I wondered how much of Roddie's strength, his will to win, he owed to that cheeky polarity.

He hauled up the rope and jammed it back into his duffle. "I've hired a couple of climbers to field test it and I'm tagging along, and speaking of tag-alongs, what am I going to do about Kyle Froy? Jerko filed his papers, and now he's slapping bumper stickers on every pole in town."

"Who *is* he?" I unlocked my office, and Roddie followed me inside.

"Carpetbagger. He and his wife just moved to Newton, apartment on Baden Street."

"Wait a minute, Roddie. You're in Ward nine. I'm almost certain Baden's in ten." I poked among my collection of municipal maps and spread Newton across the conference table. My finger traced a ward line. "I'm right. Froy can't run against you."

"Must be an old map. City's always fine-tuning the boundaries."

"Well, play it safe and check with the clerk."

We got down to the voter survey which Roddie loved… except for everything he hated, and the changes took an hour to hammer out. When we finished, I printed a fresh copy for him to review one last time. "If Huston gets the file no later than tomorrow, your order should be ready early next week."

"But I was counting on Friday." Roddie slumped in his chair. "See, this is my chance to hook Lauren. She's agreed to handle the mailing. The kids want to help too, even Delia. I'll be home Sunday in time for the finish. It'll be a real family affair."

"I don't know about Friday." Small and fairly low-tech, Huston Printer was a favorite with budget-minded candidates, but rush charges were extortionate. "Twenty-five thousand is a lot of brochures, and they have to be folded. Cost you a bundle."

"Whatever he wants, I'll pay it."

This was serious. Thrifty Roddie loved cheap. "Huston usually works late, except Fridays," I said, punching in his number.

Money worked its magic. For a thirty-eight percent markup, the surveys would be ready at noon on Friday. "And don't be late. Huston closes at one."

"Think you could you fetch them and bring them to Lauren?"

"Sorry. I'll be leaving early for the Cape."

"I'll level with you," he said. "I was hoping you could use the delivery as an excuse to stop by the house and, I don't know, have coffee with Lauren." He smiled, but his voice pressed hard. "See, one on one, you might be able to convince her to join the campaign."

"Roddie, some people just don't like campaigning."

"Lauren hates it." He chuckled, but I was beginning to catch on to Roddie. The bigger his grin, the sadder his heart.

"You seem down today. Is it Froy? Trust me, he ain't gonna defeat you. No one is."

"I'm a little tired, that's all. Delia and I spent last night in the emergency room. Appendicitis turned out to be eleven zillion cookies at bedtime." With a smile that didn't come near his eyes, he said, "Susan, if anyone could fire Lauren's interest, it's you. You convinced me to run when I had so many doubts. Couldn't you talk to her?"

A candidate's morale was more important than his war chest, and I knew what I had to do. "How's tomorrow?" I sighed.

He took his BlackBerry into the hall, and when he came back, his eyes had their old liquid glow. "She'll meet you at her gym. Spaal's, off the turnpike in Newton. Is six-thirty all right? In the morning, that is."

A gym? Grunts and sweat and no privacy? But, okay. If it would help Roddie, I'd meet Lauren on Everest.

◇◇◇

Everest I could handle, but not my empty apartment, even if the price of company was a dinner I had no stomach for. I drove to Nino's after all and parked in front of Peter Lombard's brick building, draped with LOST OUR LEASE banners. The holdouts were Tavola Rustica and MediRX, the restaurant and the purveyor of antacids.

It was barely seven-forty-five, but Tavola was closed. Through the locked glass doors, I spotted Benny, forty feet away on top of the stove, an eight-burner affair inside a deep chimneyed recess lined with quilted steel. He was hopping from burner to ledge, scrubbing the firewall with a dingy rag. I knocked, and he jumped down and let me in.

"I made soup," he announced, "but we didn't do dinner."

"Why not?" I scanned for Nino who should have been darting about, rolling pasta or prepping tomorrow's vegetables. "Where's the boss?"

"Somebody smashed up his apartment." Benny scrambled back on the stove, dragging a bucket. "Nino had to fix everything and then he got tired and went to bed."

I hurried through the interior service hall to Nino's apartment behind the restaurant and found him sunk in his armchair, head drooping over a glass of anisette. "Nino!" I shouted above a surge of music from his new flat screen TV.

His head jerked up. "Susie! Don't stand there. Come in, come in."

I hiked across the room. "What's Benny talking about? What happened?"

"Not a lot. My apartment got trashed during lunch. I've been cleaning all afternoon and still not finished."

"Are you all right?"

"Right as rain. You're the one don't look so hot." He picked up the remote and turned off the set. "Gnocchi'll cure you. I baked it with rapi and gorgonzola."

Gorgonzola, the very word put pleats in my stomach. "Never mind food. Tell me what happened here."

"I'll show you." With a grunt, he got up and led me to a side room where a smashed chest of drawers and a caved-in bed took up most of the floor space. Curtains and rods lay in broken heaps under a window that overlooked the alley.

"How awful," I said, sounding even lamer than I felt. An old man's intimate space had been invaded, the place where he slept unprotected and alone, and I feared there would be no way to bring the old peace back. I tried to reassemble the curtains, but he put out a hand.

"Leave 'em. Curtains I can fix. But not my torn up pictures."

He pulled a worn album off his closet shelf and bent over pages filled with scraps, faces and fences, a shoulder, a dress. Streaks of pale scalp showed poignantly through his sparse, dyed hair. "My family was here, my past. Now it's confetti. Who would do this, I ask myself? *Lombard* is who. Wants to scare me out. *Villiaco* knows I never leave the restaurant during lunch. So while I'm busy with customers, he sends in his thugs."

"I don't believe it. Lombard's not into crime. Your neighborhood is a paradise for vandals. You should move somewhere safe."

"Don't start buggin' me about the lease again."

"What did they steal?"

"Just my peace of mind."

"Did you call the police?"

"No police. I'll handle Lombard my own way." Without another word, he waved me out and shut the bedroom door.

I wandered around like an insurance appraiser. A cup handle lay on the counter, and there were yellow stains on a baseboard, but outside the bedroom, no real damage. The vandals had ignored everything of value: silver, TV, five shelves of copperware. They'd made mischief, but stolen nothing. Scare tactics against an inconvenient old man? Was Nino right? But Peter Lombard was famous for never quite crossing the cobweb line between sharp practice and criminal behavior. He used money, the courts, but he never broke the law.

When Nino came back, he was chipper in a fresh plaid shirt, ready to shove a meal down my throat. Again I declined the gnocchi. With a shrug, he tossed a foil package from the refrigerator into the oven, and set up the Neapolitan espresso maker with its upper and lower spouts like out-of-joint noses. "Cuppa coffee'll fix you up. And a drop of grappa."

"Coffee, yes. Grappa, no."

Might as well whistle for your cat. Nino went on pouring clear liquid from a green bottle into stubby glasses set on a tray. "My own label. Hundred proof, maybe more."

The espresso pot seethed. Nino upended it and brought everything to the table. Inside the foil was a wedge of rosemary foccacia which he pulled into steaming chunks and thrust under my nose. Two pieces had me fainting from bliss. Even the espresso was good, though I knew it would turn my garden-variety insomnia into bug-eyed mania by midnight.

"Now, something's bothering you. Don't lie. I see it in your eyes." Though he didn't call it that, Nino fancied himself a psychologist, bursting with common sense, and a dollop of kindness.

With exaggerated care, I set down my cup. "I found a murdered body today."

"*Porca miseria!* What body?"

Ignoring the grappa he kept shoving at me, I told him, and by the time I finished, I'd regressed to a nine year old, reveling in the dark joy of tears.

"What kinda clients you got, killing each other?" Nino spoke gruffly but he patted my hand.

"She wasn't my client. Her boss is, and if he killed her, I'm Jane Austen. The police are investigating."

"Police." He spat the word.

I couldn't think of a reply, and we both fell silent. Gradually, Torie Moran retreated into someone else's bad dream.

"Give me your pictures," I said, still eager to do something constructive for my half-stand-in grandpa. "I know a photo lab that works miracles."

"Never mind the pictures. What's done is done. I want you to use this…" he waved his hand around his head. "…*felony* against Lombard when he sues us. And if he doesn't sue us, I want you to sue him."

I noted that cozy "us," but I wasn't up for a squabble. "Look, if you can link Lombard to the vandalism, tell me how. Otherwise, stop harping on it."

"He did it!" Nino's larynx wobbled. "And I'm gonna make sure he knows I know. I left him ten messages. Coward hasn't called me back."

"I'll talk to him tomorrow. Meanwhile, will you please stop antagonizing him with phone calls?" I inhaled my grappa, a smoked-lemon scent that was almost inviting. "Answer me something. Am I your consigliere?"

"Thought I told you to roll your r's."

"Nino, am I?"

"Yeah, yeah."

"My advice is valuable to you?"

He nodded, a grudging jut of his chin.

"Take Lombard's offer. What kind of traffic do you get here? Medical students? Office workers who go home at five o'clock every night? In Cambridge you'll get the Harvard Square crowd, tourists, people from the suburbs. Any restaurant owner would kill for that location. And Lombard is giving it to you at the Brookline rent."

Nino swallowed more grappa. The glass trembled in his hand, and I remembered that he would be seventy-four in November. I drove the thought away. Everyone's hand shakes once in a while. "I can't leave," he said. "It's not just Tavola. It's the neighborhood. I'm at home here."

An idea flitted through my mind, and I pounced on it. "Home is where you make it. What if Lombard threw in an apartment, walking distance from your new restaurant?"

"What if. What if." He rocked his hands. "What if that smoke-eating toad threw in ten million dollars? What if you married yourself a nice Italian boy like that George Cluni guy I saw on talk TV?"

"George Clooney is not Italian."

"You sure? He looks Italian."

"Well he's not."

"You're how old? Twenty-five?"

"I'll be thirty in September, a regular old maid."

"Thirty! By thirty, I was divorced five years. How come you don't bring the cop guy around anymore?"

"We're not talking about Michael Benedict. I saw him today, and he wouldn't even look at me. Anyway, I thought you didn't like him."

"Hey, old maid, he's better than nothing."

Yeah, I thought. Lots better. "All right, Nino, maybe I'm not going to get married. Well, boo hoo for me. But you're wrong about Lombard." I sipped my grappa, which wasn't half bad once the esophageal spasm burned itself out. "Lombard is not a toad."

Nino grinned. "Yes, he is. He's a sneaky toad."

"Okay." I laughed into my glass. "But a smart sneaky toad."

He leaned over and tapped his glass against mine. "*Ti salut, Susanna,*" he said, no smile in his eyes. "Lombard is a smart, sneaky, fat, rich toad, but he's not gonna get my restaurant."

Chapter Five

Alone In The Cold Room

Bluesy music drifted like musk across the front porch, and through an open window I could see my landlords slow dancing in the parlor. Miles' hand lightly strummed Martha's spine, and while I fumbled for my key, she kissed a spot behind his ear. My heart gave a smart little rap against my ribs. Envy. Longing. In four months together, Michael and I had never once danced like lovers.

Inside my apartment, I listened to the emptiness I usually covered with bustle. The music had stopped, and I guessed M 'n M were going to bed early tonight. From the kitchen, I called Deirdre and checked my messages. "Not a one," she said, "but what's wrong? You sound terrible."

I told her, and unlike Nino, who was, after all, a guy, Deirdre understood that Michael's presence had affected me as much as finding Torie's body.

"Not to be callous," she said, "but this woman meant nothing to you. Michael eased your way."

"Her dress was soaked in blood."

Silence. Then she murmured, "I'm sorry, Susan. I didn't mean you don't care. Its just that Torie Moran is beyond healing, and you've got to focus on life."

"You're right about Michael," I said. "I do miss him."

After a long hot shower, I dried off in front of the fan, letting the air rake over my body until I shivered, my mind flooded with images I couldn't drive away: Michael's stony face. Chaz's taw marble eyes. Torie's foot, toenails painted a fashionable blue.

Spaal's gym was crowded, rock 'n' roll blasting, dozens of early birds pumping to the beat. When I spotted her, Lauren was stepping onto a treadmill, an ancient unmotorized model off by itself in a corner, the only private space in the gym. She was wearing shorts and a tee shirt and a twisty metal necklace. Tortoise shell clips held her hair off her face. The clips made me think of Torie.

I walked over. "Lauren? Remember me?"

"I'd know you anywhere. That serious face." Not hostile, but not friendly either, Lauren bewildered me. Exercising while she talked seemed a not-so-subtle way to put me and Roddie's campaign in our place at the bottom of her do-list.

She began a slow walk, both hands gripping the bars, the roller belt rumbling under her feet. "Roddie told me you wanted to discuss something urgent."

Thanks, Roddie. Shift the burden *and* the blame to me. "He's worried about the voters surveys," I hedged. "Carrier-sort mailings get kind of tedious. One mistake, and the post office won't deliver."

"I think I can handle it."

Somber, indifferent, she walked faster, treading in place and moving miles away from me. I suddenly wanted to disrupt her journey. "Oh hell, Lauren. It's not about the mailing. It's about you."

"Me?" An eyebrow went up.

Another day, I'd have launched into a ramble about the importance of family, how it could lift flagging morale. Now all I said was, "Roddie told me he needs your support."

"He has my support."

"He needs something less tacit. He wants to discuss strategy with you. Go over the issues."

"Isn't that why he talks to you?" Her voice was innocent of irony. I couldn't catch her eye.

"I'm just a hired hand. Roddie needs *you* to be happy about what he's doing."

She stopped in her tracks. "Happy? Of course I'll help with the campaign, but what's happiness got to do with it?"

"Look Lauren, all Roddie wants is a tiny show of…enthusiasm. If you started going to parties with him, going to debates, helping him define himself for the voter, you might even find a speck of joy in the campaign."

She began to jog, hair clips bobbing, necklace bumping her collarbone "You are very young, Susan."

A woman dressed in yellow spandex strutted our way, ankles and wrists bound in velcro weight pouches, dumbbells in her hands. A chastity belt affair crawled between her thighs and up around her waist.

"Lauren, see that girl over there?"

"Uh huh." She answered in a breath-saving way, turning her head where I pointed.

"What's that thing riding up her backside?"

"Butt harness," she gasped, trotting very fast now.

"You are kidding me. What's it for?"

She slowed her pace slightly. "Helps her professionally."

I looked at the muscled body, legs spread, weighted arms flapping up and down in front of a mirror. Snowboarder? Mud wrestler? "How so?"

"She's a lawyer."

My antennae perked up. "Oh?"

"Harness keeps that stick up her ass."

A wit, our Lauren. Eyes closed now, she broke into a run, and I sensed she was zoning out. Roddie had clearly overestimated my persuasive gifts.

On my way out, I asked the spandexed lawyer for directions to Ladies. She hoisted a velcro-wrapped wrist toward the coatroom, which was empty except for a few metal racks. And little Delia Baird, asleep on a sofa, arms and legs curled around her pink security blanket. A frown creased her petal skin. While I watched, she sighed and rolled on her side, thumb veering back toward her cheek. Lauren had babysitting problems this morning, I guessed. I gently untangled Delia from her blanket and covered her with it. I assumed she was safe, all alone in the cold room.

From my car, I returned a call that ended with my driving to Hudson, New Hampshire, to confer with a candidate. By eleven I was back in my office, where Peter Lombard had left an early morning threat. I punched in his number, and before I finished saying my name, his secretary put me through.

"Your nutso client's been leaving *ugly* messages on all my phones."

"Hello to you, too."

"Nino Biondi is a harasser." Lombard coughed juicily. "*Harasser!*"

"Peter, his apartment was vandalized. He thinks...well, he doesn't know what to think."

"Any damage to my building?" Lombard's quick anxiety rang true.

"No real damage at all." I put him on speaker and crossed to the mini-fridge where I dug out an ancient Coke, tasting of tin, but flush with caffeine.

"I gotta tell you, I'm getting tired of that old man. What're we going to do about him?"

"Make the right offer."

"I already offered him the moon."

Sloshing Coke on my desk, I slumped down in my chair. "Try an apartment."

There was a silence of cigars. Lombard had played out the scene so many times in my presence I could see him at work, snipping the end, firing up, pinching a shred of tobacco off his lip. "Whatta you mean, an apartment?"

"Sweeten the pot one more time. Add an apartment, walking distance from the new restaurant, and he'll accept your offer. I'm ninety-nine percent sure." I wasn't even ten percent sure, but a free apartment in Cambridge would be an astounding concession. Nino was stubborn, but not a fool.

"Ninety-nine percent is not a guarantee."

"It's close. Shall I bring him the offer?"

"I gotta look at the numbers. We're talking a lot of money for a place near Harvard Square." Now he was inhaling, a nicotine smile gliding across his face. "What the hell. Okay. But it's my final offer. I need everything signed by Friday."

"I'll do my best."

"So far, your best hasn't been good." That did it for good-bye.

I immediately relayed this conversation to Nino, who listened as far as "free apartment," but cut me off when I got to "lease."

"No time to talk. Benny's minding the stove."

I swiveled toward the arched windows and stared at the sky. "Lombard wants your answer by five o'clock today." That fib would give Nino a way to come out on top by dickering past the deadline. "Think about it."

"Have supper with me," he said. "Benny can run things while we eat."

"I have plans for dinner."

"Susie! You got a date?"

"It's business. I thought you couldn't talk now."

"Here's what you do. Bring this…this…"

"Client."

"Bring the client here."

"Mr. Renfrow won't want to socialize. He's the one whose assistant was murdered."

Nino *tsked* a brief note of sympathy, then said, "Beh, the client can wait at the bar while you and I talk private."

I sighed, every inch a battle. "Nino, if I come in with my client, I want you to say hello and goodbye and nothing in between."

"Have I ever interfered in your life?"

"You hated Gil and let him know it."

"Gil was a bum."

"He wasn't." He was the love of my life.

"Sorry," Nino spoke softly, for him. "But I never said a bad word to that new guy."

"You cross-examined Michael like he was a crooked cop. Twice burned, thrice shy."

"What's that supposed to mean?"

"It means lay off my date."

"I thought it was business."

"It is."

He chuckled.

I picked up my laundry, the purple dress and a couple of business suits on hangers, the rest compressed in bundles suggesting mail-order treats. The reality was thin and worn and out of date. In two years of solo practice, I hadn't bought anything new except emergency duct tape for hems and safety pins for buttons.

Back at the Beemer, I dumped everything on the seat, and in the muzzy interior light the purple dress glimmered like phosphorescent mold. Releasing the brake, I headed for the Chestnut Hill Mall. A businesslike dress for dinner with Chaz shouldn't be too expensive, and chances were good I'd be keeping his fat retainer. What did a few bucks matter in the end? Torie's Jaguar hadn't saved her.

Near the corner of Grant Street, I slowed to a crawl. From here, I could turn right for the mall or continue on home, leaving plenty of time for a soothing soak in my clawfoot tub. I shifted to first, riding the clutch and arguing with myself.

The case against shopping: life is short, use it wisely.

The case for shopping: life is short, go for broke.

I turned right and drove fast, before the contradiction paralyzed me. A shower would soothe me enough and, what the hell, so would new underwear.

I parked illegally and sprinted for the shops where I charged up khakis and skirts, blouses and tops, designer shoe knockoffs, plain cotton briefs and a few frilly ones. I even found a faux-biker shirt with cunning zippers, and an ice blue dress that wasn't totally unbusiness-like. By five I was ready for bed. On my new Porthault sheets. Sleeping alone, I needed top quality *something* wrapped around me.

On my way out, I drove past a dumpster and wrestled with an impulse masquerading as thought. Why not give myself a completely fresh start? I parked, and pulled my laundry off the back seat. At the dumpster I paused with my hand on the lid. I was in Chestnut Hill, a choosy place where expectations and entitlement ran high. Maybe my old things weren't good enough for *this* dumpster. An iridescent fly buzzed past my head. Oh, hell. I tossed everything in and drove away. Light and free.

Chaz arrived promptly at seven, his SUV so high off the ground I had trouble climbing up in my new five inch Louboutin knockoffs, even with his arm steadying me. I asked how he was coping, and his dark linen jacket wrinkled softly around his shoulders when he shrugged. As we drove, I broke a silence that threatened to become awkward, as if going out for dinner was a game-changer I needed to thwart. "Any progress on the investigation?" I said, and we both relaxed.

"My CFO's in the clear, if that's progress. Bart Bievsky. Did you meet him at Johanna's party?"

"Red suspenders? Drove Torie home?"

"He says he left her inside her condo, five sheets to the wind, but very much alive slumped on a sofa. On his way out he passed two of her friends who stopped in to say hello. I call that cast iron."

"Unless he went back later and did her in. Or do the police think she was murdered at NGT? Someone put her body in the Jaguar, maybe even killed her there."

"They found signs of struggle, and blood, in her condo, so that's where they're focusing. Lieutenant Benedict admitted as much. Wasn't giving anything else away though."

No. Michael rarely gave anything away, a useful trait in police work that in our relationship had double-locked my heart.

Chaz glanced at me. "I told him you and I were together until one-fifteen or so."

"What did he say to that good news?"

"Not a blinking word, Susan. Just jotted a note and lit a cigarette."

Smoking again, after four months on the wagon. For some reason this pleased me.

Implicitly, after talk of struggle and blood, we agreed to stop discussing the murder. Chaz patted his pocket, the crooked-tooth smile back on his face. "Brought my nominating papers. Picked up quite a few signatures. I'll show you at dinner. Have you thought of a good Italian place? I passed one on Boylston, on my way to your house. Tavola, something."

"Tavola Rustica. One of my clients owns it and, actually, I hope you don't mind, but I promised him I'd stop by."

"Is your client the chef?"

"Chef-owner. Nino Biondi. He's fantastic, but I'd rather not have dinner with him looking over my shoulder. He can be, shall we say, difficult."

Nino was waiting by the door, Tavola almost bare of customers at this hour, which would be peak near Harvard Square. Three couples shared a window table. A solitary man hunched over a paperback, occasionally forking up a strand of badly rolled spaghetti.

After introductions, my oldest and newest clients shook hands, and for several long seconds Nino stared up at Chaz, no doubt reading intentionality into every move Chaz made, including breathing. As they walked into the bar Chaz tilted his head toward Nino who was talking nonstop with his voice and his hands. Benny was barkeep tonight. On that front, at least, all would be well, as long as Chaz didn't order anything more complicated than Scotch, no rocks.

"Where'd you meet up with this one?" Nino said when he joined me at his table, bringing wine and stuffed mushrooms on a tray. He looked tired and annoyed, and I regretted coming here.

"I did not 'meet up' with Chaz Renfrow. He's a new client, and let's talk about your lease." I tasted the wine and recognized Nino's best Barolo, his usual peace offering, though we hadn't yet quarreled. A preemptive move, no doubt.

"I don't like his eyes."

"What's wrong with his eyes?" I briefly closed my own.

"Cold."

"He's a businessman. They all have cold eyes." Except Nino himself of course, and Roddie Baird.

"What's his business?"

"Biotechnology."

"What's that?"

"Gene-splicing. You know, putting different parts of a cell together to make something new."

"Beh." Nino stared sourly at the mushrooms. "Who needs something new?"

Italian folk music played softly through the speakers, cheerful tunes that didn't improve anybody's mood.

"Your lease, Nino. Let me tell Lombard you'll consider moving if he finds you an apartment."

"That man is lying to you."

"Lombard doesn't lie."

"Not Lombard. That one." He jerked his thumb toward Chaz, in deep conversation with Benny, their heads almost touching over the bar. "I can read his face. He is not telling you the truth."

"About what? What are you driving at?"

"I know a liar when I see one. And a user. He wants what they all want, only he don't want to give you nothing back. Pretty young girl like you."

When it came to sex, my half-stand-in grandpa was a suspicious prude. I stared at his hands, freckled with grave spots, clutching medieval ideas that had died out even in Naples.

"And he wants something else besides." Nino went on beating the horse, and I was tempted to tell him Chaz Renfrow didn't interest me. He was too remote, I wanted to say, attentive only on the surface. But my new candidate was none of Nino's business.

"Mr. Renfrow wants advice. He consulted me because I'm a consultant."

"You're a patsy."

I crushed a mushroom inside a napkin and pushed it aside. "Why don't we stick to the lease. I assume you want me to tell Lombard to go fuck himself."

With a sound that startled even the spaghetti twirler two tables away, Nino smacked his glass on the tray. Wine slopped over the side, about five dollar's worth at the eighty dollar price of the bottle. "You are getting a bad mouth, you know that?"

"That's your answer?" I stood up. "Okay. Give me a call when the papers are served. I'll help you find an attorney."

I bent for my bag, but Nino reached over and grabbed my arm. "Sit down till I finish talking to you."

I shoved the table, and the glasses teetered. "You *are* finished, Nino."

In a flash, he dropped his hand. "*Mi dispiace*, Susie. I think I had too much wine. I worry about you."

"Don't. I can take care of myself. I'm leaving now. Anything you want me to say to Peter Lombard?"

Nino blinked his eyes, soft as blue water. "Tell him to go fuck himself."

◇◇◇

Chaz decided the North End wasn't swell enough for my new dress, so we ended up in Charlestown at Marella's, a trendy place I'd never visited. A reed-thin girl in saggy brown silk led us to a table near the door. While we waited for our order, we sipped wine and talked briefly about Telford's political life.

"I'm new to this." Chaz smiled an apology. "It's harder than I thought, concentrating on the campaign after what happened. But I kept my promise." He brought out his papers. "Three hundred signatures, I'm halfway home."

There were six sheets, filled on both sides.

"I'm impressed. How did you do it?"

"Friends in high and low places." He folded the papers back into his breast pocket. "I've got more circulating."

"Just don't cut it too close. Remember that margin for error."

A waiter brought bread and a bowl of olives steeped in fragrant oil. Chaz poured more wine. "This is going to sound crazy, Susan. I know you want to strategize, but I'm suddenly afraid that if I look beyond the nominating petition, I'll jinx myself."

"I stand in awe of the jinx," I confessed. If a hard science man needed a little luck in his life, it wasn't for me to naysay him. I'd start earning my pay after he filed his papers.

Dinner was a two-hour gasp of delight, and when we walked back to the Lexus, my new shoes clicking on the cobblestones, Chaz took my hand. It was after ten, the air superheated and so humid it pressed against my face. The sky was cloudless, the July moon a few days away from full. I'd have to check my Farmer's Almanac for the name. Full Hot Moon, it ought to be. Maybe *I* wanted it, Nino. But it was Michael, not Chaz, that I wanted.

At the car, Chaz surprised me by handing over his keys. "Will you drive? That last glass did me in." He didn't seem tipsy, but he *had* drunk most of the wine, finishing with a double brandy, on top of whatever Benny had served him. I was stone sober, as befitted a lawyer/consultant on a business date.

Compared to my BMW, the Lexus was a soft ride, everything power assisted, automatic transmission. "Shall I take you back to Telford?" I was being polite rather than honest, behavior that had gotten me in trouble more than once. I did not want to drive further than my front door.

"How would you get home? Tell you what. Drive me to the Brookline Marriot. I'll come by your place first thing tomorrow for my car."

If he was disappointed that I didn't offer him a bed, he hid it well. For a man in his cups, he seemed no different than he had Monday night, a little more forthcoming perhaps. While I swung the steering wheel, jumping lanes and sinking into the ride, he told me how much he had enjoyed his chat with Benny. "That was damn good grappa."

"I'm amazed Nino brought it out. He doesn't like you." We were stopped at a light, and I watched for Chaz's reaction. If he could smile off Nino's dislike, he could take on the crabbiest constituent in Telford.

"I gathered as much from the bill. Charged me a cool hundred for two glasses of the stuff. Luckily I had a credit card on me."

I groaned. "Probably thought he'd be cute and put my wine on your tab. See, he teased me about having a date. In Nino's world, the man always pays. I'll fix it."

"Don't. I like your Nino. Feisty old fellow, very protective of you. He warned me off, told me about your jealous boyfriend."

Damn Nino. He had interfered and lied, just because he didn't like Chaz Renfrow's eyes. "There is no boyfriend."

I was shy of telling Chaz my old flame had interviewed him yesterday, as if it would put a wedge between us. Or between Michael and me. Cars began honking, and I absently tried to shift the automatic stick. "The *former* boyfriend dumped me. Sweet, reliable me."

"Throw it into drive," Chaz said. "If he dumped you, guy's a loser."

Chaz's compliment pleased me; too bad I couldn't let the loser know. "I apologize for Nino," I said. "We've become close over the years. He was my first client out of law school, and when I left the firm he came with me. I handle all his business affairs, which naturally makes him think he can boss me around."

"Don't let it bother you, Susan. Nino's old, set in his ways. He seems like a decent man. Benny told me how Nino gave him work when nobody else would hire him. Benny brought out the grappa, by the way."

"Nino *is* decent. Benny's a slow learner, so Nino finds him little chores and does all the rest himself."

"And exhausts himself in the process. My father was a lot like Nino. Salt of the earth, but stubborn, unable to delegate."

A thumbnail sketch of my client.

"I saw Nino bully you tonight, and I think I know why."

"It was about my cussing." But of course it had been about Chaz, all of it. With age, Nino was slipping into stereotype, the enterprising first generation American losing ground to the suspicious Italian tyrant. "He's easily irritated after a few drinks," I said, more casually than I felt. "And he does drink in the evening."

"My father did, too. He died five years ago. Stroke. Dropped dead in his garden, and nobody found his body for days."

"How awful. What about your mother? Friends? Where were you?"

"Switzerland." Chaz flicked the radio on and off, not bothering to search for a station. "My father had no friends, and my mother died when I was eleven. Melanoma, took her in six months. She's why I went into research, to find the cure for cancer. The holy grail."

My eyes held the road, but I felt Chaz's smile. It seemed always to carry two meanings: irony and tenderness, affection and indifference. I stole a glance and this time read calm, and something bitter. The radio erupted again. I hadn't noticed Chaz touch it, but as we neared Brookline he let oldies fill the air. Judy sent in the clowns, Leonard let in some light, then Crystal began to pour out the sad sticky tune my older sister had spoiled for me. Mimi had loved this song and forced me to learn the chords when I was too young to fight back. Brown eyes, blue eyes, how much moaning can a poor girl do? I reached over and turned the radio off.

When we pulled into the hotel turnaround, Chaz spoke again of his father. "Dad never remarried," he said, "and never retired. All his sorrow went into their business. One small nursery became a chain of florist shops. Not long before he died, his doctor told me he'd been weakened by a few small strokes. Instead of helping my poor father cope, I went off to a conference thinking I'd take care of things later."

He moved closer, his arm straddling the back of my seat. "You could say I let my father die. If I'd taken charge of him, he'd still be alive."

Chapter Six

Taking Charge

The bedside phone rang in my ear. Tipped off by a 911 call, police had found Nino unconscious in the alley behind his apartment. Paper shufflers from Falkman Hospital were calling because my name had turned up on documents scattered in front of Tavola's safe.

I raced down empty streets, and as I shifted and steered, the gate between my mind and my feelings swung shut. By the time I parked and pushed through the hospital doors, my lawyer's mask was firmly in place. Business first, forms to fill out, papers to sign, and I took care of it.

Now I watched over Nino, his head swathed in bandages, his skin the color of dust. Plastic tubes drifted down from his nostrils, stirring with each shallow breath. My own face was hot, and a wisp of dizziness sent me stumbling against the bed.

"I'm here, Nino." I spoke loudly because I'd read that unconscious people sometimes respond to a familiar voice.

The IC nurse encouraged me: Mary Foley, a breezy, reassuring name that matched her bedside manner. Mary's hair, freckles, eyes were all the same ruddy chestnut. A wide white headband held back her hair, a starched nurse's cap without all the fuss.

"Is this a coma?" I said.

"No, but the next twenty-four hours will be critical."

"Could he die?"

She picked up Nino's chart. "A man his age, anything could happen."

Her words stung, and I sat rigid in my chair while she checked Nino's pulse. My eye kept wandering to the shape of his body under the sheet. How could that motionless lump be Nino? I wanted to ask Nurse Foley, gatekeeper, if, in her professional opinion, there was such a thing as an immortal soul, but I could see she was too busy for philosophy.

She patted my wrist. "Anything could happen, but probably won't. The CT scan was negative for fractures. No intracranial bleeding. He's a sturdy old fellow. Keep talking to him. Do you both a bit of good."

Around six, I went to the visitor's lounge, pressed my forehead against the window, and watched early morning traffic pulse by in the street below. Someone touched my arm. I turned, astonished to see Chaz. I hadn't heard him, or noticed the sweet spice of his cologne.

"I got your message. Why didn't you have the hotel wake me?" he said.

"At two in the morning? I just wanted to make sure you knew where to find your keys. You shouldn't have come." But I was glad to see him.

"Desk clerk said something about Nino, a robbery. I couldn't go back to Telford without making sure you were all right."

I told him what little I knew from the hospital report. "Nino's unconscious. I've been talking at him. Poor guy probably thinks he's having a nightmare, his lawyer gabbing when all he wants is rest."

"No. He's grateful you're looking after him."

We stood by the window for a few minutes. Then, while Chaz got us coffee from the cafeteria, I called my friends and canceled my Truro weekend.

Back in the ICU, Nurse Foley drew the curtains, giving the space around Nino the feel of a room. Chaz stood beside my chair.

"Nino." I took his hand. "Open your eyes."

Only his tubes moved, breathing in, breathing out.

"Where will he go after he's released?" Chaz asked.

Grateful for all the question implied, I answered without thinking. "Home, of course."

"Alone?"

"I could arrange for care." An expense Nino probably couldn't bear for long.

"Does Nino own his building?"

"Hardly. And his landlord's not the nicest guy in town."

"Who's going to run the restaurant?"

"Tavola could close for a few weeks."

But I knew Lombard would be jumping all over the lease if Nino's restaurant closed. No more sweet talk and high offers. His pals in Inspectional Services would find enough wrong to shutter Tavola for months. Lombard might even sue my shoot-from-the-hip client for slander just to keep the top spinning.

And I was the top. I'd have to hold Lombard at bay. And for what? For a cause I didn't believe in? For a stubborn old paesan who lacked business smarts? Even Chaz's successful father had lost touch with reality at the end. How much more so Nino? Every instinct told me he needed my help to survive.

"Chaz, would your father have sold his business if you'd insisted?"

He moved to a chink in the curtain. "Yes, probably. One thing I am sure of. My father would have been safe living near me. He certainly wouldn't have died all alone." A tight smile drew down the corners of his mouth. "Grand thing, hindsight."

Chaz's story, his voice, began to intrude on my carefully fenced-off feelings. I looked away. I didn't want to see his eyes.

"The worst of it was, I had a chance to intervene and I let it slip through my fingers. A few months before he died, my father gave me power of attorney. He was asking me to take charge. Asking without words, which was the only way he ever asked for anything."

"Not everyone can hear that kind of asking."

A hospital quiet infiltrated the curtained-off space. Chaz let the silence go on for so long it felt like an expectation, like he was asking me for something, without words, but when I looked, there was no asking in his eyes. No irony either. Concern for me, compassion, maybe. "I know you're upset," he said. "Not only because of…" He gestured toward the bed. A bead of fluid dripped from a pouch down the line into Nino's puffy hand.

"Even before this happened I could see you were worried. Is Nino in some kind of trouble? I couldn't help noticing he had almost no customers last night."

My empty cup caught his eye, and he nested it inside his own on the bed table, a gesture that to my tired mind spoke of solidarity, shared purpose, the comfort of friendship. "What's going on, Susan? The vacancies in his building…place looks like a ghost town."

"Business problems. Nino's landlord is renovating and wants Tavola out. He's offered to buy back the lease for a sum that would settle Nino in comfort for a long time, but Nino won't budge."

"And you think he should?"

"No question in my mind."

"Do you have power of attorney?"

"Yes, but…" But what? My seventy-three year old half-stand-in grandpa lay unconscious in a hospital bed, unable to think, let alone make decisions for himself. His welfare was completely in my hands.

"Want my advice?"

I shook my head. "You've already given it to me, Chaz. I know what I've got to do."

"You've got to take charge," he said softly.

"Yes."

◇◇◇

Lombard's cigar sliced through the air, a baton at the end of a tedious symphony. "Congrats, Susan. You drove a hard bargain." He shook his head and smiled, humble, defeated. "Wish you worked for me. I could use a tough little lawyer like you."

His good humor and boorish compliments told me I might have given one more turn of the screw, but I contented myself with a few minor changes to the buy-out and the new lease. We wanted a Viking range; permission to sublet; utilities paid by landlord. I initialed every page, and so did Lombard.

In lieu of an actual Cambridge apartment, Lombard added a monthly sum equal to what he was willing to shell out for one. This money, plus the sublet value of the Harvard Square restaurant, would keep Nino in comfort for the next seven years. In seven years, Nino would be eighty, his savings untouched and ready. Beyond that, nothing.

At ten o'clock, I signed Susan Callisto for Nino Biondi and drove straight home. The Truro weekend had forced me to clear my decks, and now its cancellation left me free to skip the office today. Sleep was what I wanted.

◇◇◇

"He opened his eyes after you left," Nurse Foley told me, when I phoned her a few hours later, after the failed nap. "Closed them right away and didn't speak, but he's more alert now. Heartbeat strong and steady."

Her good news turned my exhaustion into a compulsion to clean my apartment, the top half of a "painted lady" with pointy hat roofs and bow-window bosoms, high Victorian charm for a Californian. And high maintenance. Routine scrubbings took me to cornices and nooks, and hours later, nooks took me to supper, an osso buco from Tavola, in my freezer since December. As it bubbled in the microwave, I wondered if Nino's care packages would keep coming from Cambridge, or if this were my last osso buco.

Around nine, Chaz called and praised me for taking charge.

"I'm having second thoughts," I said. "Nino's going to be royally ticked off at me."

"He'll get over it. You did the right thing, Susan. You guaranteed his future. In the long run, he'll thank you."

Guaranteed his future. I felt better after Chaz said that.

◇◇◇

Slowly, slowly, Torie raised a white-fringed arm and pointed a talon at me. Her red mouth fell open. A gull's scream ripped through my head.

I jolted awake, certain Torie's cry was a warning from my unconscious. But of what? Heart thudding, I reached over and turned off the lamp that had burned by my bed all night. Friday was dawning, pale light in my window and crunch time for Chaz, whose nominating petition had to be filed by five p.m.

On my way to the hospital, I stopped at Nino's apartment to collect a few comforts from home, letting myself in with the key he had given me after his partner died. First, without permission, I collected the photo scraps for restoration. So much of Nino's fatalism was bound up in the cost of setting things right. If I paid for the photos, he'd complain, but I was certain he'd appreciate my welcome home gift. From Tavola's freezer I grabbed a container of chicken soup, and by seven-thirty, I was back at the hospital.

Mary Foley was at her station, same headband, same freckles, as if a day hadn't passed. "He's making great progress. If everything looks good on his eleven o'clock scan, I'll bring him your soup." She patted my hand. "Didn't I tell you anything could happen?"

We crossed the room, and she poked her head around Nino's curtain. "Don't get too comfortable, Mr. B. We need your bed for someone who's really sick." Before Nino could snap back a reply, she moved off.

"Very funny," he said as I came in. "Nobody wants me out of here more than I do."

A breakfast tray took up most of the bed table, and while he worried his oatmeal with a plastic spoon, I examined his coffee. If it were any weaker, it'd be dead.

"Can you remember anything about the attack?"

"What're you, a cop now, like your dopey boyfriend?"

"Can't remember, huh?" I smirked, just to annoy him, letting the reference to Michael pass. Nino ticked off was Nino on the mend.

"I remember right up to getting bonked. No more customers came after you and that client left, so we closed, cleaned,
prepped. Benny goes home, I have an anisette, and I'm in bed
by eleven. Later, something wakes me up, and I go check it out.
When I open my eyes again, I'm stuck in this place. *Cazzo!* The
one thing I need to remember…who woke me up…and I can't.
But there had to be three, four of 'em to take *me* down."

"Did Benny hear anything? Doesn't he live across the alley
from you?"

"How should I know what he heard? Kid's probably wondering where I am. Maybe you could call him." He looked around.
"Where's that lying nurse? She promised me real coffee and toast
an hour ago."

"You're on hospital time. Ten minutes seems like an hour."

He scrunched his face. *You do it*, those wrinkles said.

I sighed and picked up my hobo bag. Twenty minutes later I
was back with crusty rolls and fresh espresso from the latte bar
across the street. The breakfast tray hadn't moved, and when I
plopped the goody bag next to the bowl of congealed goo, Nino
pounced on the coffee like a dog on truffles.

"You're a good friend to me, Susie."

His words pinched my heart. Would he still call me friend
after I told him about the lease?

"When you leave, I want you to go to the restaurant. Put
a sign in the window. Say Tavola will be open on Sunday, just
for lunch. Be sure to let Benny know." Caffeine was pumping
through his system, fueling the grandiose plans.

"Forget the restaurant. You'll be lucky to get out of here by
Sunday. They want to do more tests."

His hands sprang up and danced in the air. "No more tests!
Sunday I'll be cookin' with gas. Pasta, salad, two different soups.
Pastries from Salem Market. Benny can do most of the work.
Lunch'll be easy."

I would have to tell him; he seemed strong enough. There were
dark pools under his eyes, but apart from the bandaged head and a
few bruises, I'd seen him look worse after a night of heavy drinking.

"*Zi' Nino*, I wasn't sure when you'd wake up. You looked so...so..."

"*'Ndundolit'*."

"Crappy, I was going to say."

"Same difference. However you say it, this sucker is killing me." He touched his bandaged lump, which provoked the usual short-lived bluster. "I *know* Lombard set me up, and this time I'm gonna prove it. Feels like my memory's beginning to come back, and if it doesn't, I'll *make* it."

"Nino, listen to me. Lombard and I signed the buy-out agreement yesterday. And a new lease for Cambridge."

He opened his mouth, and I rushed on, babbling the good news before he could tell me just how bad it was.

"I really took him to the cleaners. On top of everything else, I got utilities out of him."

"I do not believe what I'm hearing." Like a traffic cop, he put up a palm, the frown on his face slowly turning to rage, and I raced through that red red light.

"You were unconscious. Nobody knew when you'd wake up. I signed without telling Lombard you were in the hospital with your head bashed in. If he knew, he'd have padlocked Tavola and put you on the street."

"I trusted you." He fell back on his pillow, hair sticking up in inky strands around his bandaged head. In a faltering voice, he asked, "Can you undo what you did?"

"Maybe. I...you could get another lawyer. But the agreement...I had authority to sign for you."

"So Lombard won. His thugs beat the crap out of me and you let him win."

"I protected your interests. There was nobody but me to take care of you."

"How much did he pay you to do me in?"

"Don't insult me, Nino." I worked my fingers through the straps of my bag. "I did the right thing. You were half-dead."

"Better I died." His chin trembled. "You're just like the rest of them. Traitor! Get outta my sight!" He pounded his fist, and the breakfast tray toppled, coffee and oatmeal splattering the blanket and my skirt. "Get out!"

I fled, my hobo bag slamming against my hip. In the lobby I wrenched my shoulder against the glass exit doors, and one of my sandals came apart at the thong. If there had ever been a gate between my mind and my feelings, a torrent of tears now washed it clean away.

◇◇◇

Work. It had sheltered me in the past and would do so now. I paid the parking lot attendant and let the car drive itself while I planned the rest of my day. Before anything, I would take physical exercise, which would lead to a Zen-like state of detachment. Instead of taking charge, my ego would take a powder, and after that, what was left of me would keep busy with clients and candidates. By midnight, sleep would capture whatever husk of self was still blowing in the wind. Tomorrow I would after all go to Truro, and by Sunday evening, I'd be my old self.

Self?

That's not what I meant.

Or was it?

I found myself in my driveway, so I used the side entrance. From the kitchen, I kept my promise to Roddie and left Lauren a message to pick up the voter surveys by noon, and that I'd drop over around five, to help her set up. Roddie would like me to pitch in. Not part of the deal, but I had no plans for tonight.

After packing office clothes in my bag, I changed into gym sweats and tied back my hair with bungee bands, yellow for cheerfulness. Like a Zen archer stringing his bow, I laced my sneakers in tight even rows, then took the first halting steps on my journey to self-abnegation. They led straight to the kitchen, where there was just enough coffee for the sixteen-ounce mug. The caffeine rush came quickly. My mind began to chug and whir, not the Zen way, but I was a novice. I ate the last banana, grabbed my bag and scooted down the back stairs, agile as a Slinky and twice as wired.

Chapter Seven

Babes and Fools

At Spaal's, I paid the day rate and went directly to the treadmill Lauren had used, stepping into a rhythm that was far too brisk for an out-of-shape desk jockey. After five minutes, my legs were flaccid bands, only pumping because I insisted. And I did insist. I intended to achieve a little Zen inner peace before I left Spaal's, if it killed me.

The piped-in music switched from sad violins to heavy metal to synthesized jazz, but I thudded to my own beat, my mind roaming to Nino's lease, Chaz's smile, Torie's nightmare cry. I began to trot, using the pain in my legs to shut them out.

Nino had asked if I could undo what I had done, and I'd given him the only answer I knew, a firm maybe. But maybe takes longer than yes, and time was Lombard's ally. I needed advice. I decided to call my old boss and mentor Al Volpe today. During my unsatisfying years at the firm, Al and his wife had taken me under their wing, and we were still friends.

Damp hair coiled down my neck, but I kept pounding the roller belt, pushing stray locks off my hot face. How had Lauren stayed cool while she sweated? Cool Lauren, warm Roddie. Opposites attract, but after awhile, the tension must be unbearable. Michael and I were alike in our armored hearts, our stubbornness. A tendency to pun under stress. But if sameness repelled, why did I miss him? There was a Zen lesson here, if I could find it.

◇◇◇

I drove to Waltham under one of those tricky New England skies, black clouds to the west, haze to the north. There were rumbles of thunder, brief bursts of sun, and for a few minutes rain pelted my roof. When it let up I craned my neck for the rainbow that sometimes arched across the sky on days like this. A pickup truck passed on my right, tires snicking down the wet road with a sound of zippers in silk. No rainbows today.

My office staff…me…had neglected to replenish the coffee, so I brewed a pot of hot water and tried to reach Al Volpe, who was not at his desk. A yearning for Michael swept over me then, Michael as he used to be, funny, wise, the loner who puzzled and beguiled me. There was enough tea for one small pot which I drank staring out the window at the busy street below. Not a single plain blue sedan looked like Michael's.

When the gentle jolt of theanine lifted my mood, I checked in with Deirdre who took a long time to answer and sounded tired. "Thank God it's Friday," she said, and I made a feeble joke about napping on the job. She actually laughed. "Odette Brenner left you a message. Wants to consult about Roddie Baird's campaign."

Disappointment threaded through my veins. "I don't suppose anyone else called?"

Deirdre understood me only too well. "Would you like to talk about him?"

"I would not. Talk is futile."

"It's a step toward health, and your Michael is a wound that won't heal."

"Michael is not my anything. I…oh never mind, Deir. I gotta go." I hung up, too abruptly, I realized, wishing I could stop using haste and humor to cover my gloom. Maybe I was Zen-proof. But I was grateful for Deirdre's concern, for her almost professional mercy. I should have been more cordial, offered her an imaginary cup of tea.

I dialed Odette.

"Susan," she said in the hearty voice I remembered from Monday's finance meeting, "you do return your calls. Roddie never does."

"Of course I do. Roddie's out of town until Sunday afternoon."

"Nobody tells me anything. Listen dear, I'll be quick. I'm on my way out. I want to move Roddie's money to a different bank. Any reason I shouldn't?"

"No, but why do you want to?"

"They don't pay interest. Can you believe it?"

Banks never pay interest on local campaign accounts, I explained. "Too little money for too little time."

"Well, I think eighteen thousand dollars deserves some interest and I'm going to get it."

"Eighteen thousand! Already? Last time I looked, Roddie had twelve hundred."

"My committee has been busy."

I guessed what was going on. Under cover of his alderman's race, Roddie was building his war chest for Congress. "You *are* keeping a record of every contribution over fifty dollars, aren't you?"

There was a silence, then she said, "I think we've been a little lax in that department."

"God, Odette. Put notes in a shoebox. You can organize later. But one way or another, keep meticulous records. You better sit down with Roddie and reconstruct."

"I will. We will. You and I should get together. I could use a little help with the paperwork."

"How about this afternoon?"

"Perfect! I've got an office at the Bibliotecque des Beaux Arts. Can you meet me there at three? We'll have coffee and *petits beurres* and you can tell me what to do."

Telling Odette what to do was not how it worked, I had a feeling. She looked like a kindly earth mother, but I suspected her warmth flowed off hot steel.

"Give me directions, *s'il vous plait*," I said.

"*En français?*"

"Better not. I don't have much French."

"That's all right. Nobody at the Biblioteque does either."

Real estate closings help pay the rent, but privacy law is my passion and it took up most of the next several hours. I was charting case law, scouring the Web, surveying the contradictions. All was in flux, but the concept itself derived from Justice Brandeis and his landmark opinion defining a right to be left alone. Lord save us from meddlers. Nino, I thought sadly, would agree.

On my way to Odette, I stopped at Waltham Color Lab where, now thinking of peace offerings, I left Nino's photographs for restoration.

Just before three, I found the Biblioteque des Beaux Arts, two pretty townhouses on Yarboro Street in a neighborhood of historic brick and stone mansions with tiny front gardens and wrought iron fences. That endangered species, the Boston Brahmin, still dwelt here, though many of the houses had been converted to condos and flats. Odette had said I could park in the alley, which turned out to be as narrow as a medieval donkey path. By the time I wedged my car between two others, I was late, and I hate to be late. It's disrespectful, my mother had instilled in her daughters, unless a meteor struck or you lost your underwear.

I marched through the leaded glass entrance, my new chino skirt flapping around my calves. "I have an appointment with Odette Brenner," I said to a surly girl at reception who pretended not to understand me. "Odette Brenner," I said twice more, then bellowed "Odette!" inner peace a lost cause for the moment.

The girl stared at me with the blank beady eyes of a *pomme de terre*. "Odette?"

I was damned if I was going to answer "*Oui,*" one of my actual French words. "Yes," I said.

"*Oooo-hoo!*" High above the reception desk, a familiar voice, lilting and assured, came spiraling down the oval stairwell. "*Su-zanne!*"

I looked up. A foreshortened Odette was leaning over the banister. "I'm on the fourth floor," she called down to me.

Comprehension dawned on the receptionist's face. "Ah, Odette!"

Her office was a small room off a narrow hall lined with dozens of cases of champagne, left over from Biblioteque events, she explained to my wondering stare. "The director is a hoarder." She shrugged, very Gallic under the circumstances.

I settled myself in an armchair near the cookies. "Do you work for the Bibliotecque?"

"I'm writing a book about my French grandfather. They've got a small but worthy research library here." Hovering over the brass table-tray, she lifted a pumpkin-shaped pot and poured the best coffee I had ever tasted. "My husband Stan gave a lot of money to the Biblioteque, so they let me use this office. Not that I accomplished anything literary today."

She took her lipstick-stained cup to a desk heaped with envelopes and papers, closing the door on her personal life. "Roddie's contributors are legion. I broke out every name and dollar I could identify."

We dug in together, and at the end of a long hour, more than half the money was accounted for, every paper tucked into a tickler file. I offered to set up a simple finance chart, using my spreadsheet software. This meant time at my office tonight, but after I paid my visit to Roddie's wife, I'd have nothing to look forward to but reading in bed, followed by insomnia.

"Susan, you're a trooper." Odette handed me the file. "I'm sure Roddie has more names at home."

"I'll get them from Lauren." I took a last look around Odette's comfy lair. "If you like, I'll manage the data until you get your own computer."

"Computer? Not in my lifetime, dear. An abacus, maybe." The slant of her brow made her look suddenly French, a Simone Signoret without the cigarette. "Print me a paper copy. No hurry. I've got a closet full of shoeboxes."

We came downstairs into the grand hall now swirling with visitors to an art opening in the salon. Gilded rooms, people in linen and silk, for a brief moment I'd stepped into a world where politics and murder were elegant abstractions, if they existed at all. What a safe place to escape to, I thought, feeling all the more troubled and insecure as we worked our way to the exit.

Odette walked with me to my car. "I'll have more names in a few days," she said. "John Snow will help me remember when he gets around to returning my calls." I tried to picture Snow, a professional money manager, from Roddie's finance meeting. Blancmange over wingtips.

"Don't forget thank you notes to every contributor, even the ten dollar sports," I said. "And please, tell Roddie no bulk mailings. People like to be thanked first class."

"Roddie can be a penny-pinching spendthrift *fool*," Odette said. Her affection took the sting out, but her insight was spot-on. The Roddie I'd come to know wore layers of leather patches over the holes in his jackets…and handmade shirts. He drank Peet's coffee from San Francisco…and no-name cola from the discount store. He adored his BlackBerry, but his chunky black home-office phone made me want to warble *oper-ay-tor* every time I saw it.

"Make him order those customized stamps from the Post Office," I said, "printed with his name and a campaign slogan." But not his picture, I was too superstitious for that. Only the dead should be celebrated on stamps.

Odette watched me advance by millimeters out of the alley. Just before I turned onto Yarboro, she called after me, "Susan, when does the chairwoman start having fun?"

"After the campaign," I shouted back. "Dining out on your war stories."

War stories. My own were fresh wounds, especially my Nino story, and in the absence of Al Volpe, I felt a sudden urge to confide in this no-nonsense woman of the law. Former judge Odette Brenner might be willing to opine about what was irrevocable and what might be undone. I yanked up the emergency brake. "Got a minute? I need your advice about a confidential legal matter."

Settled in the passenger seat, she listened while I told her about the lease, an un-Zen-like catch in my throat. "I made a huge mistake. Nino will never trust me again."

"Mistake? You signed without his permission." She put her blunt hands on her knees. "Unprofessional behavior, Susan."

This was not the weary comment of a bored judge. It was a slap that left a handprint. I sprang out of my slouch. "Nino was unconscious. I made a judgment call."

Her poker face dissolved, and her sleepy Signoret eyes brimmed with humor. "You *can* stand on your hind legs! I was beginning to fear for Roddie's campaign. And for you, dear. My advice, I am sorry to say, is to wait and see." She got out of the car and leaned in at the window. "As soon as you said his name, I remembered Peter Lombard. In my day, he was a relentless litigator."

"Still is."

"I'll give him a call. Who knows? There might be a rabbit left in my poor old hat. But unless Mr. Lombard changes his mind, I don't have to tell you, it'll be difficult to overthrow the new agreements."

So the answer to Nino's question remained a firm maybe, but I thanked Odette and headed up Yarboro, glad I'd passed her little test, eased in spite of her caution. For once talking seemed to work, better than treadmills anyway. I wondered about that French grandfather, if reconstructing him at her desk was how Odette calmed her own angst. Surely she had some behind that brilliant smile.

I downshifted, edging onto the river road. There were faster ways to Lauren's house, but I liked to keep an eye on the Charles. The way it tacked to the ocean through miles of urban clutter made me feel safe, like I had a means of escape. I chugged past sailboats, the Hatch Shell, fishermen casting just for the hell of it. The Publick Theatre materialized, and in a burst of optimism, I parked near the risers and dialed Falkman Hospital on my cell. It was time to rear up on my hind legs and talk to Nino.

"He's gone," an ICU voice, not Mary Foley's, said. "Signed himself out this morning."

"That's impossible!" An unmufflered car tore past, and I shouted over the roar. "How could you let that battered old man leave?"

"Excuse me, Miss. Patients are not prisoners. Mr. Biondi was ambulatory. He called a friend, and off he went."

"You should have notified me before you discharged him."

"Who're you?"

"Susan Callisto, his attorney." Was.

"Please hold, and I'll transfer you to the business office."

But before the voicemail wringer flattened me, I pressed "off", my anger already fading.

I punched in Nino's number, and Benny answered.

"It's Susie. Can Nino come to the phone?"

"He's…" Silence. I could almost hear Benny's brain chugging. "He's sleeping in the big chair. He can't talk to you."

"How did you get home?"

"Taxi. I paid with my own money."

Benny barely got by on Tavola meals and minimum wage. "I'm sure Nino will pay you back as soon as he's better."

"I don't want it back! I don't want it back!"

"You're very generous." Benny's emotions were loose cannons, and I spoke softly to his pride. "Nino is lucky to have a good friend like you. Will you call me if he needs anything?" I gave him my numbers and hoped he was actually writing them down. "When Nino wakes up, tell him I love him."

"I better not, Susie. He don't love you no more."

The honesty of babes and fools.

Chapter Eight

Shadow Man

The front door was wide open. Roddie's little girl, in a pink and white sundress, marched across the hall singing and waving a paper banner.

"Hello, Delia," I said.

"I'm helping Mommy." Her banner was a sheet of blank labels. With a delicate flick of her fingernail, she peeled one off and smoothed it over her shin.

"Are you mailing yourself?"

She giggled. "We drawed pictures in camp, and I mailed mine to my daddy. He's in Colorado."

"Is camp fun?"

She nodded, silky hair flying, and stuck a label on my wrist. She jabbed it with a fuchsia crayon, and the rich smell of Crayola made me wish I was a kid again.

"Susan, I just got your message." Lauren came in through the dining room, wearing a sleeveless country-print dress that showed off the shoulders-by-Spaal, the taut slender arms. "I was afraid we'd missed you. We're just back from supper."

"MacDonald's!" Delia shouted. "I had chicken nuggets." She scrawled the air with her crayon. "And *french fries!*"

"I didn't feel like cooking. The boys are with my mother in Maine. Roddie's in Colorado." Lauren's cheeks actually reddened.

"I didn't mean to nag, but I promised Roddie I'd remind you about the deadline."

"Roddie's a worrier. I picked up the surveys with an hour to spare."

"The worry wart should have left you his van. Twenty-five thousand brochures in the Mazda must have been a tight fit."

"A friend helped me. Roddie had no idea there'd be so many boxes. And now this." She led me through to the dining room where I'd already glimpsed the yew wood table covered with surveys and dozens of cartons on the floor.

"Bring the printed labels, I'll get you started." I pulled up a chair, and Delia circled the table, patting the wobbly stacks.

"You were at my house before."

She knelt on the chair next to mine, and I gave her a few surveys to mark with her crayon.

"Good job," I told her. A little encouragement now, and by the time Roddie was ready for Congress, Delia would be running the show.

She studied the slashes of color. "I know," she crowed.

Lauren and I exchanged smiles, then I groaned and got to work while Lauren went to make iced tea, a delaying tactic no doubt. From my chair, I could see most of the kitchen. Enameled pots dangled off a ceiling rack that swayed every time Lauren walked past. "Is that hanging from Roddie's mountain rope?" I asked when she returned with tea, apple juice, and three tall glasses of ice.

"Yes, indeedy." She poured juice for Delia and tea for me, ice cubes cracking when she hit them with a spout of boiling pekoe. "Before he left, he ran around the house testing it on everything in sight. He really likes the way it looks on the rack." She laughed and rolled her eyes. "Even gave some to Delia's camp for their swings. When Roddie gets obsessional, I just stand by till he lets go. Like this interest in politics."

"You think he'll let go?"

"I think he'll try for alderman, and if he wins, Congress. One or two terms each. It's the game that interests Roddie."

Me, too, I wanted to say. I loved grassroots campaigning, the analyzing, the strategizing. I even loved composing lists and thinking about the soap operas behind them: Will ninety-five year old Nathaniel Loveland be voting this year? Why are all the voters on Oakman Circle unaffiliated?

While Lauren watched, I sorted carrier routes, number by stupefying number, but before I could demonstrate how to unstick labels and attach them to surveys in a single motion, she'd devised an efficient sweep of her own. Her movements had economy and grace, two qualities that don't always go together; in minutes she'd labeled and stacked a neat pile of twenty-five. Then her cell phone rang, and she carried it into the den.

Delia and I worked steadily with our crayons and elastics, and by the time Lauren came back, we'd organized the first lot. "Um, Susan?" She gripped the back of a chair, her color high, as if she'd just chugged a secret tipple from a hidden bottle. "Are you busy tonight?"

I hedged in case she wanted a fourth at bridge, or yet more help with the surveys. "I'll be at my office most of the evening. Was there something you needed?"

"Oh, not really." Her eyes strayed from my face to Delia to the surveys. "Do you think we could delay the mailing? The boys won't be home till next week...and...well, they really wanted to help."

"Next week's okay." I hefted my bag, wondering if she'd meant to say something else. "One thing that does need doing quickly is the finance report. Odette thinks Roddie's got more contributors' names here at home."

"Let's have a look."

Delia followed us into the den, sucking her thumb with a noise like a plunger while Lauren rooted through Roddie's desk. Dozens of names turned up. "Great," I said. "I'll work them into the list."

Back in the hall, Lauren opened the front door; immediately, Delia yelled, "Don't go!"

"I'm not going anywhere, sweetie." Lauren pulled her close.

"Not you. Her." Delia pointed a damp thumb at me.

"I second that," Lauren said. "Why don't you stay?" She and Delia stood in the doorway, looking so lonesome in the waning light I almost changed my mind.

"How about a margarita? I've got organic tequila and fresh limes."

"Could I take a raincheck?" I patted my bag. "If I don't get Roddie's finances organized tonight, I'll lose my momentum."

Outside, the sun was an orange ball streaked with pencil clouds, the air more humid than before this morning's drizzle. From the steps, Lauren and Delia watched me get into my car. When I looked back, they were still there, leaning into each other. I tootled my horn. Lauren waved, then stopped to smooth her daughter's baby-fine iridium hair.

On Commonwealth Ave. something pink on a telephone pole snagged my eye: *Froy*.

At the office, I plugged Roddie into my quirky system for tallying donations and donors and manipulating the data into various purposeful lists. Some would call it a spreadsheet. I liked to think of it as my random access attic, in two dimensions. By the time I closed up shop for the night, I'd done everything but print a copy for Odette because I'd run out of paper, which was something that never happened to consultants with secretaries.

Twenty minutes later, I was in my driveway, happy to see low wattage timer-lights in every downstairs window, which meant my landlords had gone to Vermont for the weekend, or longer. Maybe long enough for me to grub up my rent without touching Chaz's retainer.

Though I could have parked in their space, out of habit I pulled beside the hedge, a dense border of evergreens that hid the bungalow on the other side. The entire neighborhood seemed abandoned tonight, dimly lit and eerily quiet. Even the cicadas were silent, and as I trudged past the lawn, I was glad for the roof lamps that popped on and lit my way.

At the bottom of the driveway a shape glimmered in the moonlight: the garden gate, as I perfectly well knew, but I halted in my tracks like Bambi scenting a lion. The evergreens started to churn, and I reared back, ready to race for my car, just as two cream-colored cats streaked down the driveway: Pasha and Soukie, the neighbors' Persians. They flickered in and out of the hedge like heat lightning, finally scuttling under the gate. Damn cats.

At the side door, I dug out my key. A familiar scent, cloves or carnations, stirred in the air near my head. I started to turn.

"Don't move." Iron fingers gripped my neck. "Unlock the door."

"Who are you? Get away from me!"

"Open the door! Do it!"

I jabbed my elbow back, and a fist punched my spine. "Susan," the voice hissed in my ear. "Do it or I'll *shred* you." Something sharp ripped across my shirt, and now my breast was on fire. The key fell from my fingers and hit the sidewalk with a sound that burned through my veins.

"Pick it up."

I couldn't breathe or move.

"Pick it up or I'll kill you!" He dug his fingers and thumb into the hollows beneath my ears, and I closed my eyes against the pain.

"Let me go!"

"Shut up! Shut up! Unlock the door!"

I grabbed his wrist and threw myself forward. "Help me!" I screamed, my life a fraying thread in furious hands. "Please! Somebody help me!"

Voices. Doors banging. "What's going on? Where's Pasha and Soukie?"

Suddenly released, I collapsed, and my attacker vanished before my neighbors made it around the hedge. They called 911, and while I waited in their kitchen, sipping coffee, pressing towels to my wounded breast, letting Pasha and Soukie nose my ankles, terror faded and survivor's euphoria seeped in. Luck was with me tonight. I had resisted and lived.

"He tried to force me inside," I told the police when they arrived.

"Can you describe him?" The droopy-jowled older one talked; the younger one took notes.

"He kept behind me. I didn't see anything." I was certain of nothing, not his height, or the scent of his cologne, or if his voice was familiar, or if he *was* a he. "I did notice that his wrists were bony. But his hands were ferocious." Had the same hands murdered Torie?

"Anything else?"

"He knew my name. This wasn't a random attack." I told them about finding Torie's body, and the note keeper wrote it down.

Though it hurt like hell, the cut wasn't deep, and I refused an ambulance. So they drove me to Falkman's ER where I cracked jokes while a harried physician gave me a tetanus booster and brought out the sewing kit. How many doctors does it take to patch one small breast? I couldn't come up with a punch line.

Back home, survivor's euphoria clung like a second skin. Even so, I roamed the apartment, checking closets and cupboards, wedging chairs under doorknobs. After I'd battened my hatches, I swallowed a pill from the hospital and crawled into bed, where my bruised spine shifted for a sweet spot that didn't exist.

While I waited for the pill to work, a scent like roses drifted in from the window, along with a faint sound of crying, and curtains like gauzy bandages billowed in a cold night wind. Shivering, I struggled out of bed and took down the fan and looked outside. The air was hot and silent and smelled like grass. Then it hit me. There was no garden on this side of the house, no roses heavy with scent, no curtains on the windows. No one crying but me. I'd fallen asleep and dreamed a Demerol dream.

And if I had died?

From my night table I took out the photo *Earth Trek Magazine* sent me three years ago, after Nepalese militia found Gil's backpack in a village hut and human bones in a stream. I studied the crowded street in Kathmandu, in the foreground Gil's tired, unsmiling face. His dark eyes drew me in. Death brought him near tonight.

Chapter Nine

Him Again

Time rattled past like a freight train, and I was the track, beaten, bruised, flat on my back. Fires raged inside my breast, and I couldn't shake off my dreams. The telephone rang, and I picked up slowly, coming fully awake at the sound of Michael's voice.

"I heard. Are you all right?" Diffident, but not altogether cold.

"I survived."

He waited a beat then said, "Why take that tone, Susan?"

"I'm not feeling too great. What can I do for you?"

"We have to talk, about the attack on you, and…look, Charles Renfrow is dead."

I stared at the bare window, the sun shining so fiercely it doubled my pain, the pressure of gauze on every tight ugly stitch. Chaz dead? It made no sense, didn't even have the logic of dreams. We'd talked yesterday, or was it the day before? Or had I been sleeping for weeks?

"What…what day is it?"

"Sunday morning," he said. "I'll be right over."

I'd slept round the clock, but sleep hadn't mended me. I reached for the Demerol, and half an hour later, when Michael rang the bell, I was able to float down and let him in. We faced each other at the foot of the stairs.

"Susan," he said. Nothing else. Tuesday's remoteness was gone from his eyes, so gentle now I might have fallen into his arms. He moved toward me.

I stepped back, my heel hitting a riser. "What happened... tell me."

There is no way to soften murder, and Michael didn't try. "He was strangled."

The pill kept me from flinching, but not from seeing the picture he sketched in quick dark strokes: Chaz sprawled across his desk, all irony gone from his eyes. I leaned on the banister, then sank to a stair. "When?" I whispered.

"We're not sure." Michael sat on the tread below mine and told me how Chaz's housekeeper had found him at six this morning. How some kind of cord or rope had abraded his neck. How the medical examiner determined he'd been dead at least seven hours, and maybe much longer. "Right now, that's all we know." He shifted, and his warm hand found my bare foot. "Ice," he said. "Let's go up."

In the living room, I nested on the sofa among pillows he propped around me. He settled himself near the defunct fireplace in the worn brown chair he'd always favored. "I have a couple of questions if you're up for it."

"Ask away, but I only met Chaz a week ago."

"He told me you were helping his company."

"Not his company, that's kind of a quibble."

"Can you give me specifics? Tyre says you refused to discuss it."

I smoothed a puckered edge of my robe. "I'll bet even the sergeant's heard of attorney/client privilege," I said. But the dead have no privileges. I told Michael about the mayor of Telford, his war on NGT. "Chaz planned to run against him, and I'd agreed to advise his campaign. In that sense, I guess you could say I was working for NGT."

"Was there a contract?"

"A handshake. Some things aren't worth pursuing in court."

Michael patted his pockets and brought out Old Golds, a sealed pack he ripped open with his thumb, the scent of tobacco as pungent as hay in the warm room. When I said feel free, he lit up, inhaling so deeply the tip grew a long ash, which he flicked on the hearth.

"Did Torie know why Renfrow hired you?"

I shrugged against a pillow. "Chaz wanted to keep it secret until he'd filed his nominating papers, but word always gets out."

"So Torie, lots of people, may have known."

"Sure, but…Michael, are you suggesting Chaz and Torie were murdered because of his campaign?" My hand hesitated over my bandaged breast. "That I was a target?"

"Let's just say I'm worried about you."

"Believe me, there were easier ways than murder to derail Chaz." Like an EPA investigation. I filled Michael in about Beauford and Chaz, the charges and counter charges. The grudge. "Chaz said NGT is clean, that Beauford Smith was spreading rumors and lies."

"What's your take on Smith? Could he have been angry enough to murder Renfrow?"

"Beauford? Forget that. He hoped the EPA, not murder, would shut down NGT. The Beauford Smith I know is essentially honest, and harmless."

"Except on ice."

"You know he plays hockey?"

"Renfrow's wife told us. We interviewed her this morning."

"Ex-wife."

"Wife. The divorce hadn't gone through. Said she and Renfrow planned to reconcile.

I felt oddly deflated. "He told me he was divorced."

"He exaggerated."

"He lied."

Michael flipped through his notebook. A line of smoke from his cigarette rose straight up and vanished near the ceiling. "Ms. Lang also informed us that your boy Beau dated Torie Moran."

"That I didn't know." Why, I wondered, was Johanna Lang keeping tabs on Torie's love life? "Maybe Torie was the source of those rumors. She could've passed Beauford gossip he misconstrued."

"The thought had occurred to me. Any reason why he'd want to kill you?"

"Of course not. And by the way, he was out of town on Monday, and flew to Brussels on Tuesday."

"We'll be checking. How long have you known him?"

"About two years." I told Michael how Beau and I had talked software at a fundraiser. "I ended up creating an interactive Flash file for him, for Web ads. After that, we were best buddies for about six weeks. When his candidate won, he sent me flowers."

"What kind of flowers?" There might have been the slightest edge to Michael's voice.

"Orchids." I smiled. "Tiny white ones." And no, Michael, we didn't date.

He crushed out his cigarette. "Think you can tell me about the attack? If it wouldn't upset you?"

"I can try."

But upset me it did, and Michael too, in a way.

"He sprang out of nowhere," I said in a shaky voice. "I can still feel his fingers digging into my neck." A couple of tears dribbled down, and Michael passed me a Kleenex. When no more words would come, he reached over and pressed my hand. "Well," I said after awhile, "at least you know it wasn't Chaz who attacked me."

"He might have. We don't know what time he died."

"You didn't like him, did you."

"Not much."

"Whoever attacked me was wearing bay rum." And then, perversely adding weight to Michael's speculation, I said, "Chaz used it."

"Bay rum? On sale at a drugstore near you?" He ran two fingers over his amused lips, avoiding the mustache. "Own a bottle myself."

"It wasn't you. I'd know you anywhere."

The look he gave me then was as unreadable as Chaz's smile. We fell into an uncomfortable silence, and I regretted my candor. Michael's Kleenex had been an act of pity, nothing more.

"Want me to make coffee?" he said.

"I'm fresh out. There might be tea." I tried to get up, but my legs wouldn't let me. "If you don't mind looking."

He practically leaped out of his chair, as if he couldn't wait to get away from me. "Still in the cupboard over the fridge? Or have you moved things around since…"

"Since you dropped out of my life?"

He stopped in the doorway. "Was I ever in your life?"

I rested a hand on my throat, the fluttering pulse. "We were learning about each other, Michael." I closed my eyes and gave myself over to Demerol. "That takes time."

"Time?" His voice was a murmur inside a shell.

Clear as a dream I saw him walking into my life, tall, a little thin, that air of reserve. A privacy conference had drawn us to the same lecture at the Copley Plaza where a professor was addressing a crowd on Internet data thieves. Michael strolled in late and took the last chair in the last row, next to me. We glanced at each other and *boing*…two kindergarten kids. I liked him right away, and he liked me, and I had yielded to my warm, fuzzy feelings. I hadn't examined them at all. I offered him a Lifesaver—he dug down for a lime—and after the lecture, we drank coffee together in the hotel restaurant. Three frozen years began to roll off my spine.

"You must feel pretty efficient," he said to me now.

I opened my eyes. He was bending over me, so close his nicotine breath warmed my cheek. My mind wandered to his new mustache. Was it scratchy, or soft?

"All the action you can pack in a day." His voice dropped in that way I remembered, when something annoyed him. His lips hardly moved. I wished he'd shut up. *Kiss me.*

"Conferences, candidates. Dinners with clients. Must make you feel like you're getting somewhere."

I leaned forward, then fell back on the pillows. "Are you telling me you resented my work? My pathetic, grubbing real estate closings and vote countings?"

"Not your work. The feeling you gave me that I was no more important…but hey, no less either…than one of your clients."

"You're being unfair. Gil never minded my work." He'd love me forever, Gil used to say. We were mates, a pair of comfortable old gloves that ought to cling to each other.

"Jesus! Him again?" Michael walked so far away his shirt and the wallpaper blended in fine blue stripes. "Don't you ever get sick of that story? Maybe Gil didn't mind your detachment because it was just like his."

"You don't know what you're talking about."

"Why don't you explain? What do you call it when two people spend most of their time apart because one of them needs to climb down volcanoes so he can feel alive?"

"Gil never climbed down volcanoes. He led responsible, ecological expeditions."

"He babysat bored rich people. You were his stopgap. You filled in the blank parts, while he was setting up his next gig. And you loved the arrangement. That's not detached?"

"You're wrong," I said, the only defense I cared to make. I had confided too much in Michael, and now he was spinning my own words back at me. "We weren't detached from each other."

"Well, you were detached from me."

"I wasn't. I needed time. I…what about you? You know what's going on here? You wanted me to fall in love with you, and you wanted to think on it."

"Psychology's not your strong suit, Susan."

He looked so sad standing there; suddenly telling the truth became more important than protecting myself. "You were completely in my life. I think about you every day."

"Then why haven't you called?"

"You're the one went away. Why didn't you call me?"

"I don't know. Pride. Inertia."

Just like me.

He pushed the pillows aside and took their place next to me, nothing resolved except his arm around my shoulder and my head on his collarbone.

"I've been missing you." He spoke into my hair, and I wrapped one of my own heavy arms around his waist.

Me too, I started to murmur, but his kiss cut me off. Scratchy.

Afraid of my own need, I pulled back. "Maybe we should have that tea," I whispered, and slowly, like a receding tide, he let go of me.

◇◇◇

I must have slept. Dimly, I heard the front door bell chime, then the crash of the knocker. By the time I tottered to the window whoever it was had gone. I got back into bed, and next time I woke, the phone was ringing. I grabbed it. Michael had said he would call.

But it was Roddie Baird. I turned on my good side and listened, amazed, while he stormed, because Roddie always kept calm, one of his strengths as a candidate. "No, I'm not in Colorado," he snarled. "I fell off the mountain, and the techies sent me home."

"Were you hurt?"

"A few scratches. My real gripe is, I come back and find that sonofabitch Froy has plastered his goddam putrid pink bumper stickers all over my street. My own street!"

"Didn't you call him on it?"

"Yes. And I'm sorry, Susan, I know it's not cool, but I blew up. I told him he won the golden asshole award, and you know what he says? 'Is that an endorsement?' he says. Susan, he laughed in my face."

"He's goading you. Wants you to complain to the media so he can get some publicity. Even negative coverage gives him a boost."

"What should I do?"

"Tear down the stickers."

"I tried that. Somebody passed me in a car and yelled, 'Shame on you.'"

I clucked my tongue. "Can't do it in broad daylight, Roddie."

"Susan, do you really expect me to creep around after dark, like a…peeping Tom?" He paused. "What if the police catch me?"

"It's not against the law to take down illegal signs."

"Not everybody knows that. I didn't know that. I don't want a run in with the cops, let alone the voters." Another loaded pause. "If only I could get some help."

"All right, all right," I said. The pills had worn off, my fears receded to a pinprick, and the prospect of a raid was juicing me up. "I'll drive, you rip 'em down. Be ready tonight at the stroke of eleven. Wear your cape and your mask."

He was embarrassingly grateful.

It was past time to get out of bed. My stitches burned, but I could convalesce on the fly. I needed to figure out which parts of Newton to hit after dark. We couldn't tear down, let alone find, every bumper sticker in a city with three hundred miles of roads. Plus, I was starving.

The fridge and cupboards were bare, so I got dressed and grabbed my hobo bag. Drugstore candy, a big box of Giggles, would hold me while I cruised around Newton, reconnoitering Froy. I left through the side door and almost missed the little white bag on the front porch, something green sticking out the top.

The green thing was florist's tissue, wrapped around a double bunch of daisies and a note. *Sorry no orchids. BeeCee's does deli better than flowers.* He signed it M. No love, and no scent from the daisies, but I pushed my face into the tissue and inhaled anyway.

Wag's definition of Boston: an island surrounded by Newtons. This is just true enough to confound a California native like me. Newton is an edgy alliance of villages with names like Newton Lower Falls, Newton Highlands, Newton Corner, Newton-by-the-T: thirteen in all, each with it's own commercial center, activist organization, parking problems. And bunches of aldermen, which is good, for the city and for my business.

I cruised through every one of those villages, the Beemer unusually cooperative at speeds of fifteen and twenty mph. By dusk I'd mapped out a route.

On the stroke of eleven I tapped the bronze *fleur de lys* against the Baird's French farmhouse door. This triggered a scuffling sound, and a child's wail: "I don't want you to go!" Five-year-old Delia up at this hour?

Roddie let me in. A crummy looking Lauren, all bare feet, stringy hair, and drooping gym clothes, drifted through the dining room, moving like a sleepwalker straight for Delia. Behind her, the big yew wood table was still strewn with voter surveys.

I offered a general hello that was generally ignored, though Roddie did raise an abashed eyebrow at me just as Delia, in yellow smiley-face pajamas, lunged for his legs. Roddie patted her hair, his hand a mass of purple scratches from his fall off the mountain. "I won't be long, sweetie," he said, but Delia sobbed against his knee.

The tension was so thick, I almost grabbed Roddie's other knee and started whining myself. "Maybe we should do this tomorrow night."

But Roddie managed to console Delia with bribes: stories Lauren would read her right now, a trip to Drumlin Farm next Sunday, "and after we feed the ducks, we'll have chowder at Legal, as much as you want." He patted his bulging middle. "Delia and I love to eat. She stays skinny, though. Like her mother."

Kid's spoiled, I wanted to say, but I didn't really believe it. Delia had the melancholy air of an uncherished child. I remembered my own status as youngest child, growing up in the shadow of a smart, successful much-older sister. I'd always felt like the family footnote.

In the car, Roddie told me Delia had left her blanket at a friend's house and was having trouble sleeping without it. Then his head swiveled right. "Stop! There!"

I'd already spotted it, a gigantic pink tapeworm: *Froy*, stuck to a tree. Roddie ripped it down, and we zapped three more on our way to the Front: intersections on thoroughfares that led to the Mass Pike and Route 9.

Like the rank amateur that he was, Froy had slapped most of his stickers on wooden utility poles, and the rough surfaces made for easy pickin's. I'd pull close to the target, scanning for nonexistent passersby. Roddie would jump out, claw down the sticker, then jump back in, keeping the door slightly open to save precious seconds next time I stopped.

For a chubby burgher who'd fallen off a mountain, Roddie was nimble, and we swept through the night like avenging politicians. By one o'clock the back seat was littered with *Froy*s. Then we cut over to Centre by way of Bellevue, and our luck ran out.

"Will you look at that," Roddie gasped as we converged on Bellevue at Claremont.

"I see, I see." As if anyone could miss the postal holding box plastered with Day-Glo pink *Froy*s. The neighborhood itself was dark, overgrown bushes on all sides, the only streetlight shining directly over the box. As I surveilled, a carriage house across the way lit up like Christmas. A scrawny woman came out, trailing an overfed beagle on a leash.

"Hurry up," I whispered to Roddie who had hit the street and was scraping his fingernails along the top row of *Froy*s, probing for a break that wasn't there because bumper stickers *mate* with metal.

"They won't come off," he moaned.

Gil's old Swiss Army knife was handy in the glove box, but before I could toss it out, the woman started to shout. "You there! What *are* you doing?"

Her oh-so-entitled voice made me want to growl low in my throat, like her dog. I eased the Beemer into deepest shadow and joined Roddie on the street. "Sweetie, I told you this wasn't a mailbox." I yanked his sleeve, and we power-walked back to the car.

"Did you put up all these horrible signs?" the woman called after us.

Her dog barked and barked.

We covered Commonwealth Avenue as far as Heartbreak Hill, and at one-forty I drove Roddie home. "Finish the job tomorrow night," I said. "Get Lauren to help you."

"Lauren." His smile was impenetrable, almost worthy of Chaz.

After he went inside, I drove straight back to Bellevue. No self-righteous biddy was going to thwart *my* candidate. This time I had the neighborhood, and the postal box, to myself. The Swiss Army knife might have worked, but the only blade I could unfold was the corkscrew, which scratched but couldn't pierce. That left the graffiti option.

With a Magic Marker from my bag, I turned an O into a frowny face with fangs. This, unfortunately, made *Froy* look kinda cute. Warping *Froy* into *Fraud* was too hard. In the end, I simply changed every *Froy* to *Frog*, and when I stood back, they looked exactly right.

Chapter Ten

Balancing Act

Just after dawn, I dialed Michael's number. I was coming to enjoy these little one-way chats; his voice mail listened respectfully, didn't make sarcastic remarks, always let me know when I'd gone on too long.

"The daisies are beautiful," I said, gazing at the vase on my night table. I touched the petals, wondering where Michael could be at this hour. Not in Tucson, and that would have to do me. "Call me at home, anytime," I said. "I'm taking another sick day." My stitches *did* kind of pinch this morning, and the only boss I had to please was me.

At eight-thirty, I went out to BeeCee's and came back with coffee, tea, two power bars, and three pounds of the apples on special this week. Back in my kitchen I scoured yesterday's *Globe*, which my vacationing landlords had neglected to cancel; in Regional News, I found an account of Chaz Renfrow's death. The story ended with a recap of the Torie Moran case and a quote from "detective in charge" Lieutenant Michael Benedict of the state police. "We haven't ruled out robbery as a motive," he'd said for the record, which was news to me.

By noon my breast began to burn, though the pain had an itch in its tail, a sure sign of healing. Last night's gallop through Newton had worn me to a nub, and I curled on the sofa for a quick nap. When I awoke, it was twenty past six. Mondays didn't get any duller than this. I suddenly wanted to chew over the attack on me, and the murders, but I couldn't think of a soul to call except Michael, and I'd done enough of that for a while.

I maundered back to the kitchen, wondering why I'd lost touch with most of my Massachusetts friends. Maybe because, to a person, they were married or in committed relationships, while I had become a skeleton at the feast. Many of them were social network addicts. After Gil died, I'd joined Facebook myself, only to spend hours exchanging banalities with people I'd friended for no reason except the body count. Virtual friends were about as satisfying as virtual lovers. So I suspended my account.

My itch to talk was inflaming like hives, and I finally fell back on my answering service. Deirdre might not be a physical presence, but she did have vocal chords. Through two mugs of coffee I talked, leaning against the counter, anticipating fuzzy words of assurance. But when it came, Deirdre's advice was strangely categorical, for Deirdre: "Put murder out of your mind."

"Easy for you to say." I poured another refill and carried it to the table.

"It *is* easy. I do it all the time. When something upsets me, I drop it in a box and lock it away till my inner balance holds steady."

"Hmmm," I said. Fuzzy was back. Inner balance sounded awfully like inner peace, and what did that mean? Ten seconds of calm before reality stormed in. I sipped my coffee, a beverage Deirdre maintained was unhealthy. I'd sooner give up breathing.

"Balance," she insisted. "Equilibrium. That's what healing's all about. You've been wounded. Literally. Once you heal, you'll be ready to open the box and look at the murders."

"That doesn't work for me, Deir. Something pushes me, I push back right away." Which was a kind of balancing act, now I thought about it. "Why would someone kill two people and almost nail me? Michael talks robbery, but I know he's got his eye on the campaign. And I hate to admit it, but that does make a kind of sense, at least on the surface."

"Everything happens for a reason."

"Okay then, answer me this: if Chaz's wife, or even his son, murdered him, how does the campaign fit in?"

"Like an onion." She paused. "The campaign could be a layer."

A layer, an onion. I wanted precision, not *pastafazool.* "And Torie Moran?"

"It's layers all the way down, Susan. The thing about layers is they both reveal and conceal. Peel them off carefully, one by one, and you'll uncover the truth." And then, rather conveniently, Deirdre had to cut me off to service a call. When she came back, she mentioned her vacation. "I'm so excited," she said. "I leave tomorrow."

"Tomorrow! You didn't say a word to me about a vacation."

"I'm sure I mentioned it. Don't worry. The franchiser will handle your calls."

Worse and worse. I hated Deirdre's substitutes, sticklers who used voice mail or machines during hours not covered by my contract. "Where're you off to this time?"

"Tiger, tiger, burning bright," she chanted, and her words rang a faint Freshman bell. "Two guesses."

"India."

"Noooo…"

"The zoo?"

"The poet. William Blake."

Of course, Blake, much anthologized, not that I knew his poems. I'd majored in English, but aside from Chaucer and Donne, I'd dabbled mostly in writers of prose…and from prose, as Jane Austen might say, it was an easy step to law school.

"There's an exhibition of his paintings and manuscripts at the National Gallery."

"You're going to Washington? In July?"

"London, eight days and seven nights."

Wow. The answering service business must be booming. In January, Deirdre had gone to the Caribbean, and in April to New Mexico. I couldn't even manage a weekend in Truro.

◇◇◇

Michael finally called at eleven. "Took a chance you'd be up." His voice was thick with exhaustion. "I just got home."

Home was Wycherly, an hour west of Boston. Michael had moved there from Tucson two years ago, coming in as chief of police. Though he worked for the staties now, he'd stayed on. Rent was low, for a converted barn whose absentee owners liked having a cop on site. "Everything okay? Your...uh, stitches...?" His words mumbled out, as if my wound couldn't be mentioned except in a hush.

"Honestly, it's just a scratch. After you left, I did some pretty active canvassing with one of my candidates." I was deliberately vague. Michael hated graffiti.

I asked how the investigations were going.

"Renfrow never filed his nominating papers," Michael said, and that sad fact, that broken promise, brought Chaz's death home to me more finally even than Michael's description of the murder. My candidate no longer existed; already his taw marble eyes, his will to win, were growing fainter my mind.

"That narrows time of death, doesn't it?" I said, as if I could justify Chaz's faith in me by helping to solve his murder. "He died before five o'clock on Friday, or he'd have filed."

"You're assuming he intended to file."

"Michael, I guarantee it."

"Let's don't speculate. I'll know more after the lab reports are in."

"Didn't you speculate about robbery? I read it in the *Globe*."

"The victims were robbed, but I didn't release the details." He confided that Torie Moran's diamond earrings had been torn from her ears, and that Chaz's Patek Philippe and his Lexus were missing.

But Michael hadn't called about the murders. "I've been thinking about us," he said solemnly, as if "us" were an inquiry, and "thinking" meant gathering evidence. He retracted the hard words he'd thrown at me yesterday: It wasn't actually a crime to care about my work, he allowed. And like him, I was entitled to my history. "I'll try to be careful about stepping on ghosts," he said.

"Me too." I meant his ex-wife, and Nancy the pretty blonde wrangler. If there were other wraiths in the woodwork, I hoped he wouldn't whistle them up.

"I'd like us to start over." He hesitated. "On neutral turf, if you're willing. I can steal a few days here and there. We could do a little mountain camping. Hike to waterfalls. Share a sleeping bag."

The image of Michael and me under the stars, snug in each other's arms, stirred me so entirely I felt disloyal to Gil, with his picture still inside my night table, so very close to the bed. By the time we said goodnight, we'd reached an understanding: Easy does it. Camping could wait. Dinner plans worked better for two tentative people, one of whom was perhaps less tentative than she cared to admit.

The week passed in real estate closings, travel in my wheezy Beemer to my out of town candidates, privacy research. Michael called, once, just to chat, nothing new on the murders, that he was sharing.

Every morning Nino's lease pecked my liver. Odette had promised to help, but pulling rabbits out of hats, not to mention strings, took time, and I knew I couldn't force the pace. When I checked in with Tavola Rustica, Benny told me Nino was too busy to talk, which meant he was open for business and still angry.

On Friday morning, a call from Roddie found me slouched at the kitchen table nursing my third coffee. "Guess what?" he said. "Froy's pulled out."

In politics, rumors spread like oil slicks. Candidates were always heisting banks, having affairs, dropping out. "Says who?"

"Trust me." He chuckled. "The name Froy will not be blotting the ballot."

"After all those bumper stickers and taunts? Why would he drop out?"

"Maybe I made him an offer his wife couldn't refuse."

The incessant chuckling annoyed me. "Don't play games, Roddie. Tell me right now what you did."

"I didn't do anything. You did."

"Me! I've never laid eyes on Kyle Froy. Or his wife."

"You urged me to check the ward lines. I mentioned it to Odette, and she called the documents clerk. The lines were redrawn all right, in January, but when Odette challenged the vote, they couldn't produce the records!" Roddie's laugh fell somewhere between a bark and a crow. "They've been misplaced. Even the audio tapes are missing."

Coffee roiled like a cauldron of acid in my stomach. "How very convenient, but the absence of records doesn't mean the old lines are valid."

"No, but suppose I sued. The burden of proof would be on the city. The old lines would hold while we dickered. Even if I lost, it'd be too late for Froy to get on the ballot."

Neat. I wondered how many more rabbits former judge Odette had in her hat, then felt guilty about my cynicism. It was not impossible that the records had fallen into a bureaucratic black hole.

"I explained the situation to Froy," Roddie said. "That was the stick. Here's the carrot: Mrs. Froy is a tennis pro at Longwood. So I found her a fabulous new job in Boca Raton with a club that bought my swimming pool system. Froy lives off her so he didn't have a choice. It's all settled."

"Roddie, you take my breath away."

"I want to win, Susan."

"And now you don't have to face a primary."

"That's actually why I called. See, Lauren's been under the weather these last few days. I was hoping we could take a breather and hold back the voter surveys till September."

"September's too late. You can't afford to slack off. Froy may be out, but there are three other wannabees who'd love to destroy you."

I spent the afternoon at the office, phone off, designing bio pieces, fund-raising invitations, targeted solicitations. And updating accounts. Around six, on replenished paper, I printed out Roddie's latest contributors' list for immediate, personal delivery to his finance chairwoman. Odette lived on West Newton Hill, not exactly on my way home, but door-to-door service was the least I could do for the woman who had spared Roddie a primary.

Before I left, I dialed Deirdre's substitute server, a woman whose voice and an Uzi had been separated at birth. The only caller, she rasped, had been Johanna Lang.

Chaz's widow. Was she grieving? I remembered how she'd recoiled from him the day I found Torie's body. Grief would have a long road to travel from Johanna Lang's heart to her eyes. I punched in the number Ms.Uzi had given me, and an elderly woman answered the phone. "Johanna is making tea," she confided, in a sweetly frail voice. "Real tea, not that herbal stuff."

I heard low murmurs, then Johanna was on the line. "You know what happened," was how she greeted me.

"Of course. I'm so very sorry."

"We buried Charles this morning."

When I apologized for missing the funeral, she cut me off. "The service was private."

Johanna's brusqueness irritated the hell out of me. She must control NGT now, and I wondered if she smiled secretly at Chaz's death.

"I'll come right to the point," she said. "Charles advanced you twenty thousand dollars to find a new site for NGT. My husband had an unfortunate habit of overpaying for services that came with a pretty face. I want the money back."

Well, that was direct. A boss lady who knew what she wanted, if not how to charm the person who stood in her way. "Actually," I said, awed by the way she made "pretty" a slur, "Chaz paid me to advise his campaign, not find a site for his company. He hadn't told many people, but he was planning a run for mayor."

"The police mentioned that ridiculous story, Ms. Callisto, but I know what you're up to. You're a real estate lawyer. Yesterday I found a copy of your contract in Charles' safe."

Michael had asked me about a contract. What was going on here? "We had an informal agreement," I said. "Nothing in writing, and nothing about NGT."

"Please don't insult my intelligence. Last week my husband signed a lease for property in the old Navy Yard. His contract with you specifically excludes that location. You are not entitled to keep one penny of the advance."

"I don't have the slightest idea what you're talking about." And I have no intention of giving you anything, lady. The money was unconditionally mine Chaz had said, assuming I wanted it, which I suddenly, fervidly did. "Is this really the moment to talk about my fee?"

"Fee? In your pocket that money is plunder."

My heart began to race. "Your husband hired me to help him win an election. He paid me the fee he felt I deserved. You're misunderstanding something here, Ms. Lang."

Another crabby sigh. "It's Dr. Lang. I'm a Ph.D."

"Ah, well, in that case you need to call me Dr. Callisto, Dr. Lang." A niggling good quibble raises pettiness to an art form, in my opinion. "I'm a Juris Doctor, see."

"Were you and my husband having an affair, Dr. Callisto?"

"*Was* he your husband? He told me you were divorced."

"Separated. About to reconcile. The affair doesn't matter. I was curious, that's all."

"There was nothing between us except his campaign, and that was iffy. He needed hundreds of signatures." *The signatures.* "There should be nominating petitions in a drawer somewhere. They're evidence of his intentions."

"Stop wasting my time. You owe me twenty thousand dollars."

"Find the papers. Then we'll discuss my fee."

Over her silence I heard a querulous voice in the background.

"I'll be right with you, Mother." Returning to me, Johanna said "All right, I'll look for your...for the papers as soon as I get back to NGT, but can't you meet me today? Now, even? It's rather urgent."

"How about my office?" I said. Oh, these power games. Whose agenda? Whose turf?

"I'm without transportation. Glenn and I drove in this morning for the funeral. He's got my car, and I don't know when he'll be back."

"Okay." I sighed. "I'll come to you." Power tripping was just not my thing. I could always fall back on the quibble. "Where does your mother live?"

"Charles' mother. She's in a retirement community, off Gardenia Road in Weston." Johanna gave me lengthy directions, which I couldn't hear over the roar in my ears.

"*Whose mother?*"

"Charles'. She's quite elderly. I'm not sure how much she understands. At the cemetery she kept asking when Charles was coming." Johanna clucked her tongue. "So terribly sad."

But Chaz's mother had died of melanoma. That's why he became a molecular biologist. Wasn't it? "Where is Chaz's father?" I asked.

"He died last year."

"All alone in his garden?"

Silence struck. When Johanna finally spoke she was furious. "That was *my* father. I don't know why you asked me that, but Charles' father died right here in Weston. He simply didn't wake up one morning. We buried Charles next to him."

"And the flower shops? The nurseries?"

"What are you talking about?"

"Chaz told me his father owned a chain of florists."

"His father was a pharmaceutical salesman."

A salesman. What had Chaz sold me?

Chapter Eleven

Blood Relative

It was cooler in Weston. The sun filtered gently though miles of trees, and at an engine-conserving speed, the drive gave me time to appreciate the tranquility. When I finally pulled into Idlebrook retirement community, I understood how fitting a place Weston was to grow old and die in. Myself, when my time came, if it came, I planned to roller blade down Route 128, middle finger raised high.

"Susan," Chaz's mother said in a whispery voice, as if my name were a secret. "How nice. Everyone calls me Cordy, more's the pity." There was no hint of mourning in her face, but I imagined I could see Chaz in the narrow nose and cloudy blue eyes.

We shook hands. Cordy was tall, thin as a finger bone, dressed in black ski pants and sweater. At ninety-one, I guessed she was entitled to feel cold in July. She drifted to an overstuffed chair and picked up a remote, aiming it at the TV on a shelf inside a false fireplace. Gigantic letters and a roulette wheel absorbed her. "Bring my supper here, will you, Johanna?"

Cordy was able to live in one of Idlebrook's condominium units Johanna explained as she led me into a kitchen/dining room that overlooked a gazebo. Apart from memory failures, Cordy had no health problems. Chaz had visited her every Sunday, and she didn't grasp that he wouldn't be dropping by anymore. "And maybe that's a blessing."

She set a dish of grilled tomatoes on a tray, next to what looked like tuna casserole and had me yearning for a taste. Cordy yearned too, to judge by her avid look when Johanna placed the tray in her lap.

"Thank you, dear. Tell Charles to bring me my blue comforter." A hint of autocrat in her voice, and then she was stirring her noodles, no more talk of comforters. Sadness touched Johanna's face, fading as quickly as Cordy's short-term memory.

"I'll buy two consonants," somebody shouted to wild applause.

We went back to the dining area. At the window, I watched shadows race across the summerhouse roof. The evening sun flared through a cloud, and I remembered how dawn had burnished Chaz's face in the hospital waiting room.

Johanna joined me, an envelope in her hand. She was wearing elliptical glasses that made her look shrewd. "Why did you ask about my father this afternoon?" Her voice was accusing, and my first impression of her, someone to dislike, came galloping back.

"I didn't know he was your father. Chaz told me he'd lost his parents in tragic ways. The question is why would he tell me those stories?"

"Negotiating tactic." She rubbed her finger across the top of the envelope.

"Nothing to negotiate." I repeated my mantra. "I signed no contract with Chaz."

"What do you call this?" She yanked papers out of the envelope.

We sat at the table, and I read over a standard agency contract: *I'll find what you want if you pay me a fee.* In this one, the agent, me, agreed to find a relocation site for NGT anywhere in Massachusetts except the Navy Yard because Chaz was aware of that location. Twenty thousand of my forty thousand dollar finder's fee was payable upon signing. It was a copy, dated two Mondays ago, the day I had agreed to advise Chaz's campaign.

It certainly looked like my signature.

"It's a forgery," I said, out of my depth and wildly calm.

Johanna shoved her glasses to the top of her head, her eggshell skin sallow in the waning light. "Why on earth would Charles forge your signature?"

"Who says he did? Maybe whoever benefits forged *his* signature, too." I aligned the pages and reattached the clip. "He paid me to advise his campaign. You're certain he didn't mention that to you?"

She leaned across the table, ready to leap for my throat. "My husband had no interest in politics. In our twenty-three years together, he never once voted."

"Maybe he changed more than houses when you separated."

"And maybe you are looking to keep money that doesn't belong to you." Her lips stretched over her teeth, nothing in her eyes except an anger that reinforced my calm.

"Your husband wanted a campaign consultant," I insisted, as if stubborn repetition ever convinced anyone of anything. "He considered twenty thousand dollars a suitable fee for my services. And I intend to keep it."

She snatched the papers out of my hand. "I'll get the money back, in court if necessary."

"Go ahead and sue me. Other reputations besides mine will be on the line."

"Are you threatening me?"

I pointed to the contract. "Who else but you benefits from the forgery?"

"I am not a forger."

Cordy's television erupted in laughter, a better reply than the one I bit back. I got up to leave. "You won't get far without the original agreement. If one exists."

"Wait, Susan." With visible effort, Johanna smothered her anger. "Let's look at this another way. What if Charles *did* come to you for campaign advice? Was whatever you did worth twenty thousand dollars?"

I walked to the window and studied shadows on the lawn, about as reasonable a way to insight as tea leaves or psychotherapy. The short answer to Johanna's question was no. A longer answer would surely tangle me in tedious quandaries about rights, honor, personal integrity, the rule of law. I went with no.

Back at the table, I said, "Got any more of that casserole?"

"Find the nominating petition and you'll see where I fit in." A few noodles clung to the rim of the pan, and I scraped up every crusty bite.

The coffee stopped brewing, and Johanna unplugged the pot. "Whatever game Charles was playing, his candidacy doesn't matter. Only the money matters. The twenty thousand he paid you came from a small personal account. It was collateralizing over a million in new loans. I've *got* to replace it or NGT will default straight into bankruptcy."

"What about key man insurance?"

"The insurers are delaying because…it was murder. They want to audit the books."

Grande finale music reached us from the library. Johanna didn't seem to notice, and Cordy probably hadn't either.

"We've got the Navy Yard lease, so our investors can't pull the plug because of that." She sighed. "There's light at the end of the tunnel. I would hate to lose everything over…an accounting glitch." She smoothed her arms and looked at me, a sincere look that, had I been a man, would surely have hinted at sex the way certain wines hint at spice. "I can tell what you're thinking," she said. "Charles is dead, Torie is dead, and I am completely focused on NGT. You disapprove."

"Not at all. Sometimes it's easier to face tragedy by being practical. I admire that in a way." A little tiny way. Peculiar people the Langs and the Renfrows, superegos fully in charge. Chaz had been eager to resume his campaign the day after Torie's murder.

"I am in shock," Johanna said. "But I can't bring back the dead. My job is the survival of NGT. Charles would have demanded no less of me. NovoGenTech was his proudest creation." She raised her cup in a kind of salute. "Now, it will be his monument."

For a moment, her eyes blazed with the same zealous light I had seen in Chaz's the night he told me about the immortality gene. I had to admit Johanna was probably correct in her assessment of Chaz's priorities. His very political campaign had been driven by NGT's need to expand.

"When do you pull out of Telford?" I asked.

"February one. Our Navy Yard site has got to be ready by then. We won't need to borrow much, just a bridge loan to keep us going till the insurance money comes in. Charles insisted on a large policy, thank God." She leaned back, her smile almost a gloat. "The police seemed disappointed to learn that NGT is sole beneficiary."

That sounded like Sgt. Paul Tyre, who would feel personally thwarted by evidence of innocence.

"Don't Chaz's relatives inherit his shares?"

"That's what the sergeant said. Yes, Glenn and I benefit. If NGT survives."

I wondered what a divorce would have done to Johanna's ownership position. "When did you and Chaz separate?"

"About six months ago. But a few days before he died, he asked me to give it another try, for our son's sake, and I said yes." Her complaisance evaporated. "Glenn may be nineteen, but he was devastated by the breakup."

I wasn't sure I believed her, but with Chaz dead, who could contradict her?

Real-time voices reached us from the library. The television volume dropped, and Cordy murmured a greeting. Seconds later Glenn and a dark-haired girl with puffy cheeks and a small, curved mouth joined us. "Mom, this is Darcy Villencourt," Glenn said. "I told you about her. We were in the same econ class last year."

Darcy told Johanna how sorry she was about Mr. Renfrow, and Johanna accepted her condolences with a quick shake of her head. An uncomfortable silence followed, finally broken by Johanna. "Majoring in Gender Studies, is it?"

"Women as victims of the process." Heavily flossed, child-sized teeth beamed at us.

"Darcy and I spent the afternoon at the Arnold Arboretum," Glenn said quickly.

"It's so peaceful there." Darcy had a face like a pansy, broad forehead, narrow chin, with a deep groove beneath her lower lip. "I wanted to show Glenn the gingko walk. I find it a spiritual place. A healing place."

Shades of Deirdre. If anyone else mentioned healing, I'd argue for pain. Whatever happened to mourning? Just plain old rending your garments and howling your grief.

In a gesture very like his dad's, Glenn put his hand on Darcy's arm. "We stopped by to see if you need anything. Otherwise, we'll be off."

"You should have called." Johanna stared at Darcy's teeth, then at her son. Perched on top of her head, her glasses looked like a second set of flashing eyes. "I was worried."

"Sorry," Glenn said. "If you want the car, I'll take Darcy home and forget the meeting."

"What meeting?"

Darcy answered. "A few friends are getting together to help Glenn meditate."

"Meditate?" Johanna managed to make the word sound like "defecate."

"Uh," Glenn studied the floor. "We want to kind of…contemplate Dad's dove."

Her face gone eczema-pink, Johanna got up from her chair and walked around the table. Standing side-by-side, mother and son so resembled each other I wondered how I'd seen Chaz in Glenn's face. "What exactly do you mean by 'Dad's dove'?"

"Mr. Renfrow's spirit," Darcy said.

"His soul." Glenn sounded so sad I wanted to pull him to my bandaged breast.

Johanna moved closer. Darcy held her ground. Glenn looked like a bare bone caught between dogs.

"We did not have a religious ceremony precisely because your father was an atheist. If you must pray, pray for NGT."

After they left, Johanna brought Cordy a dish of ice cream, and I poured more coffee which neither of us drank.

"I'll look for those campaign papers tomorrow," she said. "Names on a petition. There wasn't anything like that in Charles' house, or his NGT safe, but I haven't really gone through his office yet. He was a terrible pack rat. If I find them, you can have them."

She propped her chin on her fist. "Susan, I've told you why I need the money back, all that hinges on it. I'm willing to forget about the contract."

"I'm not. I need to know who forged it, and why."

"Take it." She pushed her envelope toward me. "I made a copy for Sergeant Tyre last night. And the original contract, the police have it. Tyre told me they found it…clenched in Charles' hand." In a moment that passed instantly, Johanna may have blinked back a tear. "Will you return the money, Susan?"

Twenty thousand dollars. For me it meant a little financial security. Debt reduction. Breathing room. Chaz had given it to me unconditionally, but in my heart I knew I hadn't earned it, or much of it. I ran a reluctant hand through my hair. "I'll calculate a fee based on time," I sighed, "and send you the balance."

Nino was right. I was a patsy. "You'll have to sign a blanket waiver of claims against me," I said, trying for a little belated intransigence.

"Certainly. I'd like everything settled before I leave for Telford. I'll be glad to come to your office tomorrow."

Although tomorrow was Saturday, we arranged a two o'clock meeting. On my way out I stopped by the library to tell Cordy goodbye. She had fallen asleep to the screech of television cars, the remote still under her veined hand. Her head was askew, her eyelids thin as gauze. A line of saliva had dried on her jaw.

Johanna saw me to the door. "What do you expect your fee will be?" she said, hesitating, but able to overcome her delicacy. "Ballpark figure."

"Not enough, Johanna." I stepped onto the walk. "Not nearly enough."

◇◇◇

Odette Brenner's white federal house sat on a country lane in the middle of dense suburbia. Most of the lights were out, and while I stood there debating whether to ring the bell or shove the contributors' list through the mail slot, the door opened.

"Susan. I thought I heard a car." Odette shooed me inside without spilling a drop of cognac from the snifter she was cradling in her palm. "Roddie's been trying to reach you. The police are questioning him about that Telford murder."

I stopped in my tracks. "About Charles Renfrow?"

"I think that's the name."

"Renfrow was one of my candidates. Why would the police be talking to Roddie?"

Odette gave me a sharp look. "He says it's some kind of mix-up and he's sure you can fix it. Mix-up!" She shook her head. "It's murder, and I want to bring in my nephew. Gordon Brenner is the best criminal lawyer in Massachusetts, but Roddie won't let me. Just because he's done nothing wrong he thinks he's got nothing to worry about."

She led me down a dimly lit hall, one stocky arm swinging against her loose cotton dress. In a little den off the kitchen, she picked up the desk phone and passed it to me when Roddie came on the line.

"Susan, don't you check with your service? I've been calling you for hours."

For some reason, Roddie needed to put me on the defensive, and he sounded so stressed, I let him. "Sorry, I had my phones off. What's going on?"

"The police found one of my surveys in Renfrow's Lexus, so they think I knew him."

"That's what this is about? Renfrow was a client. I was in his car last week with a bag full of drafts. I must have dropped one. Where are you?"

"Special Investigations Unit, Boston office."

"Who's questioning you? Put him on."

"I'll handle it now I know what to say." He hung up before I could stop him.

"Sounds like he won't be needing Gordon!" Odette had been hovering near the phone, and now her face bloomed a cheerful pink. She poured me a cognac and topped up her own. "Lauren will be relieved...I assume."

It seemed a bizarre thing to say, and her confiding tone incited my nosiness. "Do the Bairds get along?"

She hesitated. "Lauren is moody. I don't know her well."

An evasion, but except as it affected his race, Roddie's marriage was none of my business. I kicked off my shoes, tucked myself into an armchair and listened to the sounds of Odette's snug home. In the kitchen, the freezer chunked ice into a tray. The dishwasher volleyed water down the drain. Somewhere behind me, an air-conditioner hummed. House harmony, I thought, in a melancholy minor mode.

"Roddie and my husband were good friends," Odette said. "And Roddie has stayed close to me. Stan died ten years ago. I'm still not over it."

She turned on a lamp, and her broad nose and strong chin softened in the dusty amber light. She seemed to float on shadows, an old-master portrait in a summer shift. Sipping my drink, listening to her house sing, I suspected Odette, for all her optimism and brazen hair and legal connections, was lonely.

"Women mourn," she said. "Men remarry." Then she laughed, as if she'd made a wry joke. "And don't you forget it, Susan."

I promised I wouldn't.

We chatted for a few minutes about Nino and my mistake, repeated our confidence in Roddie. When she'd drained her glass, she set it on the table. "Well, I'm glad you stopped by. Thank you for the list, all your hard work."

A clear signal for me to leave. I slipped on my shoes, but before I made it to the door, Roddie phoned again, his voice wound tight. "You better get over here. Sergeant Tyre's started pushing about when I got back from Colorado."

Chapter Twelve

Sticky Strands

A trooper led me to a fifth floor office crowded with filing cabinets, every windowless wall covered with bulletin boards. Sergeant Tyre was hunched over a cluttered desk, paging through a folder. This place would give a flea the heebie-jeebies, I thought; let alone Roddie, who was sitting off by himself on an orange molded chair. He was dressed like a rugged outdoorsman, staring at his hands as if they were distant mountains.

"Time to leave, Roddie," I said.

He nodded, but didn't move. "Delta can't confirm my departure, Susan. I'm on the manifest, but after I fell I switched my flight. Then I got bumped."

"What's that got to do with the price of bananas?"

"Routine follow up, Suze." Tyre had decided to notice me. "We're interested in Mr. Baird's whereabouts at the time of Renfrow's murder." He rubbed his baggy eyelids and stretched his arms over his melon-shaped head.

"See, Delta put me up in one of those cookie cutter airport hotels, I forget which one," Roddie blabbered on. "We're waiting for them to get the name and call me back."

Some instinct told me not to press for explanations. I wanted Roddie to shut up. I wanted to get him out of here. But I needed information from Tyre. "What do my client's travel arrangements have to do with Renfrow's murder?"

"They give him an alibi."

"He doesn't need an alibi."

"We're checking everyone who knew Renfrow. Mike vouched for you, Suze." He tossed me a quick knowing smile. "That campaign paper we found links Renfrow and Baird."

"It does nothing of the sort. It's mine and I dropped it in the SUV. As you know."

"I didn't know till Baird finally got a hold of you."

"Well now you know. Let's go, Roddie."

"Hold on." Tyre grabbed his phone and made a call. "Mike, the political consultant is here. Wants to take her client home." He jerked his chin in my direction. "Mike wants to see you both. Left on your way out."

We got as far as the door before Tyre revved up his Columbo act. "Hey, Suze, this afternoon we found Renfrow's Lexus in Brookline, four blocks from your street. Any idea how it got there?"

Four blocks from my street? I managed a casual, "Nope."

"One more thing. Renfrow was your candidate. Mr. Baird here is also one of yours." He paused, possibly waiting for me to clutch my throat and confess to something. "And you're telling me they didn't know each other?"

"Do all your informants hang out together, Paul?"

Michael was waiting in the hall. He nodded at me, then turned to Roddie. "If you wouldn't mind one or two more questions?"

We followed him into another grim office. At a corner desk, a different trooper tapped on a keyboard. Mr. Coffee sizzled on a shelf, next to a stack of styrofoam cups and powdered creme. Roddie and I sat down at a small round table. "You know the Lieutenant?" he asked in a loud whisper.

"Not very well." This was pure unvarnished truth, though I might have said more if the trooper hadn't brought over coffee and fixings on a tray.

"Anybody? Fresh pot."

I accepted a cup and savored the hint of polycarbon under the burnt jockstrap taste of the brew. Michael joined us at the table, his manner cool and official.

"Sorry to keep you so late," he said to Roddie, then launched right in. "I hear you've got pretty eclectic business interests."

Roddie slitted his eyes in a yawn that looked fake even to me. "I'm a professional trend spotter, Lieutenant. Chlorine-free swimming pools. Miniature satellite receivers. Super light, super strong mountaineer's rope. Take it from me, extreme climbing is the boomers' last big adventure."

Michael leafed through his notepad. A pack of Old Golds peeked out of his shirt pocket, and his sleeves were turned back, exposing sinewy wrists and a drugstore watch that he'd already checked twice. "Ever invest in biotechnology?"

"I only invest in things I can see, touch, and feel."

"That's a no?"

"That's a no."

"How about the Cordelia Guaranty Trust?"

"What the hell are you driving at? That's a fund I set up for my daughter. I've done the same for my sons."

"You manage the trust?"

"My wife and I are passive trustees. My financial adviser looks after the trust assets." Roddie turned to me. "You remember him, Susan. John Snow."

"Sure do. I remember how quietly he sat at your finance meeting while everyone talked about money."

"Financial wizards don't need to talk. So far, John's raised most of my campaign contributions."

"Snow calls the shots for your daughter's trust?" Michael said.

"Yes. He will consult me before he tries something he considers exceptionally risky."

"Did he consult you before he invested one and a quarter million dollars of the Cordelia Trust in NGT Corporation?"

Under his dark beard stubble, Roddie blanched. "That's the entire fund! What the hell is NGT?"

I started to tell him, but Michael talked over me. "Novo-GenTech. Renfrow's company. The Cordelia Trust bought convertible debentures from NGT about two months ago. NGT gave back stock, a promissory note, and a small bank account held jointly by Renfrow and the Trust."

This would be the loan Johanna had told me about, and the bank account Chaz must have raided to pay me that hefty fee. The Cordelia Trust was beginning to feel like another sticky strand of a web with my name on it. I shifted on my butt-busting chair, a Marrakesh prison reject along with the coffee.

"Where'd you hear about this?" From a sleeve pocket, Roddie extracted a tiny compass and took a read, as if checking his emotional bearings, which were grim in every direction.

"Bart Bievsky," Michael said. "NGT's chief financial officer. According to Bievsky, Renfrow kept the loan papers in a safe deposit box, separate from other NGT documents. Bievsky reviewed the transaction, and he remembered the names Baird and Snow on the note. So far we haven't located Renfrow's bank, but Snow will have copies."

"*If* Snow invested in NGT, he didn't consult me. I'll straighten this out right now. Get him out of bed if I have to." Roddie began pressing numbers into his BlackBerry.

"Don't bother. We tried to reach him, but he's out of town and out of touch."

"Oh, yeah, I forgot. He's somewhere in Alaska, wilderness camping."

"More Boomer adventures." Michael dropped his Old Golds on the table, tapped out a cigarette, then checked his watch again, which made me wonder whether he was timing the interview or his nicotine breaks. "You're saying you have no knowledge of Charles Renfrow?"

Roddie spun his compass. "Never heard of him. Or his company."

Eyes half-closed against a phantom drift of smoke from the unlit cigarette, Michael studied my unhappy client, and then dismissed him. "Thanks for coming in, Mr. Baird. We'll want to talk with you again after we find the loan documents."

Without so much as a nod at me, Roddie snatched up his compass and barreled out.

"Wait!" I called after him. "I'll walk you to your car."

"Save your legs. I'm not up for any more company tonight." His anger shivered in the air and under my skin. And then he was gone, leaving a reluctant promise to phone me tomorrow.

"You should've let me know about Roddie," I said to Michael.

"Didn't know he was one of yours. Look, Susan, we need to talk about this." The cigarette was back in its pack, a move that was beginning to look like a tic. "There's a link between Baird and Renfrow. The survey, the trust, how many coincidences add up to a lie?"

"Roddie explained all that, and I believe him. You should focus on someone who did know Chaz Renfrow. His wife told me you found an agency contract…at the scene of the crime."

"Part of a contract, clutched in Renfrow's hand."

"Did it look like this?" I passed him the copy from my bag. "Courtesy of Dr. Johanna Lang. Says she gave another copy to Tyre yesterday."

Michael looked it over. "You signed this last Monday?"

"I did not! Last Monday I agreed to advise Chaz's campaign, and we shook hands on it. I never saw, let alone signed, that…*document*. It's a forgery. A scam. It excludes the Navy Yard, and whatta ya know, that's the very site Chaz selected. Johanna wants me to give back my retainer, which she calls a finder's fee, like I'm trying to cheat her now that Chaz is dead. She tried to bully me out of the money today, and when she couldn't, she wheedled."

He smiled. "And that worked?"

"Sort of." I edged toward the door. "I'm leaving, Michael. Talk to you tomorrow."

"What's wrong with tonight?"

◇◇◇

Rain began to fall, a few needle drops that shocked my skin. Michael wrapped his arm around my shoulders, and I hugged his waist, and we moved slowly through the night like invalids bracing. By the time we reached the parking lot, the drops had turned to mist, and every nerve in my body was on fire. We stood beside my car listening to distant thunder, while I fumbled inside my hobo bag for the key.

"Wouldn't a briefcase be easier?" Michael pushed my bag aside and kissed me.

"If I was that buttoned up..." I started to say, my words engulfed by another kiss, "...I'd never have fallen for a madman like you."

"Me, a madman?" His fingers wound through my hair, by now a crinkled mop in the saturated air. "What does that make you?"

"Happy," I admitted, against all odds and my mother's advice about discretion.

With Michael at the wheel, we made it to my house in twelve minutes and thirty-seven seconds by my cellphone clock. From the street, the painted lady glowed like a cruise ship in the night; downstairs, the light-timers were doing their two-step, and upstairs, as was my habit since the attack, I'd left on every light.

Michael handed me the car keys. "Your, uh, vehicle needs a tune-up."

"Or a miracle." Though, if the gods were grudging, having Michael back in my life was miracle enough. I could get by without a reliable car.

As we headed down the driveway, the security lamp snapped on, spreading light like smoke through the drizzle. Michael squatted by the side door and touched an invisible spot on the wet pavement. My blood? I rubbed my arms to keep the goose bumps down.

Michael blotted his fingers on a tissue and stood up. "The ER physician thinks your attacker used something extremely fine-edged. A precision razor."

Precision razor...knives, box cutters, even chain saws were somehow less fearsome.

"M.E. on the scene said the same thing about Torie Moran, only he called it a microtome blade."

"Microtome...?"

"Lab tool, used to slice tissue for slides. It's basically a blade on a handle."

I forced myself to picture it. "Like an X-Acto knife?"

"More like a straight razor. We found three in their cases. That's every blade at NGT, accounted for."

"Did you search Lab 45?"

"We searched the entire building. What do you know that I don't?"

"Plenty," I said, to tease him and to relieve my own anxiety, and succeeding in neither. The memory of Chaz's blank face as he urged me to explore the lab while he dealt with Torie remained as vivid as a recurring dream. "The night Torie was killed, I saw a tool on a shelf that looked like a weird pasta scraper. Tapered handle, wide edge."

"I'll check with Evidence, but if there was a microtome blade or anything like it in Lab 45, they wouldn't have missed it. The ones they found were in locked labs, by the way. Only a few researchers, and Renfrow, knew the entrance codes."

A raindrop trickled down Michael's cheek. I reached up and brushed it away with my fingertips. He kissed my palm and held my hand just long enough for me to feel that no harm could come to me now, outside in the rain, on the spot where I'd been attacked. "Tyre thinks Renfrow and Torie were having an affair that went sour," he said, all business again.

"Sergeant Tyre would suspect a pair of mismatched socks. How many affairs end in murder? And why would Chaz come after me? We sure weren't having an affair." It was suddenly, overwhelmingly, important to me that Michael understood this.

"I offer a possibility, Susan."

"How's Johanna for a possibility. She knows the entrance codes, and if Tyre's right, maybe she was murderously jealous."

"Jealousy, greed, revenge...yeah, yeah, but something else is going on. Why *were* you assaulted?" Michael's face was closed, his emotions scribbled in a language only five people on the planet could decipher. Was I one? "Brookline police said the guy who attacked you crashed through back yards to get here, breaking fences, flattening shrubs. But, amazingly, nobody heard or saw anything."

"It was late. Maybe they didn't hear anything till I yelled."

In law school, I'd read about Kitty Genovese, stabbed to death in full view of her neighbors' apartments while she *screamed* for help. Eventually, one person out of the dozens who heard her called the police, far too late to save her. My aged, cat-loving neighbors had rushed out at my first shriek and delivered me from evil. I vowed to never again make jokes about cold-hearted nosy New Englanders.

I unlocked the door, and we loitered at the foot of the stairs. "I'm not sure it was a man who attacked me," I said. "The voice was a...whisper."

"Him. Her. Whoever it was probably picked up plenty of scratches along the way."

I knew where this was leading, back to Roddie's bruised hand. "Won't you please forget about Roddie Baird? He's a good man. He would never hurt me, or anyone. And he didn't know Torie Moran."

"Baird's in the clear for Moran. The night she was killed, he was at Children's Hospital till dawn with his daughter and her appendicitis, which turned out to be too many cookies at bedtime. If whoever killed Moran attacked you, he's off the hook there, too."

"But not for Chaz?" I had a queasy realization. "Are you saying there are two different murderers?"

"Looks that way to me. Two different murders, two different weapons. I'm convinced Baird knew Renfrow."

"Even if he did, he had no reason to kill Chaz."

"Maybe he lost his shirt on NGT. How's that for a reason?"

"Revenge wouldn't bring back his money, and under the dreamy-eyed mask, Roddie is completely pragmatic. What else have you got on him, besides a few irrelevant scratches?"

"That unconfirmed alibi."

I had no answer to this.

We climbed the stairs and went in through the pantry, thinking our separate thoughts. The kitchen smelled like honey, the day's heat trapped inside a friendly room I had bunkered like all the rest. I cranked open a window, and cool moist air swirled over my face. Michael came up behind me and kissed my neck, and I let go of Roddie and Torie and Chaz. Around me, on the counter, lay tag ends from BeeCee's: apples in a copper bowl, sugar cubes on a flow-blue plate, a box of China tea. Something like happiness surged through me.

"Want some?" I lifted the box, covered in cryptic strokes.

"Later."

Somehow, we made it to the bedroom without knocking over any chairs.

From the night table lamp, the leaded glass dragonfly perched on an emerald leaf, topaz eyes fixed and appraising. The rain was heavier now, coming out of the west, a whistle in the wind. Christ, I could hardly believe it. My love in my arms, and I in my bed again.

While I lolled on embroidered sheets, coffee brewed in the kitchen. I pictured Michael hunting for cups, his bony knees bumping the cupboards. Last night's rain had washed away two weeks of muggy heat. After breakfast we planned to walk by the Charles, maybe stop for lunch, leaving just enough time for me to keep my appointment with Johanna. Unless I decided to retain my retainer, as any self-respecting attorney would do.

The phone rang.

"Susan?" The voice was faint, but I recognized the soft Southern tones.

"Beauford? Where are you?"

"Lobbying the pope."

"You're kidding."

"When in Rome...Never mind. I've been worried about you. Did you take my advice and drop Renfrow?"

How could Beauford know? I sat up and folded my pillow against the headboard. "It never came to that. I...he was murdered last week."

"Really." Beau sounded so laid back I wondered if he'd reinserted his ear stud. "Glad I'm out of the country. I'd be suspect numero uno."

I hesitated, then spilled out the rest of the story. "Look, Torie Moran was murdered a few days before he was. I'm sorry. I know you were friends."

A long silence, then his voice, hard now, completely engaged. "Renfrow killed her."

"I think somebody wanted them both out of the way."

"He killed her! I told you about NGT's polluting. Torie caught a spill on her cellphone camera and burned a disk. When the time was right, she planned to go public."

"Torie a whistle blower?" The Torie I'd met seemed far too self-absorbed to worry about a little poison in the aquifer. More to the point, Chaz told me she had a financial stake in NGT: stock, a piece of a patent. "What spilled? Did she show you the video?"

"She gave me a back-up copy after Renfrow bankrupted me. Said one of these days she'd use it to bring him down."

"Maybe she was just trying to make you feel better, show a little solidarity. She was fully invested in the company."

"Torie had a conscience!" He was shouting again. "I screened the video. It's unmistakable. A bucket of stuff spills, and everybody in the lab clears out in about three seconds except a guy in a jump suit with a hose. He washes it down the drain. Torie told me it was radioactive material, and it happened all the time. And Renfrow condoned it."

"Beau, you've got to tell the police."

"Police? I'll hold a press conference! I'll organize a lawsuit! Torie Moran was a crusader. Before I'm through, NGT's going to be paying goddamn reparations!"

"Slow down," I said. "Where's the video?"

"My apartment. I'm...hold on a minute." I heard voices, Beauford murmuring to someone. When he came back, he'd shifted emotional gears yet again. "Susan, I'm running very late here. Gotta go."

"Wait! Tell my...tell Lieutenant Benedict. He's investigating the murders. Here, I'll put him on."

"No time. People are signaling me."

"Give me your number."

"Palazzo Spirito, room 247." His voice came in a staticky whisper I strained to understand. "I'll call you again later."

"Beau, can I go to your apartment and borrow the video?"

A few garbled words, then our connection broke. On caller ID his number came up zeros, fourteen of them, and when I dialed his cell, it went immediately into voicemail.

Over breakfast, Michael said he'd track down Beauford at his hotel.

"What if you can't?"

He shrugged. "We'll wait till he gets back. The video might be useful, but without Torie to account for it, it's really just a kind of visual hearsay."

While I dressed for the day in my faux-biker top and a wrap-around skirt, Michael took a call of his own, in the kitchen. Five minutes later, he rejoined me in the bedroom, as dispirited as yesterday's jeans, which he'd put on again after his shower. "The Captain has invited me to lunch. At his house, no less."

"It's your day off!" In the back of my mind, I realized, a plan had been hatching: After our stroll by the river, Michael and I would drop in for lunch at Tavola Rustica where Nino would welcome Michael and forgive me. "Do you *have* to go?"

"The company store, Susan. We'll still have tonight."

"What about our walk?" Was I actually whining?

"We're good for that, as long as you get me to my car by noon."

Some of Michael's clothes had languished in my spare room since April. He changed again, out of the jeans into wrinkled but clean chinos and a faded shirt that put blue in his sea-gray eyes. He caught me watching. "What're you staring at?" A wicked smile lifted his mustache and gave him a Rhett Butler air. I suddenly felt all Scarletty. He reached out and tugged the looped zipper that ran from my neck to my waist. "Maybe you should wear something simpler for a walk by the river."

"Depends," I said, "on what you mean by river."

The zipper glided silently down, fingers untying me, river washing over me. Bad girls go everywhere.

Chapter Thirteen

Greed

I parked near the bridge, and we headed for the woods, away from joggers and bicyclists. At river's edge the path petered to cinders, and I stopped to watch a scull glide by. Michael pushed ahead, as if he had a destination. When I caught up, he was standing on a concrete platform a few hundred yards from a boathouse surrounded by skiffs and canoes that rocked gently in the current. I sat down and pulled him next to me. I was feeling so happy I wanted to shout, but Michael wanted to talk shop.

"If Beauford Smith is right about toxic spills, Renfrow may have had a helluva better reason than a botched affair to kill Torie."

"So would anyone involved in a cover-up." I got to my knees and sank back on my heels. "Take the man with the hose. What if he found out about Torie's video?"

Michael kept his face to the river, at this point wide enough to harbor a miniature island covered with scrub. "Until I get my hands on it, this is just so much speculation."

Why did Michael's speculations always lead back to my candidates? Frustration overwhelmed my joy in the day, and I struggled to shake it off. "You're ignoring others with motive."

"If you mean Johanna and Bart Bievsky, the night Renfrow was killed they had dinner in Boston, in full view of the restaurant staff. They stayed over at the Copley. Room service brought drinks. Housekeeping brought towels. Everybody vouches for everybody."

"Maybe a little baksheesh changed hands. Where were they when Torie was murdered? Where was Glenn?"

"We're looking hard at all the alibis, Susan. I'm not ruling anyone out." He selected a flat stone and shied it into the river. Three little skips, then it sank. "I don't know if Renfrow and Baird are murderers, but it's no coincidence that both were your candidates."

"You mean it's no coincidence that two intelligent men looking for a political consultant would settle on me." Carefully balancing the chips on each of my shoulders, I got to my feet. "I am easy to work with. I am not too expensive. I have never lost an election."

"How many campaigns have you advised?"

"Four. And three in progress." Not counting Chaz. "I know it's not a lot, but numbers don't matter, just results." If I didn't stand up for myself who would? But numbers lie, I well knew. If my campaigns were medical trials, the sample would be too small to count.

Wind gusted off the river. From a fringe of island weeds, a mother duck and a trail of ducklings glided out, the water so clear I could see their feet paddling. "I wonder where the term 'lame duck' comes from?" I said.

Michael had no eyes for ducks. "One of your candidates loaned over a million dollars to another of your candidates. You really believe that was a coincidence?"

"*If* the money was loaned. I'm with Roddie on this. You still haven't proved it."

"We will. Renfrow and Baird are connected somehow, and you're in the cross hairs. Was it really your talent for winning aldermen's races that brought Renfrow to you?"

He was stirring up all my old doubts. My eyes roved after the ducks as they meandered across the river. Life was better for ducks.

Back in Boston, I idled the engine while we discussed the evening's possibilities. Michael tossed his cigarette lighter from palm to palm. "I don't know if that's such a good idea," he said.

"But I *want* to cook. I'll be back early. I'm meeting Johanna at two. How long can it take to hand over seventeen thousand dollars?"

"Lawyer giving back her fee?" The lighter bounced off his knee, and he bent for it, not quickly enough to hide the smile. "We better eat out. You're going to need consoling."

"Staying home and being frugal will console me." For once, I wanted to fire up the old hearth, though Lord knows, the frugality wasn't optional. The three thousand I'd decided to keep was earmarked for overdue rent. "I'll make something easy, tuna noodle casserole."

I could see Michael weighing my offer against his desire for a decent meal. "I don't mind staying home," he said, stepping out of the car. "But let's be fair. Whoever gets back first cooks. Deal?"

"Deal," I said, grudgingly, because I knew he'd manage to rush back ahead of me.

As I drove off, I caught a glimpse of him in my rearview mirror, unlocking his plain blue sedan. The cigarette was already lit.

With two hours to kill before my appointment with Johanna, I knew exactly where I needed to go while I waited. Tavola Rustica, without Michael to deflect Nino's anger. Traffic was light and, like a migrating swallow, or a lemming, I drove on automatic pilot, using the miles to frame a question that had been tugging at me for days: Was the attack on Nino somehow linked to me?

Just after twelve I parked in the municipal lot and walked down Boylston along Lombard's building, past the drugstore to Tavola. Through the window, I could see people talking and laughing, flowers in vases, elbows on napkins. I entered to an airy infusion of basilico, lemon, and Neapolitan folk songs. Inside, family life ruled. A toddler whimpered to his smiling mother. Three tables over, a little girl poked a daisy in her father's hair. I was the only spinster in the place.

From the pastry case I watched Nino tap menus against the stand. Up close, his eyes were dull, and there were purple bruises on his face and neck. A surgical pad was taped to his forehead. When he was ready to notice me, he pushed the menus into a holder. "Whatta you want?"

"I saw stracciatella on the menu."

"No tables." He walked away from me.

"Nino, wait. I need to talk to you. Your lease, and…"

He kept on going. When he reached the kitchen area, he shouted something to Benny, who was shaking a skillet over blue flames that curled up the sides. Benny abandoned his station and came over to me. "Nino wants you to wait there." He pointed to the deserted bar.

Very quickly after that, generosity overwhelming his rudeness, Nino brought me stracciatella. He glanced at his watch and sat down at my frisbee-sized table. "Five minutes."

Steam rose off the soup, so hot I couldn't touch the bowl. "Remember the woman I told you about?" I said. "She was murdered with some kind of blade. Then somebody used one on me." I gave him the details, and he listened impassively. "So I'm wondering if the guy who attacked you had anything like that blade on him."

"Blades, clubs." He rubbed his bandage. "I don't remember nothing. I'm old. Whatever happened, it's gone."

"Not because you're old. A head wound can wipe out anybody's memory. If it comes back, you might help solve a murder."

"Solve nothing." He waved invisible flies off my soup. "I don't remember, but I *know*. I'm taking care of Mr. Fat Rich Toad my own way."

"Oh? Did Lombard admit something?"

"Mind your own business. Time's up! That's all I got to say to you."

Instead of making awkward goodbyes, I sipped my soup. Fiery strands of egg bonded to the roof of my mouth. "Look, Nino," I burbled through ice I'd dug out of my water glass. "I'm worried about you. Two people associated with me are dead. I've been

126 Angela Gerst

hurt. What if you're wrong about Lombard? You could still be in danger. Maybe because of me."

His face seemed to soften, and he gave my wrist a little tap. "Watch out for yourself, hear me? You trust too much. Like that guy you brought here, drank all my grappa."

"But...haven't you heard?" My surprise faded. Nino didn't keep up with the news, said it depressed him. He put his hands on his knees, and I told him what I knew. When I finished, he shook his head.

"Bad things come with that man. I warned you." Quintessential Nino logic: a nugget of reason surrounded by chaos.

"But I'm not dead, Nino. Chaz is."

"You got lucky for once." He stood up, something final in his stance. "Finished?"

"I'll leave," I said. "Just want to tell you I'm working on getting your old lease back."

"I got it back."

Surprise licked my face. "I...wonderful! What happened?" But I knew. Judge Odette's magic hat.

"The toad said I could stay."

"So you won after all."

"Yeah, I won." He picked up my bowl. "I got a new lawyer. I want my papers back."

My hand froze on the table. "I...I'll put everything in the mail."

We left the bar together. I tried to pay, but Nino wouldn't touch my money. The ball was in his court now. No way could I come back again with my hat in my hand. At the door I waved to Benny who held up a spatula and rocked it back and forth like a tiny rubber flag. From Tavola's hidden speakers, a tenor began to soar. Just what I needed. Puccini, and sobbing.

Outside, I paused at the MediRX window display, walkers, portable potties, crutches, guaranteed to set your heart aflutter. An arrangement of plastic braces looked oddly festive trimmed in pink and white velcro. I thought about Spaal's gym and physical fitness. How maybe I should join while I was still continent and ambulatory. How infinitely preferable was the treadmill to the walker.

My left eye began to throb. I went inside for aspirin and almost fell over a stack of *Saveur* magazines, August issue, I noted, transfixed by a cover of flaky raspberry jewels on a crystal platter. Impulsively, I decided to bake whatever that thing was for dessert tonight. I grabbed a magazine, along with two rolls of Lifesavers, and a jumbo bottle of generic aspirin.

Next to the pharmacy counter, a persimmon-haired woman was bent over a ledger making pencil checks. Her fingernails were green, her eyelashes Betty Boop. To my surprise, the word "Pharmacist" was stitched on her dustcoat lapel in thread that matched her nails.

"Hi," I said, and she looked up, eyes a glittering, contact lens blue. I dumped my selections on the counter.

"Beautiful day, isn't it?" she said. "After all those scorchers." She closed the ledger and whipped her nails across the register keys.

I paid her, astonished that, in a world awash in sugar, Lifesavers cost more than aspirin. Luckily, I had more headaches than sweet teeth. "Get much business these days?" I asked, feeling particularly human after lunch with Nino.

"Used to be busier before the building emptied out. Restaurant still brings us a few customers. But I gotta tell you, on Saturdays, by three o'clock this whole block is dead."

"Where did everybody go?"

"Landlord's getting ready for a major new tenant."

"Any idea who?"

"It's been hush-hush, but we think one of the hospitals is coming in." She tilted her head toward the medical district just up the road. "This building is perfect for outpatient clinics. It's got the square footage. Parking, and public transportation a block away."

It made sense, and it explained why cheapskate Lombard had bought out his tenants with such a free hand. A hospital would make valuable improvements to his building and then, the clincher, pay him ten times his current rent.

"Are you moving?" Like Alice in Wonderland, the more I probed, the curiouser I got.

"We stay. Headquarters hinted we're part of the deal. My guess is, whoever's coming in will either buy up our parent company or give us a service contract."

"Why all the secrecy?"

"Wondered myself. Maybe the new tenant wants to get all his ducks in a row before the neighbors find out. Zoning is a patchwork around here."

For all her green nail polish, the lady seemed aware and informed, someone I might after all trust to fill my prescriptions, though maybe not to shut up about them.

"Tavola Rustica hasn't moved," I said, an assertion I hoped would draw out more canny speculation.

"I'm betting the new tenant wants it," she obliged. "There's a trend away from cafeterias in hospitals."

In my car, I opened the Lifesavers, curiosity unsatisfied. If Nino had still been my client, or even my friend, I'd have called Peter Lombard and asked why he changed his mind about Tavola's lease. Not for a minute did I believe that a satellite hospital was interested in Nino's restaurant. On the other hand...I crunched into gear and headed for Waltham...who cared what I didn't believe?

Not even Boris' Bakery did business on weekend afternoons in July, but here I was, juggling my hobo bag and two towering coffees from Freddie's. At the end of the hall, bedpans and walkers fresh in my mind, I veered away from the elevator and galloped up the stairs. Coffee beaded through the little holes on top of the cup covers.

News of today's temperature drop hadn't reached my office, so steamy my hair puffed out like chestnut cheese doodles. I carried the coffees to the kitchen area and at last watered my long-suffering plants. At my desk, I cut Johanna a check for seventeen thousand dollars, and that simple act relieved the uneasiness I'd felt since I'd let Chaz woo me with largesse. I remembered how he'd stood over me while I deposited his check, how I'd shivered to the ATM machine's eerie hum. *Radix malorum est cupiditas.* The root of all evil is greed, as we English majors learned from *The Canterbury Tales*; law school notwithstanding, accepting Chaz's money had made me feel greedy and sad, proving that even lawyers get the blues.

Now I stretched out on my screened-in sofa with *Saveur,* sipping coffee and yawning over fish stews and lemon pies and hand-rolled noodles. I tried to visualize my mother's pasta scraper. What *had* I seen in Lab 45? Michael said he'd check with his Evidence crew.

A pleasant heaviness tugged at my lids. Beside me, the fan stirred my hair. Fingers…how dreamy…scar on his cheekbone, taw marble eyes. No. Chaz was marble eyes, blue like Cordy's. I closed mine. The minutes stretched out like taffy. *Saveur* slipped from my hand. I thought about lemon pies and Delia's eyes.

I woke with a start to find Johanna standing over me, an over-night bag in her hand, something floral in the air. "I knocked, but you didn't hear me," she said.

A moment of fuddled panic kept me from speaking. Had I sensed her presence and pulled myself out of a nightmare? In this shadowy corner of the room, her bony nose and short dark mane gave her a Delphic look. I half expected her to launch into prophesy.

"Um…" I said, as she stepped away from the sofa and gave me breathing room. The little creatures scrabbling in my gut settled down. I rubbed sleep from my eyes.

When I was fully awake, I offered to reheat the spare coffee, but Johanna declined. "I don't have time. I'd just like my check." Her expression was not quite avid. In ivory linen and bitter-sweet silk, everything spotless and eggshell smooth, Johanna was dressed to chair a board meeting. Next to her, I was a bag lady in training.

"How did you get in?"

"Through the side entrance."

"I mean my office."

"When you didn't hear me, I turned the knob and came in."

"I could swear it was locked." I walked over and checked the button bolt. Down, but not all the way. I pressed my palm against the door and listened for the click, then led Johanna to a client chair.

Her hands settled in her lap, not clenched exactly. She glanced around. "Is this a loft?"

"Some call it a penthouse."

She didn't crack a smile.

I adjusted a standard waiver-of-claim, and after a close reading, she signed. Then I gave her the check, which she examined long enough to be sure of the comma and decimal point.

"Thank you," she said. "It's a small amount, but kingdoms have foundered for want of a horse."

Very poetic. Should have alluded to Shakespeare myself and taken a round twenty percent.

By two-thirty she was ready to leave. "Do you have a phone book? I need to rent a car. Glenn has mine. He and Darcy stayed overnight in New Hampshire. Some kind of sunrise ceremony on top of a mountain, I gather." She seemed embarrassed. "I thought it would be simple to rent a car in Weston. It wasn't. I took a cab here. Cost me the earth, and now I'll have to pay again. I can't afford to lose another day at my lab."

With seventeen thousand in hand was Johanna angling for a ride? While she searched Yellow Pages, I had a noble impulse, only a little tainted by ulterior motive. I wanted Chaz's nominating papers to wave in Michael's face. I especially wanted another discreet look through Lab 45. If I forgot about raspberry pastry, I could Beem her back to Telford and still be home in time for dinner.

"Don't bother renting a car. I'll take you," I said, and told her why, the part about my kind heart, and the part about Chaz's nominating papers. Lab 45 was not mentioned.

To my surprise, she declined. The rental company had a customer pickup service, and she gave them my address. Glancing a last time at the check, she zippered it inside her bag. "The irony is, while I pay for cabs and car rentals, the police still have the Lexus."

"Where's the Sonett?"

"In my driveway. It's too unreliable for me to risk driving into the city. Glenn wants it, but I'll have to sell that money sponge." She hurried to the door. "I'll look for those papers," she said. "If I find them, I'll mail them to you."

Twenty minutes later, while I was recalculating my debt payments, Odette called with grim news: Roddie's campaign manager had jumped ship. "Because of that business with the police. I've agreed to take over until Roddie decides whether to stay in the race."

"Roddie's thinking of quitting? Without talking it over with me?"

"Losing his manager really shook him, Susan. And your, uh, friendship with one of the investigators bothers him, too."

I tossed my empty paper coffee cup at the wastebasket, and missed by a Massachusetts mile. "I don't mix my private and public lives. If Roddie doesn't understand that, I'll explain it to him right now."

"Give him time to work things through, Susan. He relented and hired my nephew, just to handle the media. They've started nosing around, and Lauren has gone into a funk. Roddie isn't sure she can stand up to the pressure. And he's worried about the children."

Reluctantly, I agreed to wait until tomorrow. "He's done nothing wrong," I said. "He'd be a fool to quit."

"Exactly what I told him. All the same, I am glad he called Gordon." She cleared her throat. "Susan, whatever happens, I want to thank you for all you've done."

"You're the one deserves thanks. I heard about Froy."

She laughed. "Well…"

"And Nino's lease. Lombard's letting Tavola stay in Brookline."

"Wonderful," she said, "but much as I'd like to take credit, I haven't called Peter yet."

"Must be Nino's new lawyer." Someone far more effective than his old one.

I locked up and left for home.

Nosing out of the parking lot, I spotted Johanna in front of the building, twisting her ring and watching traffic flow by. Her skirt was wrinkled now, and it bagged over her knees just the way mine did. She looked vulnerable, and very tired.

I leaned out the window. "Hey!"

She twisted around, her face a mix of hope and disappointment.

"What happened to your rental car?" I shouted

"They didn't come. I'll have to call a cab after all."

"Bad luck." I opened the passenger's door, and this time, she accepted the ride.

Chapter Fourteen

Visualize Whirled Peas

"Had lunch?"

"Brunch with Cordy at Idlebrook." Johanna pushed her glasses up into her hair, brown and thick, like some New England critter's winter pelt. Afternoon glare threw shadows around her head, sharpening her profile.

"Your mother-in-law's a lovely woman, beautiful eyes. Must have been hard on her, the breakup of your marriage."

"Not at all. She couldn't grasp the idea. Cordy is not fully *compos mentis*, as I'm sure you've noticed."

Compos mentis. Getting, and keeping, it together. Had I really seen beauty in Cordy's empty face? Eyes may or may not mirror the soul, but in Cordy's I had seen Chaz. Before age stole her memory, she'd probably been as magnetic as her son.

"For Cordy, nothing changes now. Every day she waits for Charles; and for all his faults, he *was* a good son. If only he'd been as good a husband, or father." Melancholy softened Johanna's voice, but not her self-possession, which made her impossible to warm to. From the corner of my eye I saw her press a hand to her cheek, though I couldn't imagine her crying.

"If you want to talk, I'm a good listener," I said. I'd be the mythical stranger who offers an insight, then gets off the bus before you do.

She found a Kleenex and blew her nose. "Charles was a monster with smiling eyes. He cheated on me so smoothly I only found out that first time when he left a draft email open on his computer. The love-mail, I called it. No address or name, just a few honeyed phrases he probably lifted from a book."

"It's possible he wanted you to find it."

She nodded. "To punish me for using his computer. For invading his space."

For snooping, did she mean? "Or maybe he invented a lover."

"No. His affairs were compulsive." She brought out a compact, which opened under her thumb. Brittle chimes tinkled out. A musical compact? I couldn't help staring.

"Present from Glenn. When he was a little boy, he used to save up his allowance and order doo-dads from those on-line catalogs." In the angled mirror, she powdered her face, dabbing her chin so fiercely I figured she'd pounced on a zit.

"Chaz was awfully proud of him," I said. "Told me how Glenn was going to manage his campaign, how he made the Dean's List at Dartmouth."

"Dean's List?" She clamped down the lid on a thin middle C. "From the day Glenn entered college, he's been on academic probation. He has so many incompletes they've suspended him."

Another of Chaz's white lies, though this one bothered me more than the lie about being divorced, which was almost the truth, give or take a quibble. Hold on, Susan, I chided myself. A lie that was *almost* the truth? That's called sophistry, and it leads to sleaze and corruption and SNL sketches of national candidates. A lie is a lie is a lie.

"As a boy," Johanna went on, "Glenn was a bundle of so-called disabilities, ADD and the like. He's still shy. Gravitates to bossy people like that Darcy."

The Beemer hesitated, but I stayed in the left lane and managed to pass a slow-moving truck without triggering the rumbles and spurts that might interrupt Johanna's narrative.

"Father and son couldn't have been more unalike," she said, circling her finger over the compact in a way that seemed obsessive to me. "Charles was a brilliant student and a gifted athlete. High school quarterback. College lacrosse. He plays… played tournament tennis. Glenn couldn't live up to his father's achievements, let alone his expectations." She stopped, but I had only to wait, to drive, to not intrude.

"Charles never forgave him. The cruelty started when Glenn was very young. Barbed jokes. Humiliations. Charles walked out on Little League games the minute Glenn dropped the ball. By the time he was twelve, Glenn refused to play any sports at all."

"Poor kid." I didn't know what else to say.

"I'll speak one good word of the dead. Charles thought his cruelty would help Glenn 'shape up.' When it didn't, Charles became more confronting. Once, he lost control and slapped Glenn in front of a friend. All this took a terrible toll. Glenn even developed a little stutter."

The highway narrowed, and within seconds traffic began to crawl. I slid into first, careful not to stall. "Johanna, you've just told me in so many words why Glenn might want to murder his father."

She laughed out loud. "Everyone wanted to murder my husband."

"Who's everyone?"

"The staff, anyone who knew him well. But Charles was more valuable to us alive. If I'd wanted him dead, I'd have done him in long ago."

"Because of how he treated Glenn?"

She took a sudden interest in the highway, half-smiling at something I couldn't see from the driver's side. "I know you're pumping me, Susan."

"No, I…"

"Oh, why the hell shouldn't I talk to you? I *need* to talk."

The car in front of us advanced, and now I saw the bumper sticker that had caught her eye. *Visualize Whirled Peas*. Peas, murders, lies, the joke was on me. For all my probing, I could visualize the mash-up, but the world on its rightful axis eluded me.

"Anyway, I've already rambled on to the police, which must make my dismal marriage a public record." A softer Johanna was speaking now. She told me how Chaz had stopped having affairs when she threatened to leave him, how after Glenn was sent off to boarding school, he'd started cheating again. Her response, an affair of her own, in effect ended the marriage. They'd stayed together for NGT. "And for Glenn," she added quickly.

"Any idea who he was seeing?"

"By then I had no interest in his love life. I accepted that our marriage had become a business deal, just like our contract with Chestnut Hill College."

"Johanna, the police think Chaz and Torie were having an affair."

"It couldn't have been Torie. She wasn't his intellectual… peer." A satisfied smile broke across her face, as if she knew her own worth. "It wasn't Torie."

We were traveling a route I recognized from my drive home with Chaz, lanes that curved between acres of farmland and encroaching suburbs. I glanced at Johanna. "Maybe they had a fling, and Chaz broke it off, and Torie wanted revenge. Beauford Smith told me she was about to blow the whistle on NGT for toxic dumping."

"That's a lie! NGT has a safety record any lab would envy. And Torie loved the company." Johanna gave her head an angry shake. "Beauford Smith is a vicious, unprincipled man."

Not the Beauford I knew. Torie's video might yet have the last word on toxic rumors. "How long were you at Chestnut Hill College?"

"Eight years. We moved to Telford after I identified the longevity enzyme."

"Is that like, uh, the immortality thing?"

"No. It's like the chicken ovary thing."

By God, in spite of everything, the lady had a sense of humor. "What is it you do? I mean, how do you get from a chicken ovary to cluck everlasting?"

"Do you really want to hear about this?"

"In easy English? Sure."

"Essentially, we insert the longevity enzyme into a chicken ovary gene for cloning. Not a single altered cell has deteriorated or died since we began our experiments. Does this mean immortality?" She lifted her hands. "Like every biotechnology firm, we hope the cloned gene leads to a cure for cancer. That would be immortality enough for me."

"Does Glenn work in research?"

"Not anymore. NGT has a small marketing department. He fits better there."

"Have the police questioned him?"

"Yes, and they're satisfied that Glenn had no opportunity to murder his father, or Torie. Bart and I didn't either." She faced me. "That's what you want to know, isn't it?"

"Johanna, the police are never satisfied. I'm trying to understand where all the pieces fit. This has touched me too." I told her about the attack in my driveway, not mentioning the microtome blade; I hoped to search Lab 45 without tipping my hand.

"How terrible," she said. "I didn't know."

We drove the last miles in a silence that was broken by a sudden *crack* like gunshot when a pebble dinged my car. I gasped. Johanna didn't turn a hair.

But in the empty NGT parking lot, she faltered. I'd parked where she told me, in her own space, three down from Torie's. Last night's rain had washed away most of the bloodstains, and what remained looked like coolant leaks if you didn't know better. We gave Torie's space a wide berth and circled to the front of the building.

Passing a corner window, I spotted the Persian violet I'd admired on my first visit to Lab 45, and the sight of it dropping like leftover salad inspired me. "Your poor plant's in trouble," I said, hoping to insinuate myself into the lab without having to lie.

"Torie's plant. Damn thing gives me the willies. No one's watered it since…"

"Let me do it. I've got a green thumb." Well, I *had* tended my plants today.

"Better you than me."

She unlocked the entrance, and turned off the alarms, and as we tapped down empty corridors, mounted cameras noted our progress. Unlike NGT's working labs, which had coded touch pads by every door, Lab 45 was open to the hall.

"Here we are." Johanna stood back to let me in. "There should be a hose under the sink long enough to reach the plant. Or, why don't you take it? Nobody wants it."

After she left to look for Chaz's papers, I examined the plant, yellow leaves listing as if weevils had struck. Persian violets must need water *every week*, which certainly ruled them out as plants for my office.

Next to a box of plastic bags the hose coiled like a comatose snake. I attached it to the faucet, but water pressure sent it careening into the sink. For a few wet moments, I tried to adjust the connector, saw it was stripped and gave up. Snoop first, then deal with the plant.

I hurried to the wide bracketed shelves where I'd first seen the pasta scraper, or microtome blade if that's what it was. The vinaigrette bottles were there, funnels. Microwave oven. Shelf after shelf of laboratory jumble. Working methodically, I'd reached the middle when, somewhere in the building, a door slammed, making hollow echoes that spooked and goaded me.

I worked faster, clearing a space and leaning into the shelf. In the weak light I made out test tubes and screens and...*there it was*, stuck sideways between shelf and wall, as if someone had jammed it there. I reached for it, and it bit my finger, and a curse whipped up my throat. Gingerly, I tugged, and the handle came out, attached to a fine steel blade. Up close and streaked with my blood, it no longer resembled a refugee from my mother's kitchen, but more like a hand-held guillotine.

Footsteps clopped down the corridor, and for an eerie second I heard the ghost of Torie's sandaled feet. I knew it was Johanna, but goose bumps prickled the nape of my neck. Should I leave the blade where I'd found it and hope it would still be there when I told Michael where it was? Should I steal it and risk breaking the evidence chain? Or had I done that already?

The footsteps closed in, leaving me no time to cross the room for my bag. I rammed the tool back against the wall and filled the empty space with lab clutter. Using the hem of my skirt, I wiped my blood off the shelf, and with half a second to spare, finger oozing, I made it to the sink.

Johanna walked in and stopped short, nearly dropping the folder in her hand, as if the sight of my blood revulsed her. "Are you all right?"

"Nicked myself on the hose," I lied, directing a blast of cold water from the faucet to my finger. Blood swirled down the drain, and the cut gaped like a fish gill.

Her eyes wandered from my finger to the faucet to the plant in the window. "How could you cut yourself on a hose?" Her expression was a mix of incredulity and concern.

"Connector's stripped—it's really jagged around the rim." I turned off the faucet and wrapped my finger in a wad of Kleenex from my hobo bag. There was a basin under the sink, which I used to slosh a little water on the dying plant, an act of mercy that made me feel better about my lies.

In the hall, Johanna handed me Chaz's nominating papers. "Are these what you wanted? They were under a box of computer paper."

◇◇◇

Something was wrong. Instead of beating me to the stove, Michael was on the sofa, staring through the big front windows at a pink and gray twilight, the snuffed stub of a cigarette wedged between two fingers. I thought about Bogart, how cool he'd looked before lung cancer wasted him. I stepped over Michael's legs, squeezed myself between his hip and a pillow, and kissed his ear, wishing I could kiss away his gloom.

"Hey, darlin'. *Que tal.*" He hugged me, and didn't resist when I pinched his cigarette and flicked it into the fireplace.

"How was lunch with the boss? Did you eat well?" Italian insight. What your hosts fed you told a story, about who they were or what they thought of you. Sometimes both.

"Turkey roll," he said.

Ah, hell.

"It's all right, Susan. Captain Shea is Irish. He put out a real spread. Pickles and potato salad. Guinness."

"So he didn't fire you?"

"Not exactly."

I'd been joking. Michael wasn't.

"He asked me to think about stepping down from the NGT cases." Michael avoided my eyes, which told me what the problem was. Me.

"Tyre brought Shea that agency contract, and thoughtfully pointed out your signature. Told him you have ties to everybody, victims, suspects, the lieutenant in charge. Your fingerprints and your nose are everywhere." He laughed, a dry little chuckle.

Lacking perspective, I couldn't salvage any humor from Tyre's treachery. "What a putz that guy is," I said, though I knew today's visit to Lab 45 would add weight to his narrative. "You must be feeling completely betrayed."

"More like stupid. And violated. But there's a wake-up call here. Shea's worried about my objectivity." He pulled me closer. "You want the truth? I'm worried too. He's leaving the decision to me."

"Sure he is. *If* you decide to take yourself off the case." I wrung a pillow. Had it been a chicken, it would've died on the spot. "If you don't, he'll force you out, and the putz will replace you."

"Screw Paul Tyre. I told Shea I needed time to decide. As of tomorrow, I'll be taking vacation days." My tissue-wrapped finger, tinged with pink, caught his eye. "What happened?"

I told him about my afternoon with Johanna and my visit to Lab 45. "That pasta scraper had very sharp teeth," I said.

"And that's your counting finger." He kissed it, and we held hands in the murky twilight. "You know, it might have been a microtome pasta scraper. They're new on the market." He actually laughed, and I managed a smile. As one of nature's born straight-men, I could live with a little humor at my expense if it cheered Michael up.

"Whatever you call it, your evidence crew missed it."

"You ought to look at an actual blade. How about a hot date at the morgue tonight?"

While Michael organized a visit, I took out the little *cafe'
presse* my mother had sent in a fit of pessimism about my unmarried state, and brewed coffee for one. After Michael tired of
teasing me, a jolt of caffeine might keep his spirits high.

He joined me at the window table in the kitchen. "Lamoth
can see us anytime after nine," he said. "That'll give me time to
stop in Boston and go through the case notes."

The coffee smelled so good I stole a nip from his cup. "You
know," I said, "Torie could have been…bashed…inside Lab
45 and dragged through the building to the parking lot, completely
out of sight until the last few feet. There's a fire door
near Johanna's office."

Michael listened with what looked like a thoughtful expression, then shook his head. "The evidence points to an attack in
her condo, and in the trunk of her car."

"The killer could've hosed her blood down a drain," I insisted.
"He could have wrapped her body in plastic garbage bags. I
found some under the sink."

"There were no plastic bags in her car, Susan, nothing to
connect Torie Moran's murder to NGT except her body in the
parking lot."

"But why attack her at home and then drive her to NGT?"

"Maybe the killer wanted something she kept in the Jag."

"Whistle-blowing evidence?"

"Or secret formulas, or love letters, or a lottery ticket. One
of her sandals is missing. And her evening bag."

"And those diamond earrings."

"Trophies," he said.

◇◇◇

Tyre ducked away when he saw us.

I waited in a computer room while Michael checked files and
worked the phones. Twenty minutes later he came back. "No
microtome blade in Lab 45 last Tuesday."

"Couldn't the crew have missed it?"

"Not likely. But we'll try to go back for another look, preferably with Johanna's permission. Getting a warrant won't be easy."

We left, and this time Tyre intercepted us on our way to the elevators. His face needed a shave, or a transplant.

"Mike," he said, breathless from all that ducking and hiding. "Shea told me about your lunch. I want you to know it wasn't me contacted him. He called me as soon as they told him Suze found Moran's body. He asked me to keep him apprised, his word."

"Is that why you didn't *apprise* me of the contract Johanna Lang gave you?" Not waiting for an answer, Michael continued down the hall.

Tyre kept pace with us. "C'mon, Mike. Shea calls the shots. I just follow orders."

An elevator slid open, and we stepped inside.

"Mike! It's a high profile case. Whatta you want from me?"

Michael moved away from the doors, and I let them close on Tyre's unhappy face.

"Maybe he's telling the truth," Michael said. "But the bottom line's the same no matter who juggles the numbers. You're someone I find it hard to be objective about, and you're intimately involved in these cases."

Outside, he lit his cigarette and inhaled all the way back to the car where he fastened his seat belt and reached for my hand without letting go of the cigarette or dropping an ash. "Let's snatch some supper," he said, "forget murder for awhile."

Chapter Fifteen

Sleep Like Death

"Don't bother." I pulled Michael away from the menu posted outside Brendan's Briar Rose. "Nothing's changed here since April." We entered through the bar, jammed with codgers and singles. Two hi-def TVs carried two different sporting events. Men playing with balls.

"Good to see you again, sirrr." The tallest and snottiest of Brendan's hostesses greeted Michael in her heavy brogue. Me she could live without. She found us a booth not far from the band. Weekends meant music at Brendan's.

A waitress, "Hi, I'm Delaney," stopped by, and we ordered from memory, tagliarini with mussels for Michael, the small white pizza for me. Verdicchio by the carafe. "Irish home cooking," Michael joked, and Delaney gave an earnest nod. The wine came, and I sipped mine, sinking into the padded booth, listening to the band tune up. Within minutes, I was as relaxed as my grandmother's girdle.

"How's Nino doing these days?" Michael liked Nino, and if the feeling wasn't quite mutual, Nino had at least tolerated my cop boyfriend.

The wine made me just maudlin enough to confess that I'd used my power of attorney to sign the lease deal Nino didn't want. "Dammit, Michael, he was in intensive care. Unconscious.

I knew if Lombard found out he'd evict Nino quicker'n you can say shy. So I bargained him into the ground and got Nino everything. With utilities! And now he won't speak to me."

"Give him time. After all the shouting is over, you Italians are a forgiving lot."

"Don't bank on it. Hell hath no fury like a woman dumped."

"I'll settle for that imitation of forgiveness you gave me last night." He reached for my hand, almost knocking over my wine. "I didn't dump you, Susan. You can't dump what you don't have."

"Michael, I was joking. Please let's don't go there again."

"You're right. I apologize." But he looked more annoyed than contrite.

The band played four notes, then stopped and conferred; a man in hi-def knee socks kicked a ball across a TV screen; Delaney brought our food. Pasta and mussels occupied every iota of Michael's attention, and when I tried to pour him more wine he declined.

"Don't sulk," I said.

"Why not?" But then he grinned over his fork and I felt forgiven, though I didn't know what I'd done except speak the truth. Maybe there was a season for lies and I'd missed it.

While my pizza cooled, I dug Chaz's papers out of my bag. "I want to show you something, lieutenant."

"Feel free to call me sir."

"Certainly," I said, and he groaned at my killer wit. I laid the papers on the table. "You doubted Chaz. Read'em and weep."

"I thought we were taking a break from murder."

"We're not talking about murder. We're talking about your lack of confidence in my judgment."

He ate another mussel, wiped his fingers on one of the big cloth napkins that always graced Brendan's tables, and finally opened the folder. After a casual scrutiny, he handed it back. "Yeah? So?"

"You don't believe Chaz hired me to advise his campaign. The signatures prove he did."

"Names on a few pieces of paper? They don't prove a thing."

"They prove his intent. Nobody who is not a serious candidate would put in the energy it takes to collect three hundred signatures in twenty-four hours. It's almost impossible, even with an army of helpers."

But something Michael had said raised the gray flag of doubt. *A few pieces of paper.*

I opened the folder and scanned the names and addresses. Six sheets. Row after neat row, every line filled. No spaces, no glitches.

How had I missed it?

In two years of consulting, I had rarely seen a nominating paper with more than thirty signatures. Never ones as clean as these. Signatures were collected piecemeal. Mistakes were made, particularly toward deadline. There should've been a dozen messy sheets in the folder, not six pristine ones.

I slid out of the booth. "Back in a minute."

"Where're you going? Your pizza's turning to rubber."

I held up the sheets. "Gotta make a few calls."

I took my cellphone to a bench in the vestibule and chose names at random, one from each sheet, using directory assistance to get the numbers. As I dialed the first, the band let loose, and I hoped blues in the background wouldn't hobble my credibility. I planned to identify myself as a political analyst conducting an astonishingly simple survey. *Did you sign nominating papers for Charles L. Renfrow?* was the only question.

The first number landed me a voice mail, the second a hang-up. I got lucky with the third, a lonely lady who didn't know Charles L. Renfrow, but was eager to denounce her son-in-law. I extricated myself and pressed in the next number. My luck held. Mary Franklyn's daughter told me her mother summered on Isleboro and hadn't voted in years. The fifth person on my list, Richard Marwick, never signed anything except child support checks. I didn't bother calling the sixth. No need to lacerate myself with any more luck. Chaz had thrown darts at a Telford census and forged the signatures.

I went back to the booth and fussed inside my bag for a very long time before I allowed myself to find my cache of aspirin.

Two tablets and a slug of wine didn't do a thing for the pain in my head or the ache in my stomach. "The signatures are fakes," I said. "Chaz Renfrow never intended to run for mayor of anything."

"I'm sorry, Susan. You couldn't have known."

"*You* knew."

"I suspected. Probably because I didn't like the man. Maybe I was jealous of him."

"You knew because you're trained to know, and you did your job."

"My job is to suspect. Yours isn't. Don't be hard on yourself."

The music was loud, but I heard every kind, mortifying word. "Hard on myself? How about smug and self-satisfied? I was sure Chaz had been murdered before five on Friday because he hadn't filed his phony signatures. I told you your business."

While I talked, Michael built a wobbly tower of shells, which clattered down on his plate. "Your method wasn't wrong," he said, stacking them again. "We use the same sort of reasoning all the time. In this case it was even simpler. We now know Renfrow was alive at noon on Saturday because he took a call from one of his scientists, and we've got the phone records. It's the other end we haven't pinpointed. He probably wasn't alive after midnight, and that's as close as we've managed to get, so far."

The shells toppled again, and this time he left them. "You're not a bad detective."

"I just don't get it. Why would Chaz pretend to be a candidate?"

"He wanted to get close to you."

"But why?" Chaz had told me so many little lies, they stacked up like mussel shells. But this lie was huge; it cut to the quick, and I'd been forewarned. My gut had spoken clearly. Why hadn't I listened?

"You're right about his forging my name on the contract." I was ready to concede everything now. "He planned to use the contract like Johanna did, to take back his retainer once he no longer needed my services, whatever they were." I tapped my chest. "Alice down the rabbit hole."

The music stopped, and applause came, a patter like rain. The waitress presented our check the old-fashioned way, at Michael's elbow. I didn't bother to protest. I let him pay. I even finished his wine.

Sax and keyboard slid into a plaintive duet. Michael left his seat and pushed in next to me, giving my shoulders a gentle squeeze. "Let's leave, Susie," he said softly in my ear. "We'll stop off at the morgue, then we'll go home, and I'll let you rub my back and bring me a beer. We'll watch ESPN, and I'll explain it to you."

Who says men can't nurture?

"What's so important it can't wait till Monday?" Johanna said when Michael served the warrant. "A commonplace lab tool? They're fungible, you know." She refused to ride with us in Michael's car, preferring to risk a breakdown in Chaz's antique Sonnet.

NGT loomed like a mausoleum illuminated by stalks of clinical light, and as we pulled into a visitor's slot, I found myself shrinking against my seat, cowed by the nighttime aura of the place. Torie had died in this parking lot, and all my powers of avoidance couldn't keep the image of her murdered body at bay.

Getting skittish will damage your credibility, I warned myself, and exited the car with such verve I beat Michael to the entrance. Johanna unlocked the double glass doors and hurried inside, keeping well ahead of us.

Inside Lab 45, I stared at the shelf I'd searched yesterday. "It *was* there," I told Michael. "I cut myself pulling it out."

"Didn't you cut yourself on the hose?" Johanna had recovered her amused reserve. She was packaged in jeans tonight. They made her look thin *and* voluptuous, like one of those illusionary drawings that shifts in the light.

"I hid it behind the vinaigrette bottles," I said, ignoring her.

"Vinaigrette bottles? Are you familiar with lab equipment, Susan?" Johanna spoke to me, but smiled at Michael.

"I know what I saw." Last night at the morgue, the assistant medical examiner had shown me an old style microtome blade on a wooden handle, the very model of the "pasta scraper" I'd cut my finger on. Sunday evening, after Johanna refused to permit a search, Michael got his warrant, and now here we all were.

Johanna pushed her glasses to the top of her head, a way to deflect her anger, I knew. "You look tired, Susan. Is your finger better?"

"Yep," I said, full of new respect for swamp Yankees and their taciturn ways. I positioned myself directly in front of her. "Did you take the blade away?"

"Why would I do that?"

She was answering questions with questions, which made me want to slap her. "Lieutenant Benedict," she said, edging away from me. "Was Torie killed with a microtome blade?"

"Very likely," I answered for him. "Maybe right here in this lab."

"The press said she was killed in her condo."

"She was attacked there. But she died in her car." My voice notched up. "Fifty feet from your office."

Johanna shook her head in mock dismay. "You're upset with me, Susan. I hope it's not because you had to give back the money."

"It's got nothing to do with the money. You *knew* I found a blade here yesterday."

"Are you sure it wasn't a trowel? Or a butter knife?"

Her sarcasm passing right over me, I went to the sink. "What about the hose? Why is the connector stripped?" I imagined Torie's killer washing her blood down the drain, and then tearing the hose off the faucet in his hurry to run water over his own bloody fingerprints.

"Lab 45 is a repository for junk." Johanna was sympathetic, but growing a *little* impatient with my shenanigans. "I have never seen a microtome blade in here. You are a befuddled young woman. You should go home and go to bed"

"Keep your advice. I want the truth." I invaded her space, sticking my face in her well-powdered face. Damn if there *wasn't* a zit on her chin.

"Where is the blade?" I spoke slowly, through my teeth. "Did you find my blood on the shelf and figure it out?" I remembered the monitors, Torie's secret video. "There's a hidden camera in here. You saw me find it."

She walked over to Michael. "I want her out of here."

"When she's ready," he said.

Voices and clatter came from the hall, and two people in green coveralls walked in trundling toolboxes and suitcases.

"Susan," Michael said, "come over and meet applied science."

The woman, Molly, was blond and stocky. Roger was narrow-flanked but chesty, and diffident, like a greyhound.

"We'll leave you to it," Michael said. "I'll want the drain pulled." He motioned me and Johanna into the corridor. "We'll be here for hours yet," he told her. "Why don't you go home? We'll reset the alarm when we leave." He turned to me, slouching in the doorway. "Susan, you go too. Take my car. I'll hitch a ride."

There was no fight left in me, only a sinking feeling that I had made a mistake.

The old emptiness rushed at me, so familiar I almost embraced it. I went to bed and buried my face in Michael's pillow. When I woke again, he was next to me. Streetlight slanted across his arm and the sheets.

"Are you awake?" I whispered, and when he didn't answer, I nudged him. "Michael. Are you awake?"

He groaned. "What time is it?"

"Three o'clock. What happened? Did you find the blade?"

He crushed a pillow under his ear and closed his eyes. "No."

"Any hidden cameras?"

"No. Let me sleep." The blanket slipped, and he pulled it over his shoulder.

"What about the drains?"

"Took 'em away."

"Think they'll find Torie's blood?"

"Dammit, Susan!" He reached across me and turned on the lamp. His eyelids were puffy, his mouth framed with heavy lines.

"Michael, all I know is the blade was there the night Torie died and it was there Saturday afternoon."

"It's gone now."

I swung my legs over the side of the bed. "Well, Johanna must have taken it. Maybe she's covering up for her boyfriend Bart. Or her son. Herself, even. *She's* the one who benefits from Chaz's death, not Roddie Baird. And she was jealous of Torie."

I got up and began opening drawers, sorting through my new clothes.

"What are you doing? Come back to bed."

"I can't sleep." Sleep was for wusses. "I'm going to mull over Roddie's prospects."

I eased my wounded self into a utilitarian bra, stepped into calf-length slacks and pulled on a top, the dusty rose with the pinwale ribbing. "He's already lost his campaign manager. If you don't leave him alone, he'll lose the election."

The quiet room grew quieter. Electricity buzzed through the bedside clock, unless it was the blood in my ears. I couldn't believe I had uttered those words, and worse, that I meant them.

Michael didn't speak until I turned and faced him. Then he said: "Are you asking me to let your client off the hook?"

A floorboard creaked, the sound of me backing off. "I like Roddie. I'm a loyal little thing and I can't help believing he's innocent. That's all I was trying to say."

"Then you'd better get out of the way and let me prove it."

I drifted uncertainly toward the door than walked back and turned out the light. "I'm going for a drive." I bent and kissed the scar on his cheekbone. "Try and get some sleep."

Michael needed sleep. For me, sleep was too much like death.

A few stars shone faintly in a patch of sky between the brownstones. I put Beauford's business card away and studied the third floor window, side and rear, where his apartment ought to be. A fire escape zigzagged down.

Before coming here, I'd mea culpa'd around town, driving up and down the Charles River, opalescent ink at this hour. Because of me, Michael had stuck out his neck on Lab 45 and found nothing. I wanted to redeem myself in his eyes, shine a disinfecting light on NGT and Johanna. While I drove, I'd devised a simple plan: Michael could use Torie's video, and Beauford wouldn't mind if I fetched it. He owed me two or three, but I'd settle for just this one.

I walked around to the entrance and scanned the tenants' directory. *Kling*, said the superintendent's name card. After three or four jabs on the buzzer, a thick voice came through the intercom. No words, just a grunt.

"Mr. Kling?"

"Mrs. Kling."

"Oh." This would be harder with a woman. "Sorry to wake you, but I'm a friend of Beauford Smith. He said the superintendent would let me—"

"Who?"

"Beauford Smith."

"You. Who're you?"

"Dina Carpenter. My bus just got in from Buffalo. Beauford said I could stay at his place while he was away."

"He didn't say nothin' to me."

"Just till he gets back from Rome." That information ought to establish my bona fides. "I know it's late, and I'd have gone to a hotel for tonight, but I lost my wallet, all my money, credit cards." In case she asked for ID. I didn't know Beauford all that well. Even a close friend might not like me poking through his things.

"Wait a minute."

She came up, a small woman in spite of her big voice, and looked me over. The weary traveler. My bulging hobo bag clinched it. Grumbling, she led me to Beauford's third floor pad. "Girls in and out of here, all hours. I told him…oh, who cares. Pays his rent on time."

I moved into the kitchenette, a tiled area at one end of the living room. "I won't need a key," I told her, as if she'd made a kind offer. "Beau keeps a spare in his freezer."

She gave me a doubting look, and I knew I had overdone it.

"Where's he staying in Rome?" she asked, one pop quiz I was prepared for.

"Palazzo Spirito. Near the Vatican." I was ad-libbing the part about the Vatican, but her jaw relaxed.

"That's right. Slipped my mind." She waited, clutching her bony elbows, while I got my bearings. The bedroom and bathroom were off a hall behind the kitchenette. There was one closet.

I hung my bag on a hook. "Well, I'm pooped."

She left, but I didn't hear her step down the hall. Trying not to breathe, I put my ear to the door. Behind me, water plinked into the sink. The doorknob turned slowly, stopped, and finally, I heard footsteps receding.

I slid on the chain and proceeded to tear Beauford's place apart, starting with his tiny bedroom, which indeed opened onto fire stairs, though not the ones I had noticed from the street. Luckily, Beau had almost no furniture. A small chest took up most of one wall, and drawer by drawer, I went through it: socks, underwear, laundry-folded shirts. No video. I looked under the bed and lifted the mattress. Nothing. I worked my way painstakingly through his closet, checking every suit and jacket. I shook out sweaters. Turned his shoes on end and tapped them on the floor.

Next I did the bathroom, dumping out his hamper, running my hand behind toilet tank and sink, both slimy with condensation. Nothing there, or in the scuzzy bathtub.

I moved into the living room. There was a lithium battery and a printer on top of a window table, but no drawers, nothing inside the printer but an ink cartridge. Quickly, holding my nose, I went through a hockey duffle, which Beauford had dropped, or maybe stored, in front of the sofa. Nothing but two sets of armor, and a stench that wouldn't quit.

The sofa cushions didn't have zippers. I put them on the floor and wedged my hand between the frame and the springs.

Beauford's sofa was saggier than mine, and he was a *successful* consultant, or had been, until he met Chaz.

A knock rattled the door chain, sending my heart on a tear up my throat.

"Hey," Mrs. Kling called.

I threw the cushions helter skelter back on the frame and tiptoed into the bedroom.

She pounded again.

I opened and closed the bedroom door and yawned like a noisy cat. "Who's there?"

"What'd you say your name was?"

I yawned again, my face close to the door. "Deirdre Carpenter."

"Thought you said Dina."

"Deirdre. I said Deirdre." By now, I'd lost track of my lies.

Without another word, she left, and in the restored quiet my alertness turned to fear. Dawn was beginning to sheer through a smudged window over the sofa. It was time to finish the job and get the hell out of here. Just one more place to search. I'd left the skeevy kitchenette for last. Suddenly thirsty, I went to the sink. Rather than use one of Beau's scurvy cups, I stuck my face under the faucet and let the water flow directly into my mouth.

Thus refreshed, I opened the cabinet and shrieked at a party of cockroaches line-dancing under a drainpipe. They didn't miss a beat in the sudden light. I had to scatter them with my sandal. My hands popping a sweat, I forced myself to explore cupboards, the oven, utensil drawers, refrigerator, and came up with the same nothing I'd already found.

Back in the living room, I checked my watch. Twenty minutes had passed since Mrs. Kling's knock. I could hear birds twitter. Traffic began to hum. Beauford had told me the video was in his apartment. Every cushion, mattress and drawer in the place had been carefully ransacked by me. I looked at the hockey bag again. Maybe I'd explored it too quickly, it smelled so bad. What's the difference between a dig through Beau's hockey bag and a dumpster dive? I giggled nervously under my breath.

That's when I heard them pounding up the stairs.

"She's in there." A key slid into a lock. "Beauford never heard of her."

Just as the door smashed the chain, I scooped up the hockey duffle and raced for the bedroom, ripping my hobo bag off the hook as I passed. The bedroom window stuck, but I put my shoulder into it and managed to drag myself and my gear over the sill.

The fire stairs groaned under my weight. By the time a voice started yelling, I'd hit the ground running. The hockey duffle thumped along the sidewalk beside me. I didn't look back, not even to see if it was cops Mrs. Kling had sicced on me.

I jumped into my Beemer and screeched toward Beacon Street. Who'd have thought Mrs. Kling would spend all that money calling Beauford in Rome and that she'd actually reach him?

Bad luck. But the duffle was snug on the back seat, and I could search it at my leisure. I started for home, then swerved for Commonwealth instead. Michael was tired, and a little morose. The sight of Beauford's hockey duffle might distress him. Better to let him sleep.

Chapter Sixteen

Delia's Eyes

I parked behind Lauren Baird's Mazda, stowed Beau's hockey gear in the trunk, and set my wristwatch for six-thirty, a not-too-unreasonable time for a conference with my candidate. Settling down on the back seat, I contorted myself into a space twelve inches shorter than my legs. Conditions were perfect for sleep: I was uncomfortable and not in my bed, and after a last shudder over my narrow escape, I knew nothing more until a relentless *tweep tweep tweep* wiped out a dream.

It wasn't my watch, it was Roddie's. He'd opened the car door and was leaning over me, a surprised teddy bear in his nut-brown terrycloth robe. "Susan, why are you sleeping in my driveway?"

I lifted my eyebrows, a move I hoped gave me an alert, knowing look. "Just passing by, thought I'd drop in."

We exchanged upside-down smiles. The *tweeeeeping* continued.

"Turn it off!"

"Oh, sorry. It's my back-up alarm." He cut off the sound, and I sat up, not inclined to speak again, or breathe much, without a cup of strong coffee. Roddie's worried eyes stayed on my face. "Is everything all right?"

"Not really. We need to talk." I combed my hair with my fingers.

He offered his hand. "Come inside. I'll make coffee."

In the kitchen, I sat at the table under the dangling pot rack while Roddie set up the Gaggia and placed a bowl of peaches and tangerines at my elbow. "Your campaign needs a spin doctor," I said.

"You came here at dawn to tell me that?"

"Friday night you promised you'd call, but you didn't. Now, Odette tells me the media's been bugging you."

"The press, cable, network TV. Nothing from the blogsphere, yet. I hired Odette's nephew to run interference. This is coming down hard on Lauren. I'm thinking about dropping out of the race."

"Want me to weigh in on that?"

"No." He walked back to the Gaggia and watched coffee dribble into the mugs which, on the watched-pot principle, seemed to drag out the process. "Everything depends on Lauren's health. And how quickly the police cross me off their list."

"When Snow gets back from Alaska, he'll explain why he authorized the Cordelia Trust loan, and that'll take care of the police."

Roddie may have heard a tremor in my voice because he interrupted the brew cycle and brought me a nearly full mug. The coffee was luscious, and the first sip hot-wired my brain.

Back at the counter, he pulled a round of bread from a jumbo biscotti tin. "Lauren's dilly-potato," he said. From the way he dawdled, slicing the entire loaf, hunting for butter and napkins, I could tell he had something to say that required careful presentation. Finally, he set the bread in front of me. "Turns out I authorized the loan. Forgot all about it."

"You?" My hand froze over the platter. "How could you forget a million dollars?"

"One and a quarter million, actually. Bear with me, because this is going to sound incredibly stupid." He tore into a slice of bread with short strong fingers that reminded me of Nino's. "Snow's old money-bags network told him NGT had a fantastic new product but was strapped for cash. He liked what he heard and decided to offer a subordinated debenture with a double payback. High interest now, big piece of the action up the road. When he recommended the investment, apparently I said sure, sure, without really listening. Not unusual for me, and two months ago I was in the thick of organizing my campaign."

He laughed, a little edgily, I thought. "So, in a way, I blame you. Susan's siren song: Newton first, then Congress. I forgot about business and began to dream."

"Oh, no you don't. Congress is *your* dream." I toyed with my bread and ended up leaving it on my plate. Too much dill, not enough salt. "So what triggered your memory?"

"The man himself, John Snow."

"But no one could reach him."

"John's got a satellite phone. I called him after I got home from the police station."

"Why didn't you give Michael his number?"

"Once I calmed down and started to think, I realized I wanted John's input *before* I talked to your friends on the force again. Isn't that the way you crafty lawyers do it? No surprises? Well I'd had enough surprises. I wanted Snow to refresh my memory, *before* I got snared in your boyfriend's bad-cop, bad-cop games again." The chair creaked under him, and he shifted abruptly, rocking the fruit bowl. There were crumbs trapped in the folds of his robe. He looked exhausted and unhappy, and I could feel his campaign slipping away.

"I hear you, Roddie," I said, trying to soothe his upset. I didn't like his jab at Michael but I let it go. "You must be relieved, about your daughter's trust money, anyway. If Snow has confidence in NGT, it's got to be a fine company."

He peered into his now empty mug. "John makes the occasional crap shoot. In this case, he felt the only real risk was the time lag between NGT's research trials and FDA approval."

"You're talking about a long time lag."

"Even if I am, the Cordelia Trust can afford to wait. Delia's only five. But the bureaucrats may fast-track this one. The way John talked, NGT's new product is going to change the world.

It's some kind of anti-aging thing." He flashed the old Roddie-smile. "Hey, Susan, that's almost as good as a bug that eats lead and shits gold."

"Better. Lots of people want to be rich, but everyone wants to stay young." I finished my coffee and refused a second cup. Any more caffeine and I'd be prancing around the kitchen like a horse with a saddle burr. "Okay, Snow is responsible for your NGT connection. That leaves your alibi. Once that's confirmed the media will lose interest, Lauren will recover, and we'll get your campaign back on track."

"Consider it confirmed." He began paring a peach the way Nino did, letting the peel loop in one long curl. "After I spoke with John, the name came back to me. Hotel Arvada. I called, and they even remember bringing breakfast to my room on Sunday."

"Great. You're in the clear. Let's move ahead."

"I've always been in the clear." He looked wistful. "I didn't kill anyone."

At just past six by the wall clock, the front doorbell rang. Roddie and I looked at each other. A second more insistent ring brought Roddie out of his chair. I gave him time to see who was disturbing his breakfast, then stepped into the dining room where I could eavesdrop from behind the ficus tree.

"Mr. Baird, a few more questions."

I recognized Sergeant Tyre's voice and rushed to join Roddie in the hall. "What's going on, Paul? Isn't it a little early even for an unfriendly visit?"

Tyre barely glanced at me. A lanky detective with faded acne scars stood at his elbow, and no one bothered with introductions. "We want to talk with you again at the station, Mr. Baird. Get dressed. We'll drive." He was brusque and peremptory, and I could see Roddie's hand moving along his terrycloth belt the way Delia's little fingers stroked her blanket.

"I'm not going anywhere. Now get out of my house before I…" He raised a fist that dropped like a stone when I tugged his arm.

"Does Michael know you're here?" I said to Tyre.

"I'm in charge now, Suze." There wasn't enough room on his face for the soup-sucking grin. "The lieutenant stepped down."

"Since when?"

"Since an hour ago."

I didn't bother to ask why. I wanted to lie on the floor and take a short guilty nap while other people sorted things through. "Paul, don't badger Mr. Baird. If you've got a question, ask it and leave, or I'll advise him to lodge a complaint against you."

"You got it ass-backwards again, Suze. We found the pilot. If Baird doesn't come voluntarily, we're prepared to read him his rights."

The fight went out of Roddie then, just as it rose up in me. "What charges?" I shouted. "What pilot? What's happening?"

"Your client knows," Tyre said.

"Susan, I wasn't—"

"Roddie, don't say another word! I'll call Gordon Brenner. And I'm coming with you to the station."

"No. If you want to help me, stay with Lauren. I'll call Gordon myself." He disappeared upstairs and came down moments later in his mountaineer's outfit, Lauren shuffling behind him in bright gym clothes that were rumpled and too loose and somehow looked gray. Hanks of hair stuck to her face. Hollow shadows sunk her eyes. In the space of a week she seemed to have dropped ten pounds and most of her sentient being.

"You'll stay?" Roddie's eyes pleaded.

"For as long as Lauren can stand me. Don't worry. You'll be home ten minutes after Gordon Brenner shows up."

Roddie hugged his wife, and she clutched him until Tyre began snapping his fingers against his palm. "Tell Delia I'll take her to Drumlin Farm when I get back," Roddie said. "Tell her we'll feed the ducks."

They left, Roddie walking between the two detectives, shorter than either of them, but more of a presence. Just before he got into the cruiser, he looked back and waved. A sound escaped Lauren, and only when the cruiser was long out of sight did she turn away, leaving the door open on the lingering after burn.

I gave her a minute to collect herself, then I said: "What pilot?"

She walked past me into the den and stood by the window, one hand gripping the sill. "Roddie came home last Saturday night. Not Sunday afternoon."

"I don't get it. The hotel verified his alibi, they brought him breakfast."

"The hotel didn't know he'd gone. They leave an early morning tray for all the airline guests. An hour after he checked in, Roddie found a pilot and chartered a jet home." She opened the casement on a hazy dawn, deliberately keeping her back to me, able to hide her face, but not the frightened stiffness of her spine.

"But he'd just volunteered to be bumped! Why the sudden switch?"

"Saturday evening, Roddie called home…and…Delia…No, I won't tell you. I'll let you hear for yourself."

Still contriving to hide her face, she maneuvered herself to Roddie's desk with its dowdy old phone and built-in message machine. "Thing's got a mind of its own. Once it starts recording, it keeps going even after someone picks up." She ejected the tape and inserted one from a drawer, playing with the switches until she found her place.

A long beep, then: "Nobody's home. 'Bye."

"Wait, Delia! Don't hang up. Where's Mommy?"

"Daddy! Daddy! Daddy! When are you coming home?"

"First thing tomorrow, bunny. I've got a present for you."

"What is it?"

"It's a surprise. Put Mommy on."

"She's not here."

"Where is she?" Tension gave Roddie's voice a fearful clarity.

"At the store. I want you to come *home*." There was a touch of panic in Delia's voice, and I suddenly felt as worried for her, alone in this oversized house, as if I were listening to her future instead of the past. I remembered her uneasy sleep in the coatroom at Spaal's, the way she lay sobbing on the floor outside Roddie's den the night of the finance meeting. This little girl spent far too much time alone. No wonder she clung to her blanket.

Roddie's voice continued to crackle. "Let's talk till Mommy gets back. Okay?"

A silence, then Delia shouted, "The bread and butterflies!" Disney music surged and faded in the background. "The flowers are singing to Alice."

"All right, sweetie. Go watch Alice. I'll call you again in fifteen minutes. If Mommy comes home first, tell her to call *me* right away. And don't open the door to anybody."

"Not even Mommy?"

"Mommy's got her key."

"What about Grandma?"

"Grandma's in Maine with your brothers."

"What about Curious George?"

Roddie sighed. "Nobody," he said. "Not even Curious George."

"Okay."

"I love you, bunny."

Delia began to sob. "The caterpillar's blowing smoke. He's going to eat Alice up!"

"No he's not. He's Alice's friend."

But Delia's sobs were turning to wails. "My tummy hurts! Come home *now*! "

"Sshh, sshh. Don't be scared. Mommy will be right back, and…*listen to me, Delia*, I changed my mind. I'm flying home now. I'll be there very soon."

"In five minutes?" she whimpered.

"Longer, but I'll call you from a special phone on the airplane, and we'll talk while I fly through the sky."

Lauren turned off the machine and put the tape back in the drawer. "I'd gone to Whole Foods for a few things." She faced me now, steely and reserved. "I shouldn't have left Delia, but I didn't expect to be gone long. Turned out the store was crowded, and then my car wouldn't start. By the time I got back, Roddie was on his way, talking to Delia from the plane. By ten-thirty, he was here with us."

"Why didn't Roddie explain all this to the police?"

Her defiant expression collapsed. She seemed unaware of the tears, which were trickling down her face. "I'm a negligent mother. It's not the first time I've left my children alone, and Roddie doesn't want anyone to know. He's very protective of them, especially Delia. And of me, our reputation in the community."

"Hang your reputation. You've got to tell Gordon Brenner that Roddie was with you from the moment he got back from the airport Saturday night. The tape explains why."

"What if Gordon doesn't believe me?"

"Why wouldn't he?"

"Roddie and I both lied."

I wasn't satisfied. Something else was going on, I was sure of it, but Gordon would have to draw it out. "Call him now. If you can't reach him, leave a message."

"I'll wait for Roddie. He'll have to agree." There was a shawl on the sofa, and she draped it around her shoulders, as if the stifling room were cold. "Did anyone make coffee?"

I offered to get her a cup.

On my way to the kitchen, I heard a sound behind me. Delia, in an eyelet nightgown, was thumping down the stairs dragging her blanket, her thumb slewed to the side of her mouth. "Where's my daddy?"

"Gone to work." It was such a little white lie, even a Jesuit might have missed it, but Delia's eyes were truth-seeking missiles.

"No, he's not. I saw his car."

"He got a ride."

"Why didn't he wake me up?"

"Does he wake you up every day?"

She nodded, pressing a corner of the blanket to her cheek. "He brings me my juice."

"He didn't have time this morning, but he's going to take you to Drumlin Farm when he gets back."

Her eyes got a faraway look, as if she could see barns and smell clover. She uncorked her thumb. "I have to get bread for the ducks. It's my *responsibility*." The syllables came out topsy-turvy, but Delia's serious face told me she knew exactly what the word meant.

"Let's go find mommy." I offered my hand, and she held it all the way to the den.

Lauren was on the sofa, cocooned in her shawl. When she saw Delia, she opened her arms. Delia ran to her, and their sadness billowed out to me.

The mastodon rocker was by the fireplace, and it creaked like old bones when I sat down. Lauren startled, then closed her eyes, keeping her face pressed to her child's. Delia's blanket had merged with Lauren's shawl, and after awhile, she peeked out at me from a muddle of pink and purple fringe. "I'm hungry," she said, probably figuring every adult could at least pour milk over cereal.

"Want cornflakes?"

"I like pancakes," she countered, not understanding who she was talking to.

"I don't do pancakes." I smiled to show that I meant it, but not in a bad way. "How about eggs?"

"I hate eggs."

"Me too," I said.

Lauren stirred. "I'll make pancakes," she murmured. "What time is it?"

"Going on six-thirty." I turned off my wristwatch alarm. "Would you like me to fix Delia some sort of breakfast?"

"I can do it. I just need another minute to rest." Her eyes stayed closed, and I wondered which tranquilizer she had taken on top of which sleeping pill, and how long ago.

Delia patted her mother's cheek. "I'll read you a story, Mommy."

"I'd like that, sweetie. When you come home from camp."

Little fingers rubbed the satin edge of the blanket. "I don't want to go to camp."

"You have to. As soon as I rest, I'll help you get ready."

"I'm not going! My tummy hurts!"

Lauren opened her eyes. "I can't take care of you today."

In a jumble of blanket and shawl, Delia pitched head first off the sofa. "My tummy hurts! I want my daddy!"

This ship was foundering, so I stuck in my oar. "Maybe she ought to stay home, under the circumstances. I'll look after her while you rest."

"I couldn't ask you to do that."

Delia studied me over her thumb. "I want Susan."

This, in spite of my culinary lacks. I was flattered.

We decided that Delia would stay with me until Roddie returned, or one o'clock, whichever came first. After she rested, Lauren would ask her mother to drive down from Maine and take Delia back with her. If not tonight, then first thing tomorrow. And she would discuss the phone tape with Roddie as soon as he walked in the door.

Forming a plan seemed to lift Lauren's mood. She managed a smile. "You're awfully kind. Delia can be a handful."

On cue, Delia began to caper and chant, "Susan, Susan, Susan," tearing around the den until I grabbed her blanket. "Sshh," I said. "Your mommy's trying to rest. It's time for you to get dressed. Come on, I'll help you."

"I know how to put my own clothes on." She raced out, blanket whipping after her.

"I hope she won't be too much for you," Lauren said.

"We'll be fine, and Roddie will be back before you know it."

"Will he?" She poked her fingers through a crocheted rosette. "If Roddie has to prove he didn't kill a man he didn't know, then we're all at risk, aren't we? Guilty until proved innocent."

It was a lucid enough comment, and I wondered if the tranquilizers, or her distress, had begun to wear off. Did she mean guilty in the abstract?

"I'd better let the camp know Delia won't be in." She pushed up from the sofa, trailing her shawl to the desk.

The Willowood directory was a flimsy production attached to an apothecary's lamp by a long orange thread I recognized as a filament of Roddie's mountaineer's rope. Lauren punched in a number, left a message, then lay down again. By the time Delia came back, dressed in overalls and pink velcro sneakers, Lauren was asleep.

"All right, kid. How's that stomach ache?"

"Better," she said. "I'm hungry."

There was no real food in Lauren's kitchen, no microwavable redi-pacs, no ten-second oatmeal. No toaster home fries.

There were elements. Flour, sugar, salt.

I'm no chemist. "Have a tangerine," I said to Delia. "I'll peel it for you."

She nibbled it segment-by-segment, dainty as a squirrel munching nuts. Watching her eat stirred my own appetite. The dilly/potato bread was on the platter where Roddie had left it, and together we finished four slices, toasted and buttered, to go with our milk.

After we cleared the table, I bent over the dishwasher, helping her load our plates and glasses. When I straightened, Nino's face flashed before my eyes, a waking vision that passed instantly. I hadn't slept much since Saturday night. I was beginning to dream on my feet.

"Want to see my brothers' toys?" Delia said, and I knew what she was up to. Let Susan explore forbidden territory with Delia the innocent bystander.

"Sure." I yawned.

The basement opened off the main staircase; Delia found the light, and we headed down to the playroom. From step to step, she chattered about this toy and that. "Josh and Sam got a truck that climbs up stairs. We got a million blocks in my camp. Me and Amanda make castles."

"Is Amanda your best friend?"

"Uh huh. We give her a ride 'cause her mommy goes to work in a different direction."

I stopped. "Amanda doesn't know you won't be at camp today. We better call so her mommy won't be late."

We went back to the den. Lauren's breathing was steady, and I left her to whatever dream was smoothing the frown off her face.

"What's Amanda's last name?"

"Lester," Delia said.

I flipped through the Willowood directory, amazed at the glamorous names the girls had: two Sophias, an Olivia, a Chloe. Delia was the only Cordelia. Cordelia, vaguely English, old-fashioned no matter which way you sliced it. I wondered if Roddie and Lauren were at the top of a new naming trend.

I dialed Amanda's number, and gave Mrs. Lester the bad news. She did not take it well. "This is third time Lauren's left me in the lurch," she said, her voice rising. "She knows I don't have my car this morning. She was going to give me a ride to work after we dropped the kids off. Can I speak to her, please?"

"She's sick in bed." My little white lies were accumulating like snowdrifts. "I don't think Delia will be going to camp at all this week. Lauren will call you tonight."

Mrs. Lester sighed. "Tell Lauren I'm sorry she's not feeling well. I'm taking the day off, so if there's anything I can do…"

Delia waited patiently while I wrote Lauren a note, which I left next to the phone.

Except for a few tarted-up Barbies, a Bratz, and a Victorian doll's house, the playroom was set up for boys being rowdy. Instruments of navigation and space travel lay scattered about the tile floor. There was an archery target, water guns, hockey sticks. A computer and a television for lulls in the action.

"Here's the truck." Delia nudged something large and black with her foot. The thing was to "truck" as "clodhopper" was to "slipper." She handed me the remote. "Wanna try?"

I pressed every button, wiggled the joystick, reversed the batteries. Nothing worked. Ten seconds later, thumb in her mouth, Delia had the "truck" spinning across the floor.

"Careful Delia," I warned as the vehicle tottered on two wheels and flipped onto its side before recovering. Watching it climb three stairs, I knew Delia had been here, done this, many times before, when Lauren wasn't looking, and the boys weren't home.

We passed an hour in the playroom, reading and singing and picking out tunes on the upright piano. I played the first five bars of *Fur Elise,* the chords for *Don't It Make My Brown Eyes Blue,* and *Chopsticks,* exhausting my repertoire.

"My turn," Delia said.

I took myself to a chair and closed my eyes. Torpor descended. Far off, I heard her flailing away at the piano, then silence, then the hum of the stair-climbing clodhopper. Careful, Delia, I wanted to say. Keep your eyes on the wheel. Your big blue eyes, Cordelia…

…don't it make my…

"Susan!"

…brown eyes blue…

"Susan, wake up!"

I felt her breath on my cheek and pulled out of my slump. Her face was so close I could see the light in her blue marble eyes.

"Cordelia," I said, not sure I wasn't dreaming. "I know who you are."

Chapter Seventeen

Another Wrinkled Truth

Delia, suddenly shy, clung to my hand. She aimed her bag of stale bread at an artificial pond ringed by woods that gave the Idlebrook grounds a mountain forest air. "The ducks are over there."

"After we visit Mrs. Renfrow."

Cordy was sitting outside in an Adirondack chair, her white hair and yellow sweater bright against the brick condo wall. Blue hydrangeas clumped around the patio, interspersed with pots of begonias and stubby scarlet flowers I didn't recognize. Johanna had told me about Cordy's "good days," when her memory held, and I wondered if she was waiting for me here in her garden.

Delia and I walked across the lawn. When we were about fifteen feet away, Cordy rose slowly from her chair. "Are you the young woman who called?"

"Yes. I'm Susan." I stepped onto the flagstone and extended my hand. Instead of shaking it, Cordy took it in both of hers, light and dry as tinder.

"I'm so glad you've come. It's lovely having visitors. Is this your daughter?" She smiled at Delia, standing close to me. "I have a son. No daughter, more's the pity."

"Delia's a friend of mine. We're going to feed the ducks, but first she wants to say hello to you."

"You won't find ducks here. Just geese nowadays."

"I want ducks!" Delia put her thumb in her mouth and glared.

Cordy stared at me, "Do I know you?" and the good day clouded over.

"I'm Susan." I looked from one to the other, from Cordy to Delia, from Delia back to Cordy. "You're Cordelia."

"Yes, that's my name, more's the pity. Everyone calls me Cordy."

"Cordelia's a wonderful name." I put my hand on Delia's shoulder. "It's my little friend's name, too. Everybody calls her Delia."

They had the same eyes.

Chaz's eyes.

His mother. His daughter. I was sure of it.

A polished and combed Lauren was standing in the middle of the den. "What do you expect me to do? Beg your silence?"

"I expect you to tell Gordon Brenner so he's not blindsided when the affair comes out. And it will come out. Of course Roddie will have to be told, but you'll handle it."

"Roddie knows. I told him right after it started."

Music leaked up from the basement playroom. I closed the door, so that Delia, who couldn't possibly understand, and who was downstairs watching a video, might not hear. "You told him?"

Humor flickered for a moment. "I don't like sneaking around."

Lauren's kind of honesty must sting, I thought. "Roddie didn't insist you end the affair? Never threatened to divorce you and take the kids?"

"I offered to leave. He said he'd rather have me this way than not at all. He asked for nothing more than my discretion. He didn't even want to know Chaz's name."

Outside, crows flew past the house, so close we could hear their wings flap. Was Roddie for real? I didn't think Michael would share me. I sure as hell wouldn't share him.

"How did you find out?" Lauren spoke deliberately, almost her old self again. Confession was *good* for her soul.

"The eyes. Delia looks like her father." And the nose, the long, slender body. The decisive manner. "Her name. I thought about the Cordelia Trust, the loan to Chaz. It took me awhile to put Delia together with Cordy Renfrow. We fed the geese together at Idlebrook this morning."

She ran a finger over her metal necklace, chunky enough to put a crick in her spine. "Why did you go there?"

"To make sure. I've been know to chase rainbows."

"Did you say anything to her?"

"Of course not. But Gordon Brenner has got to be told."

"Roddie doesn't want anyone to know."

"It's your decision, too. At least bring Gordon the tape. Never mind your negligence. The tape explains why Roddie came back a day early."

"Does it?" she said, a funny little smile on her face.

"Yes! It proves he didn't come back to murder his wife's lover. Whose name he didn't even know, or so you tell me."

"He didn't." She went to the window and began smoothing the curtain folds. "But he's always known about Delia."

What planet was I living on? "You told him that, too?"

"Yes." She said it so softly, I wasn't sure she'd spoken. "I couldn't have lived with myself otherwise. That's when I offered him a divorce."

Have an affair. Have your lover's child. But be open and honest. I ought to run that one by my mother. Or Michael. I said: "Roddie went ahead and set up a trust fund for another man's child?"

She whirled around, angry. "Delia's my child, too."

"And Roddie loves you."

"Maybe. I don't know. I wouldn't love me. But Roddie gave Delia his heart. Sometimes I think he loves her more than the boys."

Is there a feeling more tangled than love? I sat down in the mastodon chair and rocked and connected the dots. "Roddie didn't authorize the loan to NGT. You did."

"Yes. Chaz was desperate, and Roddie never pays attention to any of the trusts. John Snow and I have been working together for years. I convinced him NovoGenTech was worth the investment." She lifted her chin. "I did it for Delia, too. Investing the money seemed to link all of us together."

"Oh, yeah. One big happy family. You, Chaz, Delia, with Roddie holding the coats."

Her face took on heat, as if she'd leaned over a cook pot. Had this cool woman actually managed a blush?

"The loan documents haven't turned up yet. When they do, the police will see your signature, and you'll be dragged in. They'll find out about the affair. They always do. Promise me you'll call Gordon Brenner. Talk it over with Roddie when he gets back, but you must be completely candid with Gordon. That includes giving him the tape."

She pressed her face to the windowpane. Beyond her, the steeples of Chestnut Hill College loomed like medieval hats against a clear blue sky. "You said Roddie would be back ten minutes after Gordon Brenner got to the station. Well, it's been hours. Where is he?"

"Let's find out." I located Brenner in the Rolodex and dialed his number. His secretary told me he'd be in court until three. Another attorney from the office was with Roddie at the station. When Gordon checked in, she would tell him to call Lauren or me.

Lauren stood by the desk, an agitated hand at her throat. "They're not going to let him go. I can feel it."

Her conviction struck a chord in me. I opened the drawer where she'd stored the answering machine tape. "If you won't take this to Gordon, I will."

"No! It could hurt Roddie."

"The police have already broken his alibi. The tape mitigates his lie." I held it up between two fingers.

"Leave it!" She rushed at me, then held herself back. "Mind your own business!"

"What is it, Lauren? Are you afraid the tape will hurt *you*?"

"I don't give a damn about myself. I'd hand it over to the police this instant if I thought it'd make them leave Roddie alone. My husband did not murder Chaz."

"How can you be so sure? Did you kill him?"

"Sometimes I wanted to, when he talked as if Roddie didn't matter." She dropped her hands, her voice. Sunlight splashed across her dress. "But I don't kill what I love."

I knew how she must be feeling. After Gil died, I'd fluttered through days and months like a moth at a window. "Once everything comes out, you'll be a prime suspect. The police will want to know where you shopped. What time you got home. Who saw you."

"Maybe I'd better get myself a lawyer."

"Let Gordon advise you on that."

"I know you don't admire me much, Susan."

I shrugged. "I've come to think of Roddie as a friend."

"I love Roddie too, you know. My dilemma was wanting two men. How do I explain that to Gordon Brenner? Or the police."

For a second, I sympathized. I'd loved Gil. Now I was beginning to care for Michael, or was it love? If Gil were still alive, were to walk back into my life, would I want two men, like Lauren?

"For the last few months, I'd been trying to end the affair," she said.

"For Roddie's sake?"

She shook her head. "Not exactly. Chaz was pressuring me. He separated from his wife, and wanted me to leave Roddie. We'd agreed from the start not to injure the innocent, and now he was reneging."

"Johanna wasn't so innocent."

"That's true. She was the first to have an affair."

Another wrinkled truth. Johanna told me Chaz had cheated first.

"But Roddie is innocent," Lauren said. "Chaz's son is innocent. My sons. Why should they suffer?" She circled the room, stopping near the door. "Chaz didn't care who he walked over."

"Delia's five. You and Chaz must have been together a long time."

"We met at Chestnut Hill College. I work in Admissions. Chaz had his lab. It's been almost eight years."

"After all that time, why did he suddenly start trying to break up your marriage?"

"Because he wanted his daughter."

"He knew?"

"I told him. After she was born, he asked me to give her his mother's name, and that was the extent of his involvement. We both preferred it that way. Five years went by. Then he met her." Lauren smoothed a lock of hair that didn't need smoothing. "At Spaal's gym. On this particular morning, the sitter didn't show up so I took Delia with me. Chaz saw her there."

"Spaal's was a bit off Chaz's path, wasn't it?"

"He did a lot of business in Boston. He liked to drop into Spaal's, just to say hello, maybe grab a coffee with me after my workout. Not often, and never planned. He'd just show up. Sometimes we'd have breakfast in the diner across the street. A stolen hour." The misery that Xanax had deadened suddenly seized her face. "That morning, Delia was with us. My daughter and her father charmed the heck out of each other over buttermilk pancakes. Chaz couldn't get her out of his mind. That was the beginning of his plan to take Delia away from Roddie, have me abandon my sons, and set up housekeeping with him."

"But he gave up that plan."

"What do you mean?"

"Didn't you know he meant to go back to his wife?"

"No, but it doesn't surprise me. They were business partners. NGT was in trouble, and Chaz would've done anything to keep his company alive. He'd have seen reconciling as a temporary expedient."

"This wasn't about business. It was for Glenn's sake."

"The reason doesn't matter. Nothing would have changed between us."

But I wondered if Lauren had made the Cordelia Trust loan precisely to make sure that nothing would change.

"We'd broken it off many times. We couldn't keep away from each other. And he was determined to have his daughter." She drifted over to me, smelling of mouthwash and rose water soap. Before I could stop her, she took the tape out of my hand.

"I hate what I've become," she said, words that surprised me. She had hidden self-knowledge for so long under a crackle of honesty. "This is the first time I've talked freely about Chaz. I've opened a window, and the fresh air is hard to breathe. I'm bypassing Gordon. I'm going to the police. I'll tell them everything. When I'm through, they'll have to let Roddie go."

"What are you going to tell them? What else don't I know?"

"Just what I told you. Isn't that enough?" Her hands fluttered to her face, flushed with a look of panicked excitement. She reached behind me, scrabbling among the papers on the desk. "Where's the camp directory? Maybe Georgina Lester will watch Delia till my mother comes down from Maine."

Upstairs in the master bedroom, I sat on the bed while Lauren freshened up and changed her clothes. I'd managed, just, to convince her to consult Gordon before she went anywhere near the police. She owed that much to Roddie, was how I put it. She'd arranged to meet Gordon at three o'clock, in his office. I hoped Roddie would be finished with Sergeant Tyre and the inquisition by then.

Amanda's long-suffering mom had agreed to take care of Delia, who was traipsing up and down between the playroom and her bedroom, loading a frame pack with toys. From the adjacent bathroom, the sound of water running into a sink lulled me halfway to sleep.

When Lauren returned, her mental fog had lifted. She strode briskly across the room, pausing at her dressing table to run a brush through her hair, moving on to explore her closet, larger than my living room. "Should I dress conservatively?"

"Can't hurt."

From a color-coded row of garments, she pulled out a dull blue suit. "How's this?"

"If you want to look like a meter maid."

Next, she showed me a pinky beige straight-cut dress. "My grandmother always liked me in this. The zipper's stuck halfway. I'd wear a jacket over it."

"Not bad." I said. The idea that anyone would seek my fashion advice amused me, though of course it wasn't style tips Lauren wanted. More like demeanor tips.

While she was pulling the dress over her head, I asked a question that had been nagging at me since Delia met Cordy: "Lauren, did Chaz know Roddie was my candidate?"

Her voice came muffled through linen. "He knew Roddie was running for office, but I never mentioned you. I had no idea Chaz consulted you until Roddie told me about the voter survey turning up in his Lexus."

"Did Chaz tell you he was running for mayor of Telford?"

"Are you serious? Was he really?"

"No," I said. "Not really." Whatever Chaz had wanted from me, I guessed he hadn't confided in Lauren. She put on the compatible jacket, slipped into low-heeled pumps, added a small shoulder bag. Grandma would love it.

Delia insisted on dragging her pack out to the Mazda, but let me load it while her mother buckled her in. I hugged her goodbye.

"Tell Gordon everything you told me," I urged as Lauren slid into the driver's seat. "He'll recommend an attorney for you. Or I've got some names." I bent close to her open window. "Please don't get hung up on self-sacrifice."

She waited for me to finish, then said: "I know what I'm doing."

Troubled by her mood, I watched them drive away. Lauren had salvaged her spirit the same way I had after Gil died. She'd sketched a map for herself, assembled an emotional compass out of spare parts, and for the moment, she'd plot her course. But soon, I knew, her map would fall to dust. The compass needle would swing wildly around her heart.

Chapter Eighteen

Paper Chase

At Waltham Color Lab only one of Nino's torn photographs was ready, a three-by-five shot of a teen-aged girl squinting into the sun, cradling a puppy in her arms. Her dark hair and facial features were lost in the dazzle. Her chop-top and flares looked twenty-years out of date. Nino's daughter? Granddaughter? He never talked about his family, had confided only that he was twice married and twice divorced.

I took the photo home and settled in for a nap that might have gone on till midnight, but for a crash that woke me to a vision of Michael standing by the bed in an angel-blue shirt, looking not at all upset about Lab 45 and the ruin of his investigation. "I fell over your books," he said in a smoky baritone that rocked my heart. "Pretty tall stack considering most people read one book at a time."

"It's my sadly short attention span. Where've you been?"

"Doing paperwork." He sidled down and gave me a lingering kiss that I wanted to build on, but as my body heat soared into the melt zone, his hug turned friendly. "I'm on my way to Long Harbor Reality."

Feeling rejected, I moved to the edge of the bed. "What's at Long Harbor?"

"Renfrow's real estate broker. He's giving me a tour of NGT's relocation site."

"You're still on the case? I was with Roddie this morning. Tyre couldn't wait to tell me you'd quit."

"I stepped aside, not down. With you in the middle of everything how could I quit? Renfrow's broker may know something about the agency contract."

"That I did not sign." I grappled with my books, managing to lean over and restack them without falling off the bed. "Michael, I'm sorry I made things awkward for you."

He passed me *The Portable Sherlock*. "Don't be. You have every right to stick your nose in your clients' affairs. So come with me to Long Harbor and snoop away. There's a lobster dinner in it."

"At Lemuel's?"

"Unless you want to drive to P-town and buy 'em off the boat."

Books balanced, I walked to the closet for my new denim skirt and an old black top. "Provincetown's tempting, but I want to stay close to home in case Roddie needs me. They've been talking to him for hours. What's going on?"

"You're forgetting he lied to us."

I almost told him about Lauren's tape and her affair, but I knew he'd be bound to pass it on to Tyre. My own code bound me. The Bairds had to disclose their story, their way, in their own good time. "Do you honestly believe Roddie killed Chaz?"

"I'll let Tyre reflect on that. It's Renfrow occupies me now. I spent a few hours at the McCormick building this morning, chasing NGT paper."

"What're you looking for?"

"Anything I can find. Renfrow and his wife controlled the company, but six months ago, he transferred his shares to something called the Glendel Corporation."

Glendel. Glenn and Delia. The loving father? Or just another way to assert ownership? "What about Johanna's shares?"

"As far as I can tell, she's not involved. Six months ago they were in the middle of a savage divorce. Renfrow was probably hiding his assets. Or, if Beauford Smith's got it right, Renfrow was trying to insulate himself from corporate wrongdoing."

"Toxic dumping." I envisioned that overturned bucket, the hose. I could feel my neck flame. Beauford's hockey duffle was still in my car. Why had I bothered to swipe it? The smoking-gun video was probably under a floorboard in his living room, a trick Sherlock Holmes knew but I had forgotten. "Have you talked to Telford's biohazards people?"

"I'm focusing on Renfrow's business affairs. So far, I've come up with the names of three Glendel officers, all lawyers, and don't look so avid. I've already called them. One's out of town, and the other two stonewalled me."

"Give me the names. My old boss is still at the firm. What Al Volpe doesn't know today, he always knows tomorrow."

Michael tore a sheet from his pad and passed it to me. "It's public record," he said. "Feel free."

Like many self-confident attorneys, Al liked to answer the phone himself when he could. "Hey, Susanna banana. How come you only call when you need something?"

"That hurts, Al. I called to invite you and Kate to dinner."

"Who's cooking?" he asked quickly. Last year, Al and his wife had sampled my twelve-minute-microwave chicken divan, which let all of us down rather badly. Looking back, I realized that squat earnest casserole did have more in common with a sofa than a meal.

"I'm having it catered."

From the doorway, Michael laughed out loud.

"Of course! Tavola Rustica!" Al said. "Nino Biondi. I haven't seen him since you left us and took him with you. How is the little guy?"

A joke about dinner died on my lips. "Not so good, Al. He's not speaking to me."

"Wanna tell me about it?" Twenty-five years my senior, Al had been my confidant as well as my boss at the firm.

"It's a long story," I said, and immediately Michael walked back into the bedroom, tapping his watch. To appease him, I made it fast, giving Al the essence of what I'd done, but sparing him extraneous details, such as the splattered oatmeal and Nino's hypertensive rage. That Al didn't gasp or parcel out blame confirmed my almost girlish admiration of him as the very best kind of lawyer, fair-minded, preferring private chats to subpoenas, but a merciless advocate if dialogue failed.

"Look Susan, whatever's broken between you and Nino, I'm sure we can fix it. He's a nice guy. He'll come around. You know these old *paesans*. They need a little sweet talk, that's all. A show of respect."

Michael jangled his car keys at me from the hall. "I'm leaving now. You can meet me at Long Harbor, or go directly to Lemuel's."

I gestured for him to wait. "Al, I'm running late. One quick question."

"I thought so."

Michael had disappeared, so I raced to the point. "I need information about a company called Glendel." I gave Al the names Michael had dug up.

"I'll see what I can do. Call me tomorrow, after eleven."

I found Michael in the kitchen sitting at the table, drinking coffee. "We've got a few minutes," he said, "but if I'd let on, you'd still be yucking it up with Al."

Charlestown Navy Yard and Boston harbor materialized, streaks of blue-gray water between buildings and boats. Ahead were elegant brick condominiums reconstructed from old warehouses, and to our left, old warehouses. True to its name, Long Harbor Reality fronted the harbor, even had its own dock. Inside, the floors were old wood, spar varnished and spotted with Turkish carpets.

A silver-haired woman greeted us. "Jay will be right with you."

Michael sat down with a magazine while I ambled as far as the door to the dock where I loitered, inhaling a mix of powerboat fumes and dank sea air. At twenty past five a plump blond man, with a tight youngish face, goatee, and no apparent eyebrows, came over to us. "Lieutenant Benedict? I'm Jay Jennings."

He shook Michael's hand, but not mine, though when Michael said my name he tossed me a nod over his shoulder as he led us to his office. "Here's a copy of the lease." He slid it across his desk. "Fifty thousand square feet of unfinished space. Runs for fifteen years. All improvements paid for by NovoGenTech."

Michael flipped through the document. "Any finder's fees involved in the deal?"

"Just my broker's fee."

"When did you sign?"

"Week ago Saturday." Jay pointed to the bottom of the third page, and his jacket sleeve rode up, exposing a two-sided cufflink, artfully monogrammed.

"What brought Renfrow to Long Harbor?"

"Our June ad campaign. He thought one of our properties might suit." Jay nodded toward the lease. "That one was virtually spoken for, but as soon as he saw the building, he offered me more. Nearly cost me the sale. My first client walked away, then Mr. Renfrow got cold feet. The Monday before he signed, he called after hours and put our negotiations on hold."

The Monday before Chaz signed was the day he'd hired me. "What time did he call?"

"I just said…after hours. His call rang through to my cell at the exact moment I sat down to dinner with friends. Couldn't have been more inconvenient."

"So you didn't spend the evening together looking at harbor island property?"

"Certainly not. We did that in June."

Another whopper unmasked, though by now I'd grown numb to Chaz's dodges and double-dealings. While I'd pontificated at Roddie's finance meeting, he'd probably stolen a few hours with Lauren, then lied about standing me up. "Your boat," I said. "I don't suppose it broke down?"

"The launch. It's called a *launch*, Ms. Callisto."

Well, bite me brother. Luckily I hadn't called it a rumrunner or, God forbid, a dinghy, or Jay might have leaped over his desk and throttled me. I pretended to stifle a yawn, which I hoped made my irritation look like boredom. "Launch. I'll make a note."

Jay stirred his goatee with his fingers and rambled on in a vaguely English-accented voice that lapsed only once into townie Boston-ese. "The launch stalled for a few minutes, yes. We'd gone to Cutters Island, which happens to be one of the only private islands in the *hah-bor*. Totally unsuitable for NGT, but Mr. Renfrow insisted on viewing it. He hadn't put a penny down on the Navy Yard building, mind you. Something awfully grandiose about the man." Weeks after that event, and despite Chaz's death, Jay's annoyance seemed fresh.

"Did he say why he cooled off on your deal?" Michael asked.

Jay began arranging his peripherals, fluffed his pocket square, brushed his lapel. "No."

"Gave no reason at all?" Michael prodded.

Jay noticed my tiny smile and scowled at me. "Mr. Renfrow might have said something about needing a lower price. Lower price! What could I do? I ate humble pie and went back to my first client. A very angry client, I might add. In so many words he told me to drop dead. He didn't sue me for damages only because we'd had a gentleman's agreement. Nothing in writing." The desk phone rang and gentleman Jay snapped a few words into the handset, then slammed it down. "So. Where was I?"

"Drop dead," I said.

"Lower price," Michael clarified.

"Oh, yes. On Saturday morning Mr. Renfrow came back to the table. Acted as if nothing had happened. Only now he was offering much less. Told me he'd sign for a different property if I didn't play ball. He actually expected me to roll over, but I've got a stubborn streak. I do." Jay slapped his starched shirtfront. "I almost held out for his original offer, then decided not to risk it." Jay's face flushed at the memory. "As it turned out, it was all a high-risk ploy."

Michael moved to the edge of his chair. "As it turned out, Renfrow was murdered a few hours after signing your lease."

Jay's neck pinked up like a stringy stalk of rhubarb. "You can't think his murder had anything to do with Long Harbor. Or me."

"Are you sure Renfrow called *you* Saturday morning? Is that your best recollection?" How kind of good-cop Michael to put it like that when he suspected Jay Jennings had told a big fat lie, easily uncovered through phone records, as Jay must have realized.

"I may have left a message on Mr. Renfrow's voice mail."

"What message?"

"I…oh hell. I *had* to lease that building. It was our show-place. Our anchor. Other contracts depended on it. In the end, I offered Mr. Renfrow such a low price, and threw in so many perks, he drove in from Telford and signed before I could change my mind."

"Did you sacrifice your commission?" I asked, knowing he must have.

"Yes, I did. And Long Harbor's profit."

Snapping at me must have restored Jay's confidence because he consulted his Rolex and stood up. "I'm running late. If you want to see the property, we'll have to hurry."

It was at the far end of the Yard, well back from the water. Jay had called it unfinished space. He meant raw emptiness. The building had been used by the Navy to store munitions, and when we peered inside, I thought I smelled gunpowder. The interior had been gutted, Jay explained, in case we hadn't noticed the absence of ceilings and floors. The foundation had been reinforced. There was a new brick facade and a spiffy slate roof. The rest was up to NGT.

"Any idea how much it will cost to turn this place into laboratories?"

"Millions."

"What about Boston zoning? Any restrictions on biotech-nology?"

"Mr. Renfrow looked into everything. This site conforms."

By the time we drove away, it was well past six. In spite of my nap, I was too tired for lobster, and Michael didn't argue. "When we get home, I have to check in with Gordon Brenner," I said, melancholy stealing over me. "I don't know what's going on with Roddie."

"While you pursue justice, I'll fix supper."

I wanted something homey, easy to chew. Preferably white. "Will you make tuna noodle casserole if I make the salad? We can do a quick shop at BeeCees."

"Anything you want, Susie." Michael smiled and patted my hand. I could tell he was going to be hatefully cheerful tonight. So much had gone well for him today: He had enjoyed his tour of the Navy Yard. He liked the ocean. He undoubtedly had an idea about the investigation that he wasn't going to share with me. Or anyone else, I realized. By stepping aside, but not down, Michael was free to pursue justice his own way.

"You never call me Susie. That's what Nino calls me." Used to call me.

"Don't you like it?"

"No." My mood, which had been dipping, now took a dive.

"What did you think of Jay?" Michael said.

"He's a liar with a face like a turkey bum."

"I mean the inner Jay."

"Let me see. Where did I bury my woman's intuition?" I rested my eyes, and shades of Delia, my stomach began to hurt. Appendicitis? Ulcers? Was I developing an eating disorder?

"He seemed nervous," Michael said, not noticing my sullen misery, which deepened it.

"Probably thought you were accusing him of murder."

"Why would he think that?"

"Because he showed anger." I pulled my hobo bag off the floor and hugged it tight. "What do I think of him? He's a screw-up who wants to play let's-make-a-deal. He's afraid of you because he's a coward. He disdained me because my clothes aren't right. Jay Jennings is a prick."

"Geez, Susan. He really zinged you with that launch business, didn't he?" Michael's smile was almost as obnoxious as Jay's.

"Not at all," I said. "Launch, boat, the difference is a snob thing and the nuance is crucial to him. I find that hard to take in a man."

"Come on. Jay's humorless, not too bright, but give the guy a break. He's got a living to make. Nuanced people pay his bills."

"I oughta find me some clients with nuances. Big nuances." Not sure I had enough fingers, I totted up my afflictions: Two of my candidates were murdered, or suspects. My dearest, and former, client hated my guts. My landlords were conspiring to raise my rent. I was sleeping on sheets owned by MasterCard. Even my damn underwear was owned by MasterCard.

"Snap out of it, Susie." Michael reached over and squeezed my knee. I jerked it away, surprised by the force of my mood. An ominous calm began to spread through my core, and as we drove, I let my mind drift where it would, to sleep, oblivion.

Next thing I knew, we were parked in front of my house, and Michael was on the sidewalk, opening the car door for me. When I got out, he closed the door on my skirt. I tugged and it ripped. Damn Michael's country-boy chivalry. I headed down the driveway to my car where I hauled Beau's hockey gear out of the trunk.

Michael came up behind me. "What's that?"

"I stopped by Beauford's apartment." I spilled out the story, even the chapter on cockroaches. "Mrs. Kling chased me down the fire stairs, but I managed to grab this on my way out." I upended the duffle, and a can of wax hit my foot.

"You raided Smith's apartment?" Michael's pissed-off voice told me he had deliberately, willfully misunderstood.

"Beau gave me permission, but I didn't have a key."

His cold eyes made me explain too much. "Yes, yes, I lied my way in, but in about two minutes you're going to thank me." I hoped.

I plopped down on the driveway and emptied the bag. Piece by piece, I tore into the equipment, even probing behind the foam pads inside the helmets and under the skates' grungy tongues. Michael watched in a silence that seemed to shout. After awhile I gave up. "Okay, video's not here. Satisfied?"

He bent and began putting helmets and leg guards back into the duffle. "Susan, why don't we go inside?"

"Please don't condescend to me."

A puck dropped from his hand. "Maybe I've been crowding you these last few days," he said in the same low voice.

"And maybe I've been expecting too much." I rested my head against the car, letting warm metal soothe the back of my neck. "You should go home."

"I'd rather stay. You need me to fix your supper."

His voice seemed to smile, but where I wanted tenderness, I saw only tolerance and resignation on his face.

"You left me alone for months. What if I'd needed you then?" I scrambled to my feet. "Well, I didn't. And I don't need you now."

At last I understood how angry I had been all along.

Chapter Nineteen

Alibi

Alone in my kitchen, I tried to reach Gordon Brenner and ended up leaving messages with his answering service and voice mail. Next, I called Lauren who wasn't home, or wasn't picking up. I told her machine to please say I'd called.

Supper was peanut butter on toast, as meager as my spirits. An hour in my clawfoot tub wizened my fingers and toes, and now I was shriveled inside and out. I changed the gauze on my breast, and got into bed with Count Tolstoy. Quick as the turn of a page, I forgot about Roddie and Chaz, though it took three chapters to shake off Michael. By chapter five, I'd lost myself too, and *that* was a relief. The uses of literature.

At midnight, the telephone jangled me out of a dream that dissolved before I opened my eyes. My heart thudded, not sure whose body it occupied tonight. "Yes," I croaked.

It was Gordon Brenner. "They've charged Roddie with murder," he said. "His wife's not home so I'm calling you."

As soon as he said it, I realized I'd known it would happen. "Why?" My croak became a hoarse whisper. "What changed?"

"They linked the murder weapon to him. Renfrow was strangled with mountaineer's rope. Doesn't look good, Susan. Lab report came back. They found microscopic fibers embedded in Renfrow's neck."

"They charged Roddie over a hank of rope?"

"They found lengths of it in Renfrow's Lexus, along with that campaign brochure. They're saying the rope wasn't on the market yet and could only have come from Roddie."

"Lots of that rope out there; it was field tested. And Roddie's been giving it away like candy. Any fingerprints?"

"Nothing useful."

"So where are we? No fingerprints. And no firm time of death: Chaz could have died as early as one p.m. when Roddie was unequivocally in Denver."

"Or as late as midnight, when he wasn't."

"That doesn't sink my point. All they've got is a handful of circumstantial evidence."

"Yes, but the circumstances are narrowly focused. The rope. The trust loan. The lies. Tomorrow the D.A. will hammer them home. Arraignment's at nine o'clock. Where the hell is Mrs. Baird? She never showed for our appointment and hasn't returned my calls."

"I'd guess she's gone to Maine with her little girl. She'll get back to you." I spoke with more hope than conviction.

"She ought to get back to her husband. Roddie's worried sick about her."

"I'll come to the arraignment." As if the sight of his campaign counselor would calm Roddie's fears. "What room?"

Gordon told me, and I hung up, feeling as helpless as if Roddie had died. Once Lauren's affair was exposed, Roddie's motive for murder would lock into place. And if she talked to Tyre today, the police already knew.

No handcuffs. That was the good news.

The rest made a front-page story in the *Boston Globe,* Section B, above the fold. I pushed my oatmeal aside and laid the paper flat on the table. Roddie was grinning from a campaign photo I'd blitzed to the media back in May. The headline was two columns wide: *Newton Candidate Suspect in Murder.*

Most of the story rehashed what little the police had already released about "the NGT slayings," names of the victims, a few gruesome physical details, including an update on the rope. Sergeant Paul Tyre was quoted: "*The ligature used to strangle Charles Renfrow was manufactured by a company owned by Rodney Baird.*"

Lauren was mentioned in a sidebar about NGT and its products: *The biotechnology company had been experiencing "growing pains" at the time of Renfrow's death. Sources told this reporter that Lauren Baird, Renfrow's close friend and financial advisor, recently made a substantial loan to NGT from a Baird family trust.*

Close friend. Substantial loan. Sources. Dammit all. Against my advice, Lauren had talked to Tyre, who Michael had long suspected of courting the press. Why didn't the reporter just spell out Tyre's innuendo: *Lauren Baird and Charles Renfrow were lovers.*

The breakfast crowd at Freddie's, the plumbers, contractors, office workers, were drinking in the news with their coffees, and the sight of all those *Heralds* and *Globes* made a knot in my throat. I grabbed my cellphone and called Lauren. As it had last night, her analog voice invited a message. I complied, warning her about the media coverage. I told her about Roddie's arraignment and begged her to call Gordon. "And please get back to me? We're very worried about you." I hung up, sorry I hadn't thought to send Delia a hug.

Breakfast now looked like a lost cause. The gelatinous gruel, so full of buttery comfort a few minutes ago, had gone nearly cold; but I forced it down. To my surprise, the very bulk of it quelled my anxiety. I finished my coffee and added up my check, a few easy numbers whose sum kept eluding me. It was seven-thirty; time enough to stop at my office for Nino's files which I'd decided to return to him after the arraignment.

◇◇◇

The usual villains, traffic and parking, delayed me. By the time I hurled myself up the courthouse steps and found the right room, it was twenty past nine. Lauren, I noted with dismay, was not

"That your candidate in the *Globe*?"

"And the *Herald*, and probably the regional press, and the online news." I gave Al a sketchy account of the arrest and the two million dollar bail. "Gordon Brenner's optimistic," I said, sounding like Eeyore.

"And you're looking on the dark side. Don't. Brenner's one of the best." Al's low voice soothed like menthol. "Listen, I've got a few things on Glendel. I'll show you this afternoon, at your convenience, as long as it's around three o'clock."

"I'd rather not come to your office, if that's all right."

"I know, I know. Lexophobia."

"Actually, I'm afraid the firm might start looking like lost horizons."

"Anytime you want to come back, kid. You know that. But my plan was we meet at Caffe Vittoria like the old days."

"Sounds good." My former firm was a brisk walk away from the North End, and Caffe Vittoria had been a favorite after work stop for a few of us in the real estate department. Al's wife used to join us sometimes, and Gil when he was in town.

We settled on three o'clock, and then Al dropped his bomb. "I'm sending a cab for Nino Biondi. I played peacemaker this morning, and he's ready to listen."

"I've got nothing to say."

"Just show up and let me do the talking. What's the worst that can happen? A good cup of coffee?"

I hesitated until Al played his ace. "No Caffe Vittoria, no Glendel file."

◇◇◇

I popped open a Coke and went back to Roddie's summer schedule, mostly fluff, ice cream socials, tot lot dedications, events a politician out on bail could duck. While I browsed through autumn, a season of forums and debates, it came home to me that simply getting the charges dropped wouldn't be enough. Lingering doubt is an insidious poison. Unless they caught the killer, Roddie's campaign would wither. I put away the calendar and swigged more Coke. Like my mood, it was flat, which was better than angst. Flat, I could live with.

I decided to cultivate my plants. Though I'd watered all seven of them on Saturday, even the cast-iron plant looked peaked. I snipped a few leaves and, using my coffee carafe, I flooded them with water, which immediately rushed through the pots and drizzled over the floor. Cactuses, I decided, would fit better with my professional life. I was on my knees, sopping up the mess when someone knocked, and the door opened.

"Hi, Susan."

I jumped to my feet. "Hey, Glenn."

He was standing in the doorway, a small, dark-haired figure crowding in next to him.

"And Darcy!" I smiled, agreeably I hoped, given that they'd caught me with my tush in the air. "Come in."

I pitched the wet paper towel toward my wastebasket and watched, amazed, as it plopped juicily over the rim. I *always* missed. "Bull's eye," I said coolly, but secretly gratified.

"'Swish,' you mean." Darcy's teeth and gums had a Cheshire cat life of their own.

"I beg your pardon."

"Basketball metaphor, wasn't it?"

Why didn't I like this pansy-faced girl?

Glenn walked ahead of Darcy, and she hurried to catch up, oversize jeans bagging on top of her sneakers. They both wore blue-and-white shirts, and I wondered if that was a coincidence or an expression of solidarity. They had reached my desk, and Glenn was staring at my pencil pot much as his father had done two weeks and a lifetime ago. Darcy touched his sleeve, as if they'd been quarreling and she was offering to make up.

I switched off the plant light. "So, what brings you here?"

He turned, not quite meeting my eyes. "We, uh, we'd like to ask your advice." He helped himself to a pencil, and studied it. "Ticonderoga." A dreamy look veiled his face. "My dad used to say Ticonderoga was the sound a pencil makes being sharpened. *Ticonderogaticonderoga.*"

"It's about Mr. Renfrow's murder," Darcy said in a rush. "We know who killed him."

My pulse quickened. "Let's find the soft chairs."

In a screened area not far from the door, I took the Morris chair. They sat next to each other on the sofa, Glenn jiggling my pencil until Darcy put out a hand. Her backpack, larger than my hobo bag but very much leaner, took up most of the coffee table.

"Have you seen this?" She brought out today's *Globe*, where the NGT stories were circled in red.

"Yes," I said. "Roddie Baird is my candidate."

"He's innocent," Glenn said, finally looking at me. "Can I speak in confidence?"

It killed me to say no, but I couldn't make a promise it wasn't ethical to keep. "If you have information about the murders, it's your duty to tell the police. Tell me, and I'll be obliged to pass it on to them." Especially if it exonerates Roddie.

"I'm not exactly sure I should go to the police."

"He doesn't want to be sued for slander or defamation or something," Darcy explained.

The pencil started twirling again. "I thought maybe I could hire you so we'd have attorney-client privilege, and I could discuss it."

I shook my head. "Can't do it. I'll be glad to refer you to another attorney." Well, not glad. Sad, actually. I wanted to know, immediately, anything that pointed to Roddie's innocence.

"Susan, my father is dead. He was your client, too, not just this Baird guy. Mom says Dad paid you very well for what turned out to be no work. Can't I confide in you, just for a few minutes?"

With his head down, Glenn looked like a Chaz clone again. The narrow face, the way he stretched his legs and slouched on his spine. He'd inherited the 'persuasive' gene too, and if he lacked Chaz's height and aggression, his mildness evoked tender feelings in me. I wanted to hear him out. Certainly for Roddie's sake, but also for his own. All of which made me wary as hell. I'd been hoodwinked once by a Renfrow.

"Let me talk, okay? I won't ask for confidentiality. I'll leave that up to you."

"All right," I said, "but no promises."

Glenn's neck was raw where he'd scraped it shaving, and his Adam's apple bobbed with emotion. "Bart Bievsky murdered my father."

Hope and excitement danced along my spine, but I quickly repressed them. Bievsky had been courting Johanna. Did Glenn have an agenda here besides a thirst for justice?

"Are you going to tell me how you know?"

When he didn't answer, I said: "Your father was strangled with mountaineer's rope."

He flinched, but the police would be even blunter.

"Was it Bart's rope?"

"I don't know."

"Bart was in Boston Saturday with your mother. They had dinner together and spent the night in town. Or did they lie to the police?"

Carefully, not looking at me, he placed the pencil on top of Darcy's newspaper. "My father was murdered before they ever sat down to dinner. I found his body."

I hadn't seen it coming. "*When?*"

"Around seven."

Without any help from my fingers, my mind calculated the time difference. Seven p.m. in Boston meant five p.m. in Denver. Roddie's jet wasn't even off the runway. If Glenn was telling the truth, Roddie was in the clear.

The misery in Glenn's eyes quelled my joy. "Tell me what you saw," I said.

He breathed in, almost a sob. "I thought he was asleep at his desk. 'Dad,' I said, 'wake up.' I touched his hand. It fell away from his face...I saw his eyes and...I ran away."

"Why didn't you call the police?"

"Because I was...I needed advice. I went back to Darcy's."

"We were together all night," Darcy said. "And most of the day."

Glenn plucked at his jeans. "After they found my dad, I couldn't bring myself to tell my mother, or anyone except Darcy. My plan was to prove Bart Bievsky killed him, or at least set the police on his trail, but now I'm not sure what to do."

He was telling half-truths. I could feel it. If Johanna knew her son had found Chaz's body, she'd know how bad it could look for him, and maybe for her. And if he really hadn't told her, maybe it was because he suspected, not only Bart, but her.

"Did your mother drive to Boston with Bart that Saturday?"

Don't be a fool, his eyes said, blue like his father's but soft like his mother's, the only soft thing about Johanna. He shook his head. "She came in with my father in the morning to take care of some real estate for NGT. Dad went back to Telford. He had meetings, with some of the researchers. And with Bievsky. Mom spent the rest of the day in Boston, shopping, going to the MFA. It was her first real day off in months."

In other words, Johanna had been alone. She might have been anywhere, even back in Telford. And Glenn might be throwing sand in my eyes. But if he was willing to tell the police about finding his father's body...sand or not, that was good news for Roddie.

I got up. "I'm going to call Mr. Baird's lawyer."

"But I haven't finished."

"Please don't say anymore. I can't keep your confidences."

Darcy whispered in Glenn's ear, and I left them to mull over their options.

"Wait! Susan!" Glenn shouted.

"What is it?"

From my desk I could hear them murmuring, their voices indistinguishable until Glenn's rose above the whispers. "Will I be arrested for not reporting the murder?"

I walked back and put my head around the screen. "We'll get you a lawyer. You'll be fine. But Roddie Baird has already spent one night in jail."

"What about my mother? I don't want her dragged into this. Smeared in the press like...like that Lauren Baird. The newspapers made her sound like some kind of...*slut*." He quoted from the *Globe* story in a singsongy voice: "'Renfrow's close friend.' What's that supposed to mean? I don't want them saying my mother is a 'close friend' of Bart Bievsky."

"I won't tell Roddie's lawyer anything except the time you found your father's body. But you'll have to talk to the police."

"I need to think about this," he said.

"Just tell the truth," I shot back on my way to the phone. "Your mother can handle the fallout."

I phoned Gordon and learned that he'd be in court all day. "Have him call me the minute he gets back. Tell him I have information that clears Roddie Baird."

Three stories below, lunch hour traffic was beginning to clog Moody Street. Gordon's cookie had tided me over, but now I was hungry, and Glenn and Darcy had a starved look about them. "Glenn!" I called. "Darcy! Want some lunch?"

No answer.

"I could order calzones from the bakery downstairs!"

Another thirty seconds blinked by.

"Glenn?" I walked back to the screen.

They were gone.

Chapter Twenty

Truth And A Bluff

Far away, an exit door slammed, and I realized chasing after them was pointless. I couldn't force Glenn to tell anyone else what he'd told me. I had a sudden desire to hear Michael's voice. Passing over yesterday's childish scene in my driveway, I went back to my desk and tracked him down at the Framingham barracks.

"I was about to call you." He was cool, cutting right to the chase: "Forensics examined the drain from Lab 45. They found a strand of silk fringe. Thought you'd like to know."

"From Torie's dress?" I paced the length of the window wall.

"Looks that way."

"That's fantastic!" Fantastic. Torie was dead, and I was capering over a clue. "Now do you believe I saw a microtome blade?"

"I'd have told you if I doubted."

"But you stepped away from the investigation."

"Nothing to do with you. Nothing much, anyway. Shea and I have our differences. Always have."

"You mean Tyre is a bumswipe and you're not."

"I mean maybe you were my pretext for letting go." I could almost hear him smile. "Don't get too worked up about the fringe. Could have fallen off Torie's dress any time."

"Like she always came to work in a flapper outfit."

"Fringe isn't all we found. The drain's mildly radioactive. EPA's been notified."

"So Beauford was right. Maybe his video will finger Torie's killer."

"That would be Renfrow," Michael said, and I didn't contradict him. Chaz was dead, and if Michael was right, maybe a primitive justice had after all been served. Justice for Torie, but so far, not for Roddie.

I told Michael about Glenn and Darcy's visit. "Glenn knows something about his father's murder that will clear Roddie Baird," I said. "Someone should talk to Darcy Villencourt, too. Glenn seems to confide in her."

"I'll pass it on to Tyre."

There came a silence neither of us knew how to fill. Then Michael said, "That Persian violet you like so much? Somebody severed its roots."

"Torie's killer?"

"Or someone with a grudge against houseplants."

On my way to coffee with Nino and Al I detoured past the Coast Guard base. Patrol boats, troop carriers, sea gulls, flags, anything that streamed, fluttered or flew held my eye. A sentry blocked access to the piers, but he was friendly, and we exchanged pleasantries before I strolled on to the *USS Constitution*, a three masted frigate ready to sail in 1797 now anchored forever in place. Destiny without destination…the thought depressed me.

I plowed across Atlantic Avenue and cut through an alley that opened like a portal onto the exuberant anarchy of Hanover Street. The North End is a little knob of Boston lapped on three sides by hubbub and water. In this enclave, commerce and cheer stand in for destiny, and now the spirit of the place took hold of me. Tacking around women on sun-chairs and men in fedoras, I ambled toward Caffe Vittoria. For the moment, murder and the meaning of life were mere motes in my eye.

Like the harbor, the caffe hadn't changed since I stopped coming to town; there was one door for evening crowds and one for the neighborhood, which I opened. Nino and Al sat at a table in the smoking alcove, drinking espresso and clipping the ends off cigars.

"Wuzzup, guys?" I said, choosing a tone I felt appropriate for the occasion.

Al circled his palm in the air, and the waiter seated me. "I'll have *exactly* what they're having," I told him, and Nino frowned because he knew I meant the cigars.

"You sure?" The waiter, an old man from an old land, glanced first at Nino, then at Al who had folded his arms on the table and was dimpling at me.

"Okay," Al said, after the waiter left. The dimples disappeared, and he gave his cuffs a dramatic push up his wrists. "I want you two to make up. How about it, Susan?"

I locked my hands under the table. If Nino extended his, I'd think about it.

The waiter brought coffee only, forcing me to ask pointedly for my cigar.

"Bring *ossi di morte*," Nino told him, maybe hoping to distract me with dead men's bones, my favorite cookie, light as air, as nutty and dry as, well, old bones. Non-Italians like Michael have been known to call them punishment cookies.

I stirred sugar into my cup.

Al shook Splenda into his.

"So," Nino said.

"Well," I said.

The cookies arrived. No cigar.

"Come on," Al said, and everybody started speaking over everybody else. "...free rent...*villiaco*...wait, wait..."

The first round went to Nino. "I don't want to talk about it," he said.

"Me either." I started to get up, but Al put one hand on my arm and the other on Nino's shoulder.

"What's going on here? What'd she do to make you so mad?"

Nino rattled his tiny cup. "While I was in the hospital, she betrayed my trust. That's all. Nothing much."

"I negotiated a fabulous deal!"

Al cut me off. "Neen, you're misunderstanding something. Susan cares about you."

A fake smile began to work around Nino's mouth. "Ah, it's finally getting clear in my mind. She betrayed me because she likes me."

"You are impossible!" I snapped a cookie in half and dropped both pieces on the table. I would have said more, but Al jabbed a finger at Nino.

"Your landlord loves to sue. What do you think would've happened if he got a judgment against you while you were sick?"

"I wasn't sick. They beat me up."

"Thank you. That's my next point. You think it was Lombard's people who beat you up?"

"I know it was."

"Good, good. Then don't you think Mr. Lombard would've finished what he started?" Al puffed his cigar, waving smoke away from his eyes. "Bribery fails, somebody trashes your apartment. Violence escalates, and you end up half-dead in the hospital. Enter Susan."

Like an impresario introducing his diva, Al flourished a palm at me. My hidden face crossed its eyes and stuck out its tongue. "Before Lombard can sue your comatose ass off, she uses her power of attorney and gets you the moon."

"Hey, Mr. Volpe. She didn't convince me, and neither can you."

Al threw up his hands. He had rekindled all the old anger, not worth a good cigar. "All right, all right. Susan made a mistake. Can't you forgive a mistake?"

"No mistake! She knew what she was doing." Nino's chin quivered, stirring my pity.

Why stand on pride? I had bigger problems than this little old man who needed me whether he knew it or not. Unconditional surrender would appease him, and I suddenly came close to giving it. "Look," I started to say, not at all sure what would follow.

With a sound that froze my next thought, Al scraped back his chair. "You are a tough customer, Nino. For argument's sake, I'll concede that Susan betrayed you."

"Al, don't you dare—"

"Shut up, Susan." Al's voice swept over the table and stirred the cookie crumbs. "Okay, Nino. Let's assume Susan deliberately signed your rights away. But that was then. Now Lombard wants you to forget about the new lease and stay in Brookline. So you're back where you started."

"So what?"

Like the sun after a storm, Al's dimple appeared. "So why not forgive her?"

Nino sifted crumbs, crushing them to powder between his moody fingers.

"Come on, Neen. Whatta you say? You always did have a hard head."

"Maybe the hard head saved my life." Nino's hand strayed to his bandage. "Beh," he said at last. "I always thought Susie was the best lawyer in town."

I came up with a few weasel words of my own: "I only meant to help, Nino."

He closed his eyes for a minute, an old man taking a New York nap. When he opened them, I passed him the files I'd brought in case peacemaking failed. "You wanted these."

He pushed them away. "You keep 'em."

"Your new lawyer will need them."

"What new lawyer?" he said.

And that was as close as he came to forgiving me.

"See, that wasn't so hard, and here comes Susan's reward." Al brought out his briefcase and handed me a folder. "Here's what I got on Glendel so far. Hope it helps."

"You're an angel," I said. "Thank you. For everything."

I finished my coffee, pocketed two cookies, and looked around for the waiter. "Excuse me," I called, as he ducked behind a pillar. "I really would like my cigar."

To my astonishment, he brought it.

"How much?" I pulled out my wallet.

"Twenty-two dollars," he said.

"Oh, forget it." There had to be cheaper ways to tweak the *paesans*.

"My treat," Al said, calling my bluff.

Nino snorted.

Tucked off Hanover was a shaded courtyard with a gurgling fountain, and a bench just long enough for me and my hobo bag. I opened Al's folder and quickly scanned the ranks of Glendel officers, minority shareholders, creditors. Was one of them a murderer?

The next page listed Glendel's holdings. With handles like GenEra and MediGen and Prototech, they sounded like part of the biomedical industry, a nice fit with NGT. Were they having "growing pains" too? I read the names over, and this time, one of them leaped out at me: MediRX. Betty Boop's drugstore.

MediRX and Tavola Rustica were the only tenants left in Lombard's building. Was Lombard a missing link in the chain of lies Chaz had forged around me? I found Lombard Associates in my address book and dialed. His secretary answered in her precise, slightly hostile voice, and I asked for her boss. She put me on hold. When she came back she'd discovered that Mr. Lombard had unfortunately just left for the day.

My watch said four-forty, and since I knew that Peter Lombard rarely left his office before seven, I said, "Tell him it's an emergency!"

Without a word, she put me on hold again. Seconds later she was back, stiff as an outhouse door. "I couldn't catch him. I suggest you call tomorrow morning, around eight."

"Maybe you can help me. I need information about his Boylston Street property. What's the square footage?"

"Mr. Lombard owns several properties on Boylston."

"The Tavola Rustica building. It's about ninety thousand square feet, am I right?"

She hung up on me.

Next, I called Long Harbor Realty. Gentleman Jay himself answered, which proved my luck wasn't always out to lunch. Jay was about as effusive as you'd expect him to be toward someone who didn't know a boat from a launch.

"Quick question," I said. "Is Long Harbor being sued by Lombard Associates?"

There was a long silence, followed by an irritated sigh. "That's really none of your business."

"Look Jay, in a day or two, the police will be asking you the same question."

"When the police ask me, I'll answer. Now, if there's nothing else?"

If the answer had been no, Jay Jennings would gladly have said so. I decided to track down Nino's landlord.

I parked behind the nondescript two-story building from which Peter Lombard ran his real estate empire, *Lombard Associates* painted in gold letters on a second floor window. It was the only commercial property in a manicured area of brick houses and chemical lawns. I headed for the entrance, certain that Nino's landlord was hard at work, plotting lease buy-outs and rent increases at his mahogany desk.

At the far end of the lot an engine sputtered to life. A maroon Mercedes of roughly the same vintage as my BMW was chugging backward out of its slot, leaking diesel fumes into the air. Cheapskate Lombard probably replaced his cars every forty years, or maybe his wife drove the new ones. The Mercedes rotated like a groaning old battleship until it pointed at the exit. Long fingers protruded from the driver's side window and flicked ash off a cigar.

"Peter!" I trotted toward the car, which ground to a halt at the sound of my voice.

Lombard stuck his head out. "What is it? I'm running late."

"About Nino Biondi's new lease." I stood close to the car with my hand on the roof. A wisp of cigar smoke rose toward my face, a pleasant smell, though Lombard probably thought I disliked it. "Why did you change your mind?"

"Because I found out you didn't have his okay when we talked."

This was a lie, but I didn't call him on it. He shifted into drive and the Mercedes lurched forward. "Everything's hunky-dory," he said. "Mind your own business. Biondi's gonna stay where he is."

"With all the goodies you gave him for Cambridge, why should he stay in Brookline?"

"Talk, talk, talk. Step aside, Susan. I gotta go."

I kept pace with the rolling car. "We didn't just talk, Peter. We switched horses midstream. Nino's old lease is dead. I've got two notarized copies of his new one. With all its valuable perks."

The Mercedes hesitated, the engine wavering between a growl and a scree. "You looking for walking around money? I don't make payoffs, kid." The car inched forward again, my hand still fixed to the roof. At the exit, Lombard nosed into the street. "You had no right to sign for Biondi."

"I had every right."

"I'd leave it alone if I were you. You negotiated against your client's wishes. That's fraud in my book. Biondi's happy. You stir up trouble, you might find yourself on the wrong end of a lawsuit." A faint electrical odor mingled with the smell of cigar as his window began to rise. Near the top it whined to a stop.

Careful of my nose, I spoke into the gap. "I'd be happy to meet you in court, Peter. We can talk to the judge about Charles Renfrow. Was he a tenant of yours?"

Slowly, without taking his eyes off mine, Lombard detached the cigar from his face and placed it in the ashtray. "No."

"I just spoke to Long Harbor Realty." Truth and a bluff blended like coffee and cream in my voice. "Why are you suing them?"

He started to speak, then wrestled the steering wheel sharply right and pulled away. A sound like cherry bombs erupted from the tailpipes.

I ran back to my car, glad I hadn't locked it. Seconds later, I was following a trail of visible fumes, the Mercedes itself nowhere in sight. A familiar headache unfurled behind my left eye. I had to catch up, had to make Lombard talk to me.

At the second cross street I spotted the Mercedes wheeling around a distant corner. I hit the gas pedal, and the Beemer hesitated, then streamed ahead. The Mercedes picked up speed too, and Lombard wound through streets that were clones of each other while I tagged behind like an obnoxious kid sister.

On Hammond he swerved into rush hour traffic. Four cars whipped past before I was able to dash out in front of a fifth. Arrogant sod, thrusting her middle finger at me. I leaned on my horn, and like a contrary child, the Beemer faltered again. Carefully, steadily, I bore down on the pedal but the speedometer sank, from forty to thirty to twenty to twelve.

Ahead, the Mercedes coughed and shuddered. Cars darted around us. Ms. Middlefinger charged ahead. Lombard and I chugged past the Longwood Cricket Club. I couldn't narrow the gap between us. Lombard couldn't widen it.

Just before Route 9, the Mercedes cut right and lumbered into the retail foods end of the Chestnut Hill Mall. My BMW limped behind. Right away Lombard found a parking space and hustled his blue-blazered self into the supermarket. I dithered briefly through the lot, then grabbed a handicap space and tore after him.

Inside, I thought I saw his gray trousered leg disappear down the soda pop aisle but when I got there, he was gone. The front of the store was packed with after work shoppers. All the men wore blue blazers. None of them was Lombard. I ran back and forth, making two complete circuits, studying people hunched over meat coolers and dairy cases, picking over the grapes. My heart sank. Lombard had snookered me. In the classic dodge, he had walked in one door and out the other, while I chased after shadows.

As long as I was here, I decided to grab the makings for tuna noodle casserole. With Michael on hold, my yen for comfort food had become a desperate ache. The only available cart had a wheel that splayed out at the least provocation, with a sound like maracas. I took it and pushed ahead, torquing gently toward canned soup in aisle three.

And then, *there he was* at the deli counter, penned in by shoppers, pointing an elegant finger at a shrink-wrapped prosciutto. I left my cart by the noodles and pressed through the crowd until I was standing behind him.

"Half a pound," he was saying. "Cut it real thin. So my wife can read the newspaper through it."

"The world through ham-colored glasses," I said, and he stiffened at the sound of my voice. "Was NGT going to be your new tenant? Is that why you wanted Tavola out?"

He didn't turn around. "Stop," he said to the deli man.

"Only got a couple ounces here," the deli man said.

"Good enough."

"Did Charles Renfrow promise to pour millions into your… let's face it…decrepit Boylston Street building?"

"Never mind the cheese." He stepped back from the counter. The heel of his shoe touched my toe.

"Was Renfrow planning to convert Nino's kitchens to condos for critters…I mean, biotechnology labs?"

"Got it right here." The deli man held up a cream-colored brick.

"Skip the cheese. And the prosciutto. All of it." Lombard turned and, not looking at me, rammed his cart through the crowd.

I hurried after him. "You were counting on those NGT millions, weren't you? That's why you offered Nino so many incentives."

At the end of the coffee aisle, he tossed a vacuum bag into his cart, turned right and vanished. I found him outside the florist's walk-in cooler. "Peter, I'm not going away until you answer my questions."

He stepped inside, and I scooted right behind. Except for his succulent wheeze, it was dead silent in the chilled room.

Buckets of numb flowers were stacked floor to ceiling along three mirrored walls. There was almost no scent. From a mass of plastic-shrouded bouquets he plucked out anemones, a choice that surprised me. I'd figured Lombard for a brash red rose man.

I touched a speckled lily. "Did Long Harbor Realty interfere with your NGT deal? Think lawsuits will bring back the millions Renfrow promised you?"

He turned and faced me, both of us reflected in the walls, clusters of Peters and Susans glaring at each other through the cut flowers.

"My wife called with a list of things for me to pick up on my way home," he said. "She's a difficult woman, my wife, and I've already left the cold cuts behind. See this?" He held out the anemones. "Flowers fix everything. Now I am going to pay for my groceries." He pushed past me and put his hand on the glass door. "What you're doing here is stalking me. Don't stalk me, Susan. Don't harass me. Renfrow is not a tenant of mine."

"Not now. He's dead."

"I read the papers."

He opened the door, and sound rushed at us, voices, the rumble of carts, the beep-beep of cash registers. I breathed in the fragrance of fresh-baked bread.

"Charles Renfrow was murdered just hours after he signed a lease with Long Harbor Realty. You are threatening to sue Long Harbor. For contract interference, I'll bet."

"Harassment," Lombard said.

"Renfrow walked away from your deal, didn't he? He left you with an empty building and no rent coming in. *Renfrow shafted you!*"

He pushed his cart toward the eight items only checkout lane. "Say another word, and I'll call the police."

I let him go, a pudgy man in creased trousers, shielding himself with flowers. He wouldn't have to call the police. Soon enough, the police would be calling him.

I found my cart and added three pears. My credit card paid for the groceries, and a little later, for the gas and oil and coolant the pump jockey fed my strung-out car. The handicap parking ticket, I'd have to pay from my checking account.

Not until I was pulling into my driveway did I remember the tuna. Oh well. I'd make tunaless casserole and life would go on. I hoped Michael had called. I couldn't wait to tell him where Glendel had led. Michael had been right to chase paper trails.

Nino had been right, too. Lombard's thugs had put him away. And me? I must have been Chaz's backup plan: Get close to Susan with a phony campaign. Then sweet-talk her into taking charge of Nino's affairs, into signing away his old lease…in case the Navy Yard deal fell through. Chaz's last lie, peeled away like a layer of onion. Tears welled up, but the sulfur stink of betrayal passed quickly. Charles Renfrow had been no friend of mine, but like a kung fu master, he had used my own inclinations to topple me.

Now the question was, had an angry Lombard toppled Chaz?

Chapter Twenty-one

Frenzy

I put on the pasta pot and made a series of fruitless telephone calls trying to track down more information about Roddie's release. Where possible, I left messages. Gordon, Lauren, Odette, they all knew how to reach me, and sooner or later, one of them would.

While the noodles cooked I rounded up the rest of my ingredients: the cast iron skillet, the tin foil, the can opener, the can. Seven minutes later, I flipped the drained noodles into the skillet, whacked the opened can until the mushroom soup slid out in a gelatinous lump, and added enough water to make a kind of sauce. Everything took on the same gray tone, nothing a toasty oven wouldn't fix.

Pleased with my kitchen efficiency, I washed pot and spoon and rinsed the can for the recycling bin. My mother spent hours at the stove. I'd assembled and cleaned up in ten minutes flat. Good theme for a cookbook.

While my casserole baked, I showered and changed and tried a last time to get through to Lauren. This time the line was busy. Good. She was finally home, maybe talking to Gordon. I decided to eat quickly, and then drive to Chestnut Hill. We could wait together for Roddie's return.

I turned off the oven and peeked under the foil. Something was wrong, I could see at a glance. The gray tones had deepened, the noodles developed an odd sheen. I replaced the foil and left the casserole on the counter. Tomorrow, I'd figure out how to rescue it, or maybe Michael would call and give me a few tips. I wolfed down a protein bar, grabbed an apple, and ten minutes later, pulled around the circular drive behind Lauren's car.

The evening sky was full of Easter-egg colors, clearer than it had been all day. But it was fully dusk under the portico, a few lights showing through downstairs windows. I rang the doorbell and waited for Lauren to let me in. From a distance came the *shussh* of traffic, and quarter chimes from Chestnut Hill College. Eight-fifteen. I rang again, then banged the knocker. The door swung back under my fist.

"Hello?" I stepped into the entrance hall and listened for Lauren, who could be anywhere in the sprawling two-story house. "Anybody home?"

A sound, soft as a beating heart, made my skin prickle with watchfulness. "Lauren? It's me. Have you heard the good news?"

"Susan." The voice was so faint it might have been the whisper of my sandals on the rug as I moved through the dining room.

I halted just inside the kitchen, no longer an epicure's heaven, but a blur of shapes and colors in the halogen light. Details jumped out at me: A white stool flat on its back, a green tea kettle missing its lid. The overhead rack had collapsed. One end dangled from the ceiling, the other rested on a table strewn with copper pots, iron hooks, a poesy of dried flowers. There were dark smears on the wall, a pile of rags near the Aga cooker.

I edged toward the rags…that were Lauren…curled on the French country tiles, her small face framed in a burst of yellow hair, her swollen eyes searching me out. Everywhere I looked, at her arms, her neck, her sleeveless dress, I saw blood. I had to hug myself to keep from falling. "Oh, God," I said. "Oh God, Lauren."

"I grabbed his knife…" She seemed to be gathering and holding her breath, then forcing it out. "…tried to fight him… but he ran…" She lifted a hand, and I looked where it pointed, at a trail of blood from the Aga, across the room, to the open side door. I envisioned it dripping like candle wax down the steps to the driveway. Had Lauren really fought him off? Or had he heard my arrival and figured it turned the odds against him? The thought shook me. I started for the door, but Lauren whispered my name.

"I'm cold," she said, and I stumbled into the den, then back to the kitchen with her shawl, which I tucked around her, hiding some of the blood. The wall phone was hanging down. I reestablished a connection and punched in 911. Then I sat on the floor and held her hand. "Ambulance is on its way," I told her closed white face.

Footsteps hurried up the back steps. A shadowy figure filled the doorway. "What the hell's going on?"

Roddie.

He rushed at me, wild-eyed, and I shrank away from him.

"What happened?" His mouth was slack, his voice shrill. "*Who did this?*"

"I found her here." My words stuttered out. "I called an ambulance."

He dropped to his knees and touched Lauren's foot. "Sweetie, can you hear me? Lauren? I'm home. Wake up."

She managed to open her eyes. Her hand stirred in mine, then she fell off a cliff, to sleep. I hoped it was sleep. I got up, and Roddie took my place. "Don't quit on me, Laur." Suddenly, he glanced around the room, a new urgency in his eyes. "Where's Delia?"

"It's all right. She's with Amanda Lester, they had a sleep over last night."

We heard sirens, a squeal of tires, and in seconds the house filled with first responders. Medics stabilized Lauren, shifting her to a wheeled cot while I spoke briefly to the police about what I'd seen. Then I accompanied Roddie and Lauren to the ambulance outside. "I'll call the Lesters on the way to the hospital," he said, patting his pocket for his BlackBerry. "Dammit, I don't have their number."

"I'll call them." I squeezed his hand, but he did not look reassured.

"Her name's Georgina, husband is Bill. Ask if Delia can sleep over another night. Explain what happened, but play it down. Or no…tell them the whole story, just make sure they don't tell Delia." He climbed in beside Lauren, still giving me orders. "I'll find somebody to drive her to Maine tomorrow. Be sure to tell them that."

"Roddie, let it go. I've got your back on this."

Back inside, I went straight to the den, but couldn't find the camp directory, and had to dial information. Georgina Lester picked up in the middle of the first ring, as if her hand was welded to the receiver. "I agreed to *one* sleep-over," she said. She'd been trying to reach Lauren all evening, had left message after message, would never have believed she could be so irresponsible. When she came up for air, I told her about the attack, and she wound down. "How terrible. Of course Delia can stay."

She promised not to say a fearful word about Lauren in front of the girls, and then Delia was on the line.

"Where's my daddy?" were the first words out of her mouth.

"He's with your mommy. She's a little sick, and they're going to see the doctor."

"When will she get better?" I thought I heard the skepticism of a child who had learned not to trust, but I'm no mother. I was probably wrong.

"Your daddy will call you first thing tomorrow." I changed the subject before she could cross-examine me. "Are you and Amanda having fun?"

"We weared our same camp shirts today. And Fluffy sat on my lap!"

"What's a Fluffy?"

She giggled. "Amanda's cat. My mommy's allergic to cats."

A few more words about cats and daddy and feeding the ducks, then as Delia and I said good-bye, two Newton detectives intercepted me. After I gave yet another statement, Detective Bowdon, the shorter one with the shaved head that made him look hip *and* wise, asked me to walk him through the house.

"Mrs. Baird may have interrupted a robbery," he said. "Maybe you can tell us if anything's missing."

"I don't really know the house, but I'll try."

We cruised through the ground floor rooms where to my uninformed eye nothing looked amiss. Bowdon's interest seemed perfunctory. Upstairs in Delia's room, Curious George nested between two pillows on the canopied bed. Stuffed animals, dolls, picture books, filled two shelves. As far as I could tell, nothing had changed here since yesterday.

In the master bedroom, alertness crept into the detective's carefully bland face.

"The bed hasn't been slept in." I indicated the imprint of my body on the coverlet. "That's where I rested while Lauren changed her clothes."

"Speaking of clothes…" He opened the walk-in closet. "Look at this." At first I didn't understand why he was pointing to the orderly rows of Lauren's things. Then I saw that every skirt, top, dress, had been slashed to ribbons.

He watched my reaction, a moment of unfeigned shock, and his hard eyes told me that even I was a suspect tonight.

"Anything missing?" he said.

I turned away from Lauren's ruined clothes. "You don't seriously think he came here to rob, do you?"

"He may have wanted something to remember her by."

The surgical waiting room overlooked a courtyard and was filled with sofas and games and magazines, but no people except Roddie, asleep in a recliner behind a bank of ferns. He looked so defeated, I hated to wake him. "Roddie." I whispered, as if a soft voice would make consciousness easier.

Instantly, he opened his eyes, and we exchanged news. Lauren was still in surgery, but the doctors were hopeful. I told him about Georgina Lester. "Delia can stay as long as necessary," I said. "But I'll be glad to drive her to Maine tomorrow."

Without even a token protest, he accepted my offer.

"I'll pick her up at camp. Not too early. Around nine-thirty. That'll give me time to stop for her clothes and your mother-in-law's address."

"No way I can thank you." He took out his house key and stared at it. "Sure you can handle going back? Maybe I should pack Delia's things myself."

"Don't be silly. Lauren needs you here." I tugged, and he released the key. "I'm not afraid." Not *too* afraid. "I'm armed!" Gil's Swiss Army knife was inside the little kangaroo pouch at the front of my bag. I held it up. "See? It's got ten different blades." I pulled out the corkscrew, the only blade I had ever managed to open. "Wine, any time."

But my attempt at humor passed Roddie by. Using paper I found in my bag, he scrawled permission for me to pick up Delia at Willowood.

We spent a quiet hour staring out the window at colored lights and polished boulders in the courtyard before a personage in greens and clogs found us. "Your wife's in recovery," he told Roddie. "Everything looks good."

They walked into the hall, and when Roddie returned, the fear in his eyes had retreated. "She needed six pints of blood. I only wished they could've used mine." He dropped into a chair like a gray-faced old man. "Go home, Susan. It's pushing midnight. I'm going to bed down here." He lifted a poker deck off a side table and laid out a hand of solitaire, clearly a game with my name on it, if ever there was one.

"I'll stick around awhile and help you win."

He played his cards slowly, chewing his lip while he placed the six of clubs, the nine of hearts, and finally, drew three more cards.

"What time did you make bail?"

He studied the cards, missing an obvious match. "Around seven. Charges haven't been dropped."

"They will be." I touched the Jack of Clubs, and the Queen of Diamonds, and he made the play. While he continued through the deck, I told him Glenn's story. "When he found his father's body, you were thousands of miles away in Colorado."

"You really expect him to come forward when it counts?" He sounded indifferent, fatigue overriding hope.

"Glenn's scared, but I'm sure he'll do the right thing."

The game continued its sluggish progress. I dug a Lifesaver out of my bag, steeling myself for the hard question I had to ask. "Roddie? Lauren told me about her affair."

"Did she?" Though the game had looked like a winner, he swept up the cards and began a noisy shuffling.

"Did you know Chaz Renfrow was her lover?"

He laid out another hand, lining up the cards with fanatical precision, apparently too absorbed to speak. Finally he said, "Not until the police found the voter survey. That's when Lauren told me who Renfrow was. After that, I did everything I could to keep her name out of the investigation."

I believed him, and he knew it. The dam broke, and he told me how Lauren had shut down in the days following Chaz's death. How Delia had suffered.

"You've got to tell Gordon everything," I said.

"If Glenn speaks out, maybe I won't have to."

I picked up a card and helped him to another match. A weak grin lit his face. "Hey, Susan. What's the only surefire way to be rescued if you're lost in the desert?"

"Beats me."

"Lay out a hand of solitaire."

I shook my head. "I don't get it."

"Hordes of people will come out of nowhere, ready to kibitz."

I laughed, wishing I could use a hand of solitaire to gather every person who had ever mattered in my life. What a kibitz that would be.

"I'm leaving. Call me at any time, for any reason, especially if you can't play your ace." I hugged him. "Everything's going to be fine." By everything, I meant Lauren, and the charges against him. And the campaign. Odette and I would hold the fort. It was early days yet, I told myself. Early days.

◇◇◇

I pulled in close to my house, right up on the walkway. The roof lights snapped on; my key was in my hand. *Always hold your key like a weapon*, women's safety literature admonished. I looked down at the stub of brass between my thumb and bandaged finger, rounded point facing out, almost as sharp as a butter knife. If a tub of warm lard went on the attack, I'd be ready.

At the top of the stairs, I paused, remembering that Lauren's attacker had waited inside for her. The hardest part was unlocking the inner door to the pantry.

From the kitchen phone, I checked in with Deirdre who'd arrived back from London yesterday. Michael had left a message.

"He said to tell you he's out for bear in New Hampshire." Deirdre inhaled sharply. "Susan, I hope that doesn't mean guns."

"I think it means sniffing around in a focused way." If Michael was out for bear where Glenn liked to regroup, he must have taken my advice and talked to Darcy.

"Did he say why he didn't call my cell?"

"No, but I have a feeling he didn't want to be distracted. Leaving you a message was safer than talking to you."

"If I think about that long enough, I'm sure I'll find a way to take it as a compliment. Did he say when he'd be back?"

"Just that he'd be cross-hiking the mountains and would call you first chance he got."

This was not comforting. First chance could be days away.

"So how was your trip?" I asked, a little perfunctorily, unable to focus on Deirdre's vacation with my own world in turmoil.

"I didn't see much of London," she confessed. "I spent the entire time at the exhibition, or reading in my hotel room." In an odd, sleepy voice, she talked to me about William Blake. "I'd like to fall into his world," she said. "All the answers are there."

"Yeah, but what about the questions?" I chuckled and regretted it instantly.

"There's only one."

Lots of answers, just one question? Blake sounded way too complicated for me. Give me Chaucer or Justice Brandeis any day. I said good night and went to bed, but even with the lights on and Gil's knife under my pillow, I slept fitfully.

So Wednesday started earlier than I'd planned. Going against the morning rush, I made it to Roddie's house in eight minutes. From my kangaroo pouch, I took out the key, and Gil's knife, which I slipped into my jeans for the comfort of it.

As soon as I stepped inside, I could feel the absence of menace. No one was lurking. In the foyer closet, I found a canvas suitcase and took it to Delia's room, where I quickly stuffed it with shorts, bathing suits, overalls. Curious George sat lopsided on the bed pillows, his sweet monkey face begging me to take him too. I tried to jam him in on top of the socks, twisting and compressing his body, and then I saw what Detective Bowdon and I had missed: a cobweb-fine gash running the length of his back. Lauren's attacker had slashed her clothes to ribbons. He had also slashed Curious George.

Delia's Curious George.

I zippered her suitcase, my hand trembling on the verge of an insight. Why Delia? Why an innocent child? I couldn't compute, only knew I had to get her away from Boston.

As I drove to Willowood, I painted gruesome scenarios: Lauren's attacker knew where Delia went to camp. Was already there, terrorizing the children.

I parked at the corner of Hammond and found dozens of children playing on a scant acre of tree-filled grounds behind the Unitarian church. A girl in her early twenties detached herself from a circle of bubble-wand wavers. "Hi," she said. "Are you here for Delia Baird?"

Roddie had called about me this morning. She read over his permission note and said, "Mrs. Lester never makes it before nine. Want some coffee while you wait?"

It wasn't even eight-thirty. I'd allowed myself way too much time. I followed her toward the church wishing I'd collected Delia at Amanda's house. If the Lesters lived nearby, I could zip over and head them off. I tried to summon up the address by envisioning it in the camp directory. Why, I wondered, had Lauren detached it from the lamp?

Last night, Amanda's mother told me she had called a dozen times and left message after message on Lauren's machine. *Had someone listened to her irritated voice while he waited for Lauren to come home?*

"No coffee!" In a frenzy of fear I shouted after the girl. "I'll pick up Delia at Amanda's! Give me the address!"

Chapter Twenty-two

Pushing The Envelope

I steered into the driveway and inched toward a stone house fifty feet ahead. A Volvo sedan was parked in front with its doors and trunk open, Delia's backpack on the ground, ready to be loaded. I studied the house, surrounded by rhododendron in full flower. Its slate roof was quaintly pitched, doorframe arched, windows trimmed in sky blue. A storybook picture. Except Delia's pack lay too far from the trunk, as if she had abandoned it there. And was that a stuffed giraffe sprawled beside the left rear tire?

I hesitated.

Someone screamed, a shrill, little girl scream abruptly cut off, and now I was sprinting for the house, clutching my Swiss Army corkscrew. The front door was locked, something pink caught in the frame. Delia's blanket. If I could force the lock… but when I jammed in my corkscrew, the tip broke off.

Pushing through masses of rhododendron, I circled the house. Every door, every downstairs window was locked, some with closed shutters. There was a trellised patio heavy with climbing roses attached to the house, its lattices forming a lacy roof over the bricks. A bumblebee roamed through the flowers, but no sound came from the house, pressed against my back like a cliff I didn't want to climb.

"Delia! Come out!" The shout ripped through the quiet, and my head jerked up. A window above the patio was open the width of a breeze.

"Delia, where are you?" Softly now. "I've got your blanket."

Liar! A long silence was followed by what sounded like footsteps shuffling through the room directly above my head. My heart hammered in my throat. If the invader looked out, he'd see me trembling among the vines. I tried to disappear into the trellis, and thorns drove in like nine-inch nails. I didn't dare make a sound.

"Delia, tell me where you are, and I'll bring you your blanket."

No Delia, it's a trick.

The footsteps seemed to recede. The voice grew fainter, but didn't I recognize its whiskey and honey, promises and menace? *Pick it up, or I'll kill you*, it had threatened me. Johanna?

My disconnected thoughts began to gel. Yes, Johanna. Somehow, she'd found out who Delia was. Understood that Delia had rights to NGT. I remembered our telephone conversation. *Did you and my husband have an affair?* Her phony indifference to Torie. Her greedy demand for my fee.

Johanna the jealous. Johanna the liar.

I wasn't all that frightened of JoJo.

I *was* frightened of heights, but adrenaline drove out caution. Battling roses and thorns, I climbed the rickety trellis and crawled to the window. I forced up the sash and landed in a book-lined study a few feet from a desk occupied by elderly cat with fluffy orange fur. Her unblinking eyes fixed on me, she flicked her tail across a keyboard and snuggled her bony haunches against a telephone.

I rushed over and punched in 911. A hollow sound came out of the receiver, and I let it fall, cursing myself for leaving my cell in my hobo bag, in the car.

Fluffy stretched out a languid paw, jumped off the desk and followed me across the room. The study opened into a T-shaped hall lined with closed doors, the only light coming from an oriel filled with plants and from a stairwell that led to the ground floor.

At the top of the stairs I stood stock still, but all I could hear was a faint thrumming that seemed to come at me from everywhere. The sound made my flesh crawl; I tried to picture something harmless, a groaning old kitchen freezer, or no, one of those ductless air-conditioning units, vibrating against an outside wall and chilling the hell out of me.

I feared I must, one by one, throw open those closed doors and was mentally preparing myself, when the cat wound between my ankles. "Go away, Fluffy," I whispered, nudging her with my toe, and out of the throbbing silence I heard her cozy purr.

Something thumped, at the oriel end of the hall. "Delia! Let's play hide and seek. First I find you, then you find me."

Delia, wherever she was, kept still.

As quickly and quietly as my feet could move me, my eyes adjusting to the dimness, I worked my way toward the voice. The thrumming had stopped, but the knot in my stomach tightened like a noose.

"Where oh where has Delia gone? Where oh where can she be? I bet she's in the…*closet*." A door was wrenched open and slammed against a wall, then came a silence as the closet was presumably searched. "Not here, you bad girl! Are you under the bed?"

An impulse to shout Delia's name died in my throat. Mustn't alert Johanna. The element of surprise and a damaged corkscrew were my only weapons. I took out the corkscrew, and advanced on the balls of my feet, one of which came down on something that crunched. Not Fluffy, I hoped. In the light from the oriel I saw a green oblong with shiny plastic ears and a triangular red nose. As I pushed the toy aside with my foot, it emitted a weird beep. I snatched it up, ready to crush it in my palm, when I suddenly realized that the ears were antennas and the red nose a HELP button. Was it a kid's cell phone, or only make-believe? I pressed HELP, but nothing happened, so I replaced on the floor, and prayed it wouldn't beep again.

The voice began to rage. "Come out or I'll drag you out! Do what I tell you! Do it!"

I threw open the door on a bedroom with bunk beds that Johanna was crouching beside, her head buried in a black ski mask. Glenn's blue-and-white shirt hung over her jeans. I stared at the shirt, something unreal about the way the sleeve flapped off the shoulder, and then I understood: I was looking at a slashed shirt, stiff with dried blood.

"It's all right, Delia!" I shouted to the five year old child I guessed was cowering under the bed. "Stay where you are!"

Johanna stood up, swung around, and now I could see how much damage Lauren had inflicted last night. A diagonal slash ran from the shirt's left shoulder across the hollow chest and right thigh. Cloth and skin were crusted with blood. The ski mask stopped just below the chin, exposing the Adam's apple. The left hand came up in a fist. Taw marble eyes glared at me.

"Glenn. I should have known it was you."

The fist opened like a flower. "I'm not going to hurt her." His voice was soft, as low as a lullaby. "She's my sister. I've come to bring her home."

Tiny ears, a dry little nose, nudged my ankle, and the damn cat began to purr again.

"Take off the mask, Glenn. It scares Delia." And me.

He bared his face, clotted blood on a lip, a purple bruise on his cheekbone, and I sensed his calculation. He could still win this game. He took a step toward me. "I'm awfully sorry, Susan. Once I realized my father hadn't fucked you, I hoped we could be friends."

I held up my corkscrew. I'd poke out his eyes if I had to.

Fluffy twitched against my foot, and I let my glance flicker. "No, Delia!" I shouted, hoping to divert Glenn for even a second. "It's me, Susan. Don't come out!"

He looked over his shoulder, at nothing, and in that timeless space I picked up the cat.

When Glenn saw I had tricked him, he rushed me, and I heaved fat old Fluffy in his face. Fluffy clung for dear life, digging in with every brittle claw. Glenn howled, and I threw a Princess Bride and pillows at him and kicked his shins. A bookcase tottered, lamps toppled, and just as he managed to rip Fluffy off his face, I body checked him. He crumpled. His head hit the radiator, and his wounds began to bleed again. With a strength that came from some distant galaxy inside me, I dragged the upper bunk bed off its posts and shoved it on top of him.

"Okay, Delia, come out!" I yelled. "Let's go!"

She crawled out from behind a Victorian doll's house built on a thick wooden base and we ran into the hall. "My new phone!" she yelled, stopping to retrieve the little green oblong I'd abandoned on the floor.

"I pressed HELP, but it didn't work," I said.

"Got to hold it down." She made the 911 connection and handed her cell to me.

Before the police arrived, Fluffy, Delia and I freed the Lesters from the kitchen where Glenn had gagged and duct-taped them, Amanda to the iron base of the pedestal table and Georgina to pipes beneath the farmhouse sink. When I'd cased the exterior of the house, Georgina had seen me peering through the window and tried to catch my attention by rocking her head and back against the pipes. That was the thrumming, I'd heard, an old house vibe, if I'd known how to read it.

Lauren smiled me in. She was sitting up looking almost fit in a fancy embroidered jacket that hid her hospital gown, though not her bandaged neck and hands. Color suffused her cheeks; the transfusions were holding.

I pulled up a chair. "You look great," I said.

"I'm back from the edge." Her smile faded. She found a Kleenex and dabbed at her eyes. "Just like you."

I never met a tear I couldn't share. My own eyes began to fill. "Oh, I'm all right. Nowhere near the edge."

She pushed the Kleenex box in my direction. "Roddie told me everything. You saved Delia's life."

"Not me. The cat."

For a few minutes the room took on a damp, salty silence, interrupted by a little nose blowing and throat clearing.

"Well, I owe the cat more than I can ever repay."

"*De nada*, says the cat. Just keep on healing. Delia needs you. Roddie needs you. Even the campaign needs you."

"I'll stuff envelopes till the cows come home."

A hospital aide barged into the room behind a trolley of snacks. Lauren accepted a cup of tea, and I tried the angel cake.

"Where is that…Glenn?" Lauren said. "Have they locked him up?"

"Of course, prison hospital."

"What about bail?"

"A multiple murderer? Not a chance." I peeled the wrapper off my cake and chomped a little cotton in the over-air-conditioned room.

"I can't stop seeing his eyes." She touched the bandages on the side of her neck. "How could he kill his own father?"

"I don't know." I thought about Lizzie Borden, about the man who set fire to his ten-year-old son. Family life. My own family had done no worse than, from time to time, mislay me, which sometimes happens to a redundant much-younger sister. Now that I live back east relations are affable. My mother and sister send me thoughtful gifts while observing me through the wrong end of a rose-colored telescope. A tiny grateful Susan glows in the distant light. We mean well by each other, even love each other, which is more than Lizzie or Glenn could say.

Visitors with voices like hacksaws strolled past the open door.

Lauren adjusted her bed jacket, pulling it tightly around her. "This is all my fault. If I had ended the affair years ago, Chaz would be alive now."

"Lauren, you are not responsible for the crimes of a madman."

"But if I hadn't talked to that reporter…"

"You? I thought it was Tyre, leaking his version of your story."

"I never spoke to him, or Gordon. My courage failed. I wasn't ready to take a step I couldn't retreat from. But I wanted to do *something* for Roddie and the *Globe* seemed like my best bet." She shrank into the pillows. "I thought I could at least counter negative publicity. The reporter drew out more than I meant to say, and twisted it."

"And then pulled more out of Tyre. The media always get the last word. That's why the rest of us need blogs and spin-doctors. You should have called Gordon."

"I needed to *act*. Even a decapitated chicken needs to act." A touch pad hung from the bed frame, and she used it to lower her mattress a notch. "So what did I accomplish? I alerted the world, and especially Glenn, to my *close* friendship with Chaz."

Lauren's incessant self-blame was demoralizing me. "Glenn could've learned about you some other way. Maybe Johanna knew, and told him. Stop whipping yourself."

But she couldn't stop. "If Glenn knew about me before I talked to the press…" Her face collapsed. "What if he'd come the night I left Delia home alone?"

"He didn't. And you weren't gone all that long."

"A minute was all he needed." Her eyes darted to the window. "And I was gone for hours."

I had to catch my breath. "Chaz?"

Her face turned an ugly red. "Yes," she said. "Yes. Yes. I didn't have car trouble. That was a lie. Chaz phoned Saturday afternoon. Begged me to meet him that evening, said he had to work out some things with me." She squeezed her hands together, jerking the drip line. "I couldn't say no, but I knew I'd have trouble getting a sitter on such short notice. I ended up leaving Delia alone with cartoons and enough junk food to last all night. Though I expected to be back sooner."

I'd thought Lauren had nothing more to say that could shock me. "Chaz couldn't wait? There was no other time he could talk?"

But I remembered how he had persuaded me to meet him that Monday night, how I'd disrupted my schedule, shortchanged my obligation to Roddie. And I hadn't been in love with the man.

"He wanted to talk on Friday, but we barely had time to pick up the voter surveys. Something came up at the last minute, he told me, so we couldn't even stop for coffee."

"Wait. You're losing me. You were with Chaz on the Friday before he died?"

"At the printer's. When I couldn't fit all the surveys in my car I called him. He's the friend who helped me. He met me there and took most of the cartons back in his SUV."

"They found pieces of Roddie's rope in the Lexus. Did they come from you?"

"I'm to blame for that, too. I'd brought a couple of coils to the printer's so I could use the roof rack. I tied up a few cartons but nothing held. The ropes must have dropped off when Chaz loaded his car."

"Glenn or anybody with access to the Lexus could have found the rope," I said, "and obviously did."

"For awhile, in my misery, I even fantasized that Roddie had killed Chaz." Her tea got cold while she brooded.

"What time did you and Chaz meet on Saturday?" I said.

"We didn't. I got to Spaal's at six and waited two hours. He never showed up."

Because he was already dead, I thought, but couldn't bring myself to say.

Lauren smoothed the orange blanket that clashed with her bed jacket. "My necklace saved me. Did Roddie tell you? He had it made for me, years ago. It's some super hard alloy from a company he'd invested in just before it went belly-up. He lost his shirt on that one." She started to laugh, then bit her lip. "Think about it, Susan. Years later, Roddie's worst investment saved my life." Her laughter came in waves, and then of course, she started crying again.

I went out and came back with more tea. Lauren pretended to drink it, and I pretended to read a pamphlet about kidney stones. My eye skipped over the pages, and when Lauren gave up on her tea, I asked, "Where did you vanish to after Tyre took Roddie in? No one could reach you until…" Until I found you bleeding to death on your kitchen floor.

"I was with Chaz's mother, at Idlebrook. It was a way to be near him. After I talked to the reporter, everything drained out of me. Guilt, love. I wanted to hide. I stayed with Cordy for twenty-four hours. I felt safe there."

Nothing made sense, but I understood.

Outside, the day looked like it would go on forever, but traffic was picking up. This morning at police headquarters, when Roddie came to take Delia to Maine himself, he'd been so worried about Lauren that I'd committed to spend the afternoon with her. There were many uncomfortable hours left on my promise.

A knock, and Odette waltzed in carrying scarlet roses in a vase. "How's the patient?" No mushy demonstrations from this retired judge, just a sage-blue shift that softened the brass in her hair. Like some extravagant goddess of summer she breezed across the room and bestowed her gift. "From my garden. I snipped off the thorns."

Lauren buried her face in the petals and came up with pollen on her chin. "They're beautiful. Thank you."

Next, the goddess turned her force on me. "Susan! I left a message with your service. That Deirdre, what a hoot! I told her I was inviting you to my house tomorrow for a working lunch, and she suggested going vegan to compensate for the horrors of eating and working at the same time. Vegan! For heaven's sake, I'm *French!*"

Before I could comment, she'd relieved Lauren of the flowers and was dragging a bench to the bedside, settling in. "So, did Roddie get Delia to Maine?"

Guilty Lauren bit her lip, to keep from crying, again. "They made it in three hours. No speeding ticket!"

"Three hours I can believe. But no ticket? Bunk. Roddie always gets caught." Odette chuckled, and Lauren's cheeks pinked up under her needy brown eyes.

"He told me you've agreed to manage his campaign," Lauren said. "I'm so glad."

"Well, well." Odette fingered her pearls. "I'm glad too."

If there was ice between them, it was fast melting. In their different ways, both women loved my candidate, I thought. Now more than ever.

"Let me tell you what Roddie was like when he worked for my husband." Odette gathered us around her and for half an hour made Roddie's early struggles sound like glorious escapades. "Even thirty years ago, he loved to 'push the envelope' as you young people say. Always ready for battle. If he'd been a medieval knight, his coat of arms would've read...what's Latin for try-and-stop-me?" Her noisy laughter made even Lauren smile, which was surely the point of the performance. "And he hasn't changed. That's why he's going to win his election."

She touched a finger to her lips. "Shh. Susan, I think you're being paged."

Garbled words filtered in from the hall: *Calypso, Susan Calypso.*

At the nurse's station a man in whites handed me a phone. I heard a double click, then someone breathing asthmatically in my ear. "Nino Biondi's gonna wake up in jail if he doesn't quit jerking me around. So's your nosy cop friend."

Peter Lombard. I recognized the rasp.

"My lawyer sent you a demand letter this morning, Susie. I'm going to sue you for fraud, slander, *and* harassment."

"Peter, what's this all about?"

"I want you disbarred."

"I'll bet you do. You have five seconds to tell me what's on your mind, or I hang up."

"If Nino Biondi tries to enforce the Cambridge agreements, I will hold you personally liable. Call off your dogs and I'll call off the lawsuit."

"What dogs?"

"That's the deal, Susie." Then the creep hung up on *me*.

Whether to leave immediately, or keep my promise to Roddie was the tricky dilemma I tried to resolve on my way back to Lauren's room. Lauren no longer required my company, and if Nino had turned tables on Lombard, I needed to prepare him for Lombard's fist. From the doorway, I watched the remorseful wife and the perceptive judge sitting together in a comfortable silence I hated to interrupt. "That phone call. I really ought to take care of it."

"Go on, go." Odette shooed me away like a farmer dismissing a chicken. "Lauren and I have so much to talk about. We'll plan Roddie's victory party. And Susan, you *will* have lunch at my house tomorrow, won't you? Or tea if you can't make lunch? Or supper. Midnight snack. Whatever it takes to reel you in. I'm wearing two hats now and the paperwork is killing me."

Paperwork? Again? But who could resist Odette? "No problem. See you tomorrow at noon." I gave Lauren a careful hug, and drove directly to Tavola Rustica, mulling over Lombard's threat.

Chapter Twenty-three

The Price Of Betrayal

Benny's sneakered feet danced on the burners and the ledge. Lost in the music inside his head, he jumped from side to side, flicking his rag at the firewall, buffing the quilted steel, making it shine. Tavola was empty and locked, and Benny danced with the abandon of shy people who know they're alone. When I knocked on the glass door, his head music stopped. Rag in hand, he climbed down and let me in. "Hi, Susie. You hungry?" He sounded like his boss, even dressing like Nino in plaid shirt and baggy pants.

"No time, Benny. Where's Nino?"

"In bed. Only gets up for lunch anymore."

Not good, but there was nothing I could do about it. With time on his hands, Nino was probably drinking himself into a coma every afternoon.

I followed Benny across the main dining room, tables set for tomorrow.

"I got soup left over."

"I *could* use a little something." I sat down at the scrubbed worktable behind the counter. Benny moved his bucket off the stove, heated the *minestra di funghi*, and served it in a bowl the size of Rhode Island. The flavor was as dusky and deep as a fairy tale forest, and the mushrooms dissolved on my tongue. "This is fantastic," I said. "Did you make it?"

He nodded and placed a crusty roll next to my bowl. "Nino showed me. I made the bread, too. Someday, I'm going to own this restaurant."

"Maybe you will." Why not? As Nino had told me, Benny was coming along. If he could cook like this, he could find a business partner, though the trick would be finding one who wouldn't take advantage of his fragile intelligence. "Do me a favor, Benny? Pop into Nino's apartment and see if he's really asleep."

He backed against a chair and fell into it. "Do I have to? If he's awake he'll yell at me. Nino's not nice anymore. I like it when he sleeps." The dread in Benny's voice was new to me. I had never seen him afraid.

"All right. Let's not wake him. Maybe you can help me."

The old eagerness returned and he put his hands on his knees, cocking out his elbows exactly as Nino did. "Sure I can."

"Do you know who Peter Lombard is?"

"Nino's boss."

"Close enough," I said. "Has Nino been yelling at Mr. Lombard, too?"

He nodded. "Lombard's got to give him thirty pieces of silver. I heard him say it."

Thirty pieces of silver. The price of betrayal. Nino wanted blood money, because Lombard's thugs had bloodied him. And ironically, the hated Cambridge deal was Nino's lever, the threat of its enforcement. No wonder Lombard had tracked me down in the hospital. "Will Nino be awake this evening, do you think?" I said.

He shrugged. "Nino sleeps all the time since that man hurt him."

That man hurt him. "Benny?" I tried to keep the excitement out of my voice. "Can you see the alley from your apartment?"

"Uh, huh."

"You just told me a man hurt Nino. Tell me what you saw."

He froze. I could hear him not breathing.

"I didn't see nothing."

"Benny? Please?"

He shut his eyes, his face at war with his heart. "I *heard* something. A big noise."

"Did you look out your window? Please tell me, Benny. Nino needs your help."

The bucket sat at his foot, dirty water with a float of suds. He wrapped his fingers around the handle. "I saw Nino on the ground. Somebody walking away. That's all I saw." He stood up and edged toward the stove.

I left my chair and crowded after him. "Did you see the man's face?"

"No!" His ears flamed. He stared at the floor. Not a good liar, Benny. "I don't know." Without warning, he leaped onto a front burner, bucket and all, sloshing water on my shoulder. "I don't want to tell you. You'll yell at me."

"I promise I won't yell. Whatever you say, I'll still like you." My hip bumped the stove, a black iron affair with enough burners for two Tavolas. I stared at him, willing him to tell me what he knew. "You'll be helping the police catch that bad man."

Tears flooded his eyes, and he swiped at them. "Your friend did it."

"Which friend?" I reached for his ankle, but the stove was immense, and the recess was deep, and he darted away. "Benny! *Which friend?*"

He clattered backward over the burners until his feet bumped the firewall. Both hands plunged into his bucket for the rag. When he found it, he wrung it out and wrung it out. "Your friend who gave me ten dollars for my tip. I gave him the good grappa, and Nino got mad."

My heart continued to beat. My eyes may have blinked. "The man I brought here two weeks ago?"

Benny nodded. "He kicked Nino. I saw him."

Chaz. Not Lombard's thugs. With nightmare clearness, I saw Nino lying in the alley, Chaz's foot slamming into his head. For a moment rage overwhelmed me and, for a moment, I rejoiced that Chaz was dead. "I'm leaving, Benny. When Nino wakes up, tell him to call me."

Fear returned to Benny's face. "It's a secret, what I saw. Don't tell, or your friend will come back and hurt me, too. Then Nino will never give me the restaurant."

"He's not my friend, Benny. And he can't hurt you. He's dead."

At the door, I turned for a last goodbye, but Benny didn't notice. His feet weren't dancing now. He was standing motionless, all but his right arm which was soaping the firewall. Back and forth it went. Back and forth, like a metronome.

Feeling vulnerable, I fastened my seat belt. The Beemer lurched ahead, gears vibrating like dentist drills. It was immensely worse than I'd realized. Chaz hadn't merely used my own inclinations against me. He had written the script.

Militantly innocent, Michael had once called me. Oh, please. Giddily naive was more like it. Chaz hadn't heard about me from *Political Notes*, or from Lauren. *Lombard* had told him that I, with my power of attorney, was the key to the treasure. Chaz's plan to hurt Nino must have been locked in from the start, while Lombard looked the other way.

Empty and cold, I drove home. There was no solid core at the center of the onion. Everything was a lie. That was the only truth. I sat in my driveway under the purple sky. Still as ice, I waited for the evening star, Jupiter tonight. Then I put truth out of my mind and went into the house.

From my kitchen, I chased after Lombard, but his voice mail held me at bay. Deirdre was my own barrier, an all too human, leaky one. I checked in to see if Michael had called, and he hadn't, anymore than he'd tried to reach me on my cell. My miserable mood got ugly then. I began by complaining about Lombard. "How could you tell that man where to reach me? He threatened me. In a hospital!" As I carped, I paced, trying to walk off my anger.

"Mr. Lombard is a wounded spirit," Deirdre said. "He lashes out because it helps him feel balanced. The sound of his own voice relieves his fear."

"You are driving me nuts with that bogus talk!"

At once she fell silent, letting me barge full steam ahead.

"Balance! Healing! Get a life, Deirdre." I hung up without saying goodbye, then regretted my surliness. Though not enough to call Deirdre back.

I carried a cup of tea to the table and stared out the window. In the shadowy garden, the foxgloves waved their delicate paws. When absolute darkness fell, I abandoned my tea and lingered with Graham Greene in my clawfoot tub. There are times when a bath and a book console more than the arms of a lover.

When I woke, it was Thursday, and I had slept for six hours, the unbroken sleep of the innocent, or the psychopath. Sleep had miraculously washed away the power of Chaz's treachery to wound me. Lauren and Delia and Nino were safe. As was I. The gods had been kind, yet again.

In the kitchen, the toast popped up and the wall phone rang and I managed both deftly. That the call was from Michael added roses to my day.

"Did you sleep well with your butt in the bushes?" I said.

"Like a baby in my clean, dry tent. I just heard about Glenn Renfrow. You all right?"

"Still in shock, but not about Glenn." I shoved the barely beige bread back into the toaster and told him all I'd learned from Benny. "Chaz put Nino in the hospital, with me and my power of attorney as backup."

Michael hesitated, clearing his throat of mountain pollen or something. "If you need me, I'll come back right now."

"Not necessary. Chaz can't hurt me, or anyone, and Glenn is in custody."

"Wait, let me start over. When they told me the risk you took, I wanted to grab you and hold you tight, and then arrest you for reckless endangerment. For chrissake, Susan—you waltzed into that house with a corkscrew in your hand?"

"Once I heard Delia scream, I *had* to help her."

"You're not a cop. You're not even a...baton twirler."

Baton twirler. For Michael, this kind of fuddlement was pinning his heart to his sleeve. I uncovered my own. "I missed you last night."

"If anything happened to you I...I'd..."

"I was almost certain the killer didn't have a gun."

"Almost doesn't even count in horseshoes."

Smoke was wisping up from the toaster, more proof that cooking is a risky affair. Still feeling heroic, I stuck in a fork and rescued the bread. "I never seriously suspected Glenn," I said, scraping burnt crumbs into the sink. "I still can hardly believe it. Torie and Chaz. Lauren left for dead."

"And you."

I touched my wounded breast. "He seemed so...*innocent*." I didn't mention Michael's two-killer theory, which I'd doubted from the start.

"We found a microtome blade in the Baird's kitchen," Michael said. "It's from NovoGenTech, but not the one that killed Torie. So far there's no physical evidence linking Glenn to the murders."

"He confessed. That ought to be worth something."

"Only for Torie. And if his mother has her way, he'll recant." Michael painted a familiar scenario: Johanna's lawyers and psychiatrists were busy. If they did a good job, Glenn might be acquitted. And he steadfastly denied killing his father.

While I cruised the kitchen, washing pears and looking for the honey jar, Michael told me about his interview with Darcy Villencourt. She'd been eager to talk, he said, because after the office meeting with me, Glenn had became so agitated she began to doubt his sanity.

"Should I take offense?"

"Well, I'm mad about you myself," Michael murmured, and all alone in the kitchen I blushed.

"Um," I said. "You better finish telling me about Darcy while I can still pay attention."

"Where are you, exactly?" he said. "We'll have phone breakfast."

"That sounds naughty, Michael. I'm leaning over the sink, eating a pear. Now how did Glenn upset Darcy?"

"I'm standing outside a gas station, eating a doughnut." He sighed and told me Darcy's story: Glenn claimed he had evidence linking Bart Bievsky to the murders—Torie's sandal, his father's watch. Other items he claimed he'd found in Bievsky's car. All safely stowed in New Hampshire. When Darcy insisted he tell the police, Glenn went wild. Started yelling that the time wasn't right, but that when it was, he was going to "get" Bart.

"So why didn't she call the police?"

"She wanted to be loyal, so she convinced herself Glenn was making it all up. Aggrandizing himself. She knew he hated Bart for dating his mother. But all it took was a call from me to open the floodgates. And now I'm in New Hampshire scouting mountain tops."

"I'm guessing you're not wandering aimlessly."

"Darcy gave me precise directions to Glenn's secret campsites," he said. "That girl is a marvel of clarity. So far I've found two, nothing stashed at either."

Over coffee, I told him about Lombard's threat. "He called you my nosy friend, which tells me you uncovered his connection to Chaz."

"Mr. Lombard and I had a smoke together the other morning."

"Learn anything?"

"He likes Macanudos."

I licked the honey spoon. "If only you could prove he orchestrated Chaz's attack on Nino."

"Be hard." Michael chuckled. "Maybe he keeps an incriminating diary."

How irritating, people who laugh at their own jokes. "I'd settle for an off-the-record admission." And thirty pieces of silver for Nino. "If Glenn didn't kill his father, Lombard could've done it. He had motive and opportunity. Chaz backed out of their deal and left him with an empty building. Cost him millions. And the rope was handy in the Lexus."

"Run that by the detective in charge. I've got a mountain to climb."

I had a moment of fear. Mt. Washington was notorious for sudden storms. Don't go, I wanted to say, as if I might lose Michael too, on a mountain they'd call a foothill in Nepal. "Be careful," I said. "Promise me."

"Worrywart. I'm taking the easy way up. Cog rail train."

Riding high after breakfast with Michael, I punched in Deirdre's number, ready to apologize for my bad temper. Last week's substitute server answered, and apologies died on the vine. "Where's Deirdre?" I said.

Ms. Uzi didn't know but put me through to Mirabelle Communications where a woman informed me that Deirdre Wilcot had taken an indefinite leave from her franchise.

"Awfully sudden, wasn't it?"

"She's back in the hospital. Had a relapse last night."

"Hospital! What's wrong?"

"Her disability, you know. Our handicap program—"

"What do you mean? How can I reach her?"

But Mirabelle couldn't give out that information. The best they could do was tell Deirdre I wanted to hear from her.

I tidied the kitchen, automatically rinsing and drying while I worried about the soft-spoken woman I'd never met, who nonetheless, I realized, had become a friend. Deirdre must have lied to me about her travels. Were they disappearing *acts*? "Boxes" where she "compartmentalized" until that famous inner balance was restored? Until allopathic medicine did what it could to heal her?

Later, when I called Nino I learned, no surprise, that Benny hadn't given him my message. He was too busy to discuss Lombard and Renfrow…until I bribed him with a trip to Russo's, greengrocer to the stars.

I found him waiting on the sidewalk in front of Tavola, string bags dangling out of his pocket. On the drive to Watertown, he rested his eyes. He looked hung over, and I didn't press him. There would be time to talk after we shopped.

Inside Russo's, Nino perked up at the sight of all those edible jewels heaped high in wooden bins. While I roamed the attached greenhouse for water-averse office plants, he filled a cart with incipient Tavola specials. Twenty-five minutes later, carrying a miniature three-pronged cactus, I joined him at the register.

"I'm quitting on a high note," he said, piling tomatoes and escarole in front of a curly-haired cashier who tallied up faster than he could unload. I thought he meant his shopping spree until he added: "Give 'em my best cooking till the end of summer, then I'm gone."

"What're you talking about? Where are you going?"

"Florida, or maybe Ischia."

The cashier handed over Nino's slice of the register tape. From a large black leather change purse, the kind moths fly out of in old movies, he extracted a wad of bills and peeled off the exact amount. Accustomed to three-figure vegetable deals, the cashier whipped Nino's money into her register, then rang up my sale.

"I'm gonna retire," he said.

"You? Never."

"Believe it. I'm not the same since that sonofabitch put me in the hospital."

"You're depressed. That's natural after a brush with death."

"What death? I'm old. Don't bounce back so high anymore."

Since the cactus was a business expense, I handed over my credit card. The curly head shook back and forth. "Can't charge less than fifty dollars."

I opened my wallet, but Nino was quicker.

"I got it." He slapped ten dollars on the counter and waited, palm out, for his change. If he heard my thanks, he didn't acknowledge it.

A crate of cherries nudged my elbow as the next person in line claimed counter space. I moved forward, so close to Nino I could smell the Brylcreme in his hair. "Zi' Neen, let's talk before you make a decision."

"I've already decided, don't you listen? Lombard's gonna pay for my retirement. If he won't, I'll enforce the Cambridge deal you made for me." He hoisted his bulging string bags and left the cart behind. "And I got one more lawyer's job for you."

"What's that?" I carried the overflow, the white eggplant, the blossom zucchini, the rapi, the melons. Wrapped in paper, the cactus fit snugly inside my hobo bag.

"I need a will."

"Al Volpe can find someone to help you."

"Just a simple will. I want it ready before I retire. Gotta make sure Benny's taken care of. And a little something for you."

"Me?" Good. That let me off the hook. "Beneficiaries shouldn't draw up the will," I said. Not that I wanted anything from Nino, who was going to live forever.

We pushed through the double swing doors to the parking lot.

"Come talk to me about it, anyway. I got papers I want you to look over."

"I can probably stop over tonight. Let me call you later."

Careful of slippery lettuce leaves underfoot, we walked down an exit ramp behind a fleet of delivery trucks. Nino refused my hand and kept three steps ahead.

"About the Cambridge deal," I said. "You were dead right about Chaz Renfrow wanting something from me, only it wasn't what you thought."

"What did I think?" He slowed, and I came up beside him.

"Sex."

"Sex." His whole face twisted around the word. "That's how much you know. Right away, I pegged your friend for a user. Saw it in his eyes. I thought he'd hurt you. That's as far as I thought."

Off the ramp, Nino quickened his pace and reached the car first.

"Well, whatever you thought," I said, "sex was the last thing on Chaz Renfrow's mind. He used me to get to you. You're the one he hurt."

"I know who he hurt." Standing by the trunk, he kept a close eye on me. "What'd he need you for?"

"To sign the deal. He wanted to lease Lombard's building, and you stood in the way."

"Why'd he want such a falling down piece of junk?"

"Location, location, location. Lombard's building is next door to one of world's great research centers, hospitals, laboratories, scientists. A natural fit for NGT. Plus, Brookline has no laws regulating biotechnology."

"*Schifoso*," he said, and a few other dark Italian words I'd never heard but understood tonally. "Your friend looked familiar the night you brought him in. When Benny told me who beat me up, I remembered where I saw him. He came nosing around Tavola couple months ago, the toad brought him." He loaded the trunk and slammed the lid, then climbed in beside me. "Your friend didn't look like muscle, or I would of figured him out on the spot."

My friend. Even in death Chaz had the power to irk me. I let out the clutch. "I didn't figure him out either. He tricked me into signing that deal with Lombard."

"How, tricked you?"

I gave him my spin on all that had happened. "Renfrow wanted you in the hospital."

Nino was sitting straight as a stick, hands on his thighs. "He wanted me dead."

"I don't think he cared either way. If you died, he was golden. If you survived…well, he took a chance on me and hit the jackpot. Persuaded me to 'take charge' of your life and sign the new lease. You have to admit, Cambridge was a very good deal for you."

"It was a good deal, wasn't it?" He turned a shoulder my way, but kept his eyes on the windshield. "A good deal for everybody."

"Still is, if you want it." We crossed Bridge Street and I drove toward Brighton along the Charles River, invisible behind buildings and trees.

"No, no. It's time to get out of the restaurant business."

"Benny acts like you've promised him Tavola."

"That's right."

"You know he's not ready to take over," I said. "He needs more time, and so do you. You reopened way too soon. By the end of summer, you'll be your old self."

He shook his head. "Things never go back the way they were. Even Lombard knows that. I already told him I'll forget Cambridge, and everything else, for the right price."

I glanced at him. "Thirty pieces of silver?"

"For such a little pitcher, Benny's got big ears. Yeah, I told Lombard fifty thousand cash. I gave him a week to think over my offer. If he's willing to do something for Benny, he can pay me less. Otherwise I'll sue." Nino folded his arms across his chest, an icon of intransigence. "Since your friend got himself killed, the toad is running scared."

"Chaz Renfrow was not my friend!" If this kept up, I'd have to put a disclaimer out on the Web. I swerved onto Boylston and Nino grabbed the handhold. "Lombard is scared," I said, "because he knows he'd be a prime suspect if the police hadn't arrested Chaz's son."

I told Nino about Glenn. "That boy was on a tear. He even attacked *me*. Nineteen years old. Unreal."

"All that violence on TV. They see it, they wanna be killers."

"But Glenn seemed so sweet, gentle as St. Francis."

"Why would a saint want to kill you?"

"He thought I was involved with his father."

"Weren't you?"

"Christ, Nino! What if I was? Is that a reason to kill?" My foot hit the gas, but the Beemer balked until I pumped the pedal. "Chaz Renfrow was my candidate. Nothing more." And a whole lot less.

I made a wide U-turn and pulled up in front of Tavola. "If you need help with Lombard, let me know. I'll negotiate for you."

"I'm lucky you're in my corner," he said, putting a foot on the pavement. "For such a young girl, you sure know how to bargain."

Chapter Twenty-four

Dire Thoughts

"Sorry I'm late," I said, but since Gordon Brenner had unexpectedly decided to join us and hadn't yet arrived, I was actually early. I was speaking to the top of Odette's head, which was bowed over a coffee table heaped with *crudités* and campaign files. "I stopped by City Hall for new lists, and political buzz."

"My buzz first." Her hand darted from baby carrots to olives to radishes bristling with stems. She selected a radish and twirled it in a dish of coarse salt. "Gordon passed me some lawyer's scuttlebutt about young Renfrow. Claims he killed Torie Moran to protect his family after she made threats at his mother's birthday party."

"It so happens I was there that night. Torie seemed drunk or drugged, certainly loose enough to put the moves on Chaz right in front of me. If she threatened Johanna, Glenn could've listened in unobserved." I explained how Glenn had sat on the shadowy porch under an open window. "Torie had some kind of smoking gun video about toxic spills. A friend of hers claims she was a real crusader, getting ready to blow the whistle on NGT."

Odette shook her head, earrings clacking against her jaw. The radish hung from her fingers. "Not whistle blowing. Blackmail."

Blackmail, so melodramatic, so at odds with Torie's financial stake in NGT. I'd considered, then dismissed it. Now I savored the word. Blackmail confirmed all my prejudices. But as I sipped my wine, an image of Torie's crumpled body pierced my memory. Bleak satisfaction eroded to pity for the hapless dead.

"Apparently Johanna offered stock," Odette said. "But Torie insisted on cash."

"Which NGT didn't have. The ship was sinking. Torie wanted to get hers and get out."

"And Glenn cast himself as white knight." Odette finally chomped down on the radish, washing salt off her lips with more wine. "Appalling! But good news for Roddie."

"How do you figure? Roddie's still under a cloud. Glenn insists he did not kill Chaz."

"Susan, you're a skunk at the garden party. Of course that young man is going to deny it. Patricide! What a horror!"

A bottle of French country red sat on a tray at her elbow, and she made a pass at my nearly full glass. When I declined, she jutted her chin at the folders and notebooks tumbling over celery sticks on the table. "Let's get rolling," she said. "Trust me. Our candidate is not going back to jail."

Her enthusiasm lifted my mood. Elections are for winning, I reminded myself. Halfway through a list of untapped prospects, the doorbell rang, and Gordon Brenner walked into the room. Odette put a glass of wine in his hand, and we retired to the kitchen for a French country lunch.

"Glenn wanted to prove he was the man his father hoped he could be, right down to the bay rum," Gordon said. Through a mouthful of *pommes vinaigrettes* he told us that after Johanna's party, Glenn broke into Torie's condo and tore the place apart while she slept. "He was smart enough to wear lab gloves."

"And stupid enough to kill." Odette tugged angrily at an earring.

Gordon patted his mouth with a napkin. "Kitchen's the most dangerous room in the house. Did you know that?"

This was something I'd long suspected, and I nodded encouragingly.

"When no blackmail evidence turned up..." Gordon paused while Odette heaped more *pate'* on his plate. "Glenn woke Torie with a paring knife. Terrorized her into admitting she kept the smoking-gun video buried inside a plant pot in Lab 45. Turned out not to be true, according to Glenn, anyway. No video under the violets, but there *was* an alarm pad behind a shelf, and Torie planned to use it once they drove back to NGT."

Gordon leaned toward me, and the *paté* gave his story a garlicky punch. Using a butter knife to stand in for Glenn and a pepper mill for Torie, he demonstrated how she had edged toward the panic button while Glenn dug up the plant. Glenn caught her in the nick of time, Gordon said, but during the ensuing struggle, Torie grabbed the microtome blade off the shelf. "Naturally Glenn turned it against her. Cut her arms, nicked her neck." Gordon toppled the grinder with the knife.

I shivered at his story, Odette's fine food catching in my throat.

Paté demolished, Gordon speared a tomato wedge, which he ate off the tip of his knife, like a pirate. "Now Torie swears the video is in her Jaguar. So Glenn drags her outside, and they both search the car. Again, he finds nothing. Renfrow must have stolen it, Torie says."

I put down my fork. "He could've. Torie got very drunk that night, and Chaz walked her to her car before we drove her back to the party. What I don't understand is how this ditz managed ten years of blackmail."

A tomato seed lodged between Gordon's teeth, and he ran his tongue over it. "*If* it was blackmail. Johanna denies it."

"She'd have to, wouldn't she?" Odette said.

"Unless she wants to admit illegal activity. Meanwhile, Glenn's begun to step back from his confession. Didn't *mean* to kill, he says. When the video didn't turn up in the Jag, he 'just lost it' and bashed Torie with the blade handle, he says. She collapsed but wouldn't stop moaning, so he dumped her in the trunk. No idea how she died, blade attacked her on its own. But, hey, she deserved it." Gordon scowled, his dark eyebrows a foil for his snowy hair. "As Glenn, with great patience, explained to the police, the bitch seduced his father."

"Seduced?" I yelped. "Does the moth tempt the flame?"

"Which one was the moth?"

"All I know is they're both dead, and Glenn believed every woman who got next to Chaz was a *slut*." Balancing dishes and utensils in one efficient stack, I cleared the table, working to distance my emotions from Gordon's narrative.

Odette cut into an apricot tarte, and soothed by the sight of dessert, Gordon's eyebrows relaxed. "Of course, your client was in it up to his neck," he said to me.

Odette held back his plate, and Gordon talked fast: Faced with a dead woman and blood everywhere, Glenn had screamed for help, calling dad on his cellphone. Chaz had galloped to the rescue, then staged a turnpike breakdown to make alibis for both of them. At NGT, father and son removed every trace of the murder. Chaz even hosed down and bleached the floor in Lab 45, just in case. Glenn hoped this teamwork would open a new era in father-son relations. Instead, Chaz was the next to die.

After lunch and more work on Roddie's files, I met with my Ashcroft candidate, and by five-thirty I was back at my desk, alone in the building except for a couple of Boris' bakers. I contributed three hours to my other candidates, then, too tired for Nino, I called to beg off. "I'll stop by tomorrow morning," I said.

Instead of annoyance, Nino bubbled with good humor. Lombard had agreed to his terms. "Fifty-thousand cash," he gloated. "And I can turn over the old lease to Benny anytime I want."

"Congratulations."

"And I told him to forget about you. Write up something says he won't sue. Bring it tomorrow. That *villiaco* will sign. He's running scared. I think the police talked to him about your dead friend."

"Chaz Renfrow was not my friend!"

Nino chuckled. "Don't matter now. He lost, and I'm still going strong."

I rolled my eyes. I win, you lose. Even old men never stopped being boys. I hung up, ready for home, where tunaless casserole and Graham Greene would take me through to bed. Before I closed the computer, I set up a cold-call file. Tomorrow, I'd mine old donor lists.

The telephone rang, and I picked up, hoping for Michael. "Hey," Roddie said, to my disappointed heart. "Glad I caught you. Odette tells me you're sorting the voters."

I managed a little laugh. "Roddie, when I'm finished, you'll be able to target every left-handed Libertarian rat catcher in Newton. Where are you?"

There was a static-filled gap. "...stayed an extra day in Maine. Lauren insisted the kids needed me, and she was right. I'll be driving to the hospital later tonight."

"Everybody okay? Delia?"

"Great, great. How late will you be at the office?"

"I'm on my way out, actually."

"Okay, catch you tomorrow."

Putting my spartan establishment to bed never took long. I shut down the machines, emptied Coke dregs into the sink. I moved about, turning off lamps, pondering Roddie. He'd sounded excited and happy. His family was safe, his campaign grinding forward. The killer was in custody. Relief must have finally taken hold.

I closed the windows. Traffic noise faded, and into the quiet a floorboard creaked. Something scratched inside a wall. On my way to the light switch I heard the elevator clank and the doors slither open. I moved faster, feeling the onset of dire thoughts. It was almost nine o'clock. I was the only top floor tenant. No one I knew would visit at this hour, unless it was Michael.

Footsteps tapped, a drag in the tread. Not Michael's walk, which was brisk and dynamic to my doting ears. I switched off the overheads, and just as the footsteps halted outside my door, I saw that the latch was up! I lurched for the door, the knob already starting to turn. I thumbed down the button and heard its *click*.

"Susan? Are you there?"

Roddie. But he'd just called from Maine. I started to greet him, but my voice shrank to a whiffle.

From the other side of the door came his prankster's chuckle, the same chuckle that had done in Froy. "I called you from my car. Wanted to surprise you. Come on, open up." He rattled the knob. "I've got a present for you."

What present? Why surprise me?

I took a step back.

What if I was wrong about Roddie? Lauren had confided so very much, and Roddie never quaked from protecting his interests. I remembered how he had raised his fist at Tyre, how he'd squeezed Froy. It was *his* rope they'd found in Chaz's car. And he *had* lied.

Ridiculous. The killer was in custody. I reached for the knob.

But Michael believed there were two killers. And I'd misjudged so many things. I crept back to my desk, prepared to wait Roddie out.

Should I call the police? No, better try Boris', where night bakers were still mixing sourdough. Maybe if I asked nicely, they'd bring me a pastry, and I could greet Roddie on my way out, and we could all take the elevator down together. I placed an uncertain hand on the phone.

"I know you're in there," Roddie sang out in the hall. "I'm parked next to your car."

I wanted to shout that I'd walked over to Freddie's for coffee. Deirdre was convinced minds could communicate, and just now, with my back to the wall, telepathy might come as easily as prayer. *Go to Freddie's*, I shrieked inside my skull. If Roddie heard and obeyed, I could sneak down to my car and make my escape.

The phone rang under my hand and I seized it reflexively. I'd tell whoever it was to come rescue me, and worry about explanations later. "Hello," I whispered.

"Hey, Susan. I knew you're there." Roddie calling me on his cellphone, and me falling for it. Again. "What's up? Let me in."

"I don't want to see you right now."

There was a fraught silence, then he said, "Oh, I get it. You too," and clicked off. His footsteps retreated. The elevator clanked its way down.

I waited ten stiff minutes, then took the stairs. A glass door opened on the parking lot, and from the safety of the building I searched every inch of asphalt with my eyes. My car was where I'd left it, a cardboard box now resting on its trunk. Roddie's minivan was gone. I hurried outside, not sure what to do about the box, which didn't actually look like a bomb. I lifted it, shook it, and finally opened the flaps. Steam wafted out. Inside were two fat live lobsters and a lump of dry ice.

I slid the box onto the back seat and slunk toward home. I owed Roddie an apology. Nino, Deirdre, Roddie...how many did that make now, anyway?

Chapter Twenty-five

Soul Fire

As soon as the second claw poked out I knew I had to get rid of Roddie's gift. I could imagine the headlines: *Lobsters devour campaign hack. Animalistas denounce politicians.* I had already hurled an innocent cat. I cruised past Tavola Rustica and MediRX, both closed, and parked under one of the fake gas lamps that dotted Nino's neighborhood. Leaving the lobsters in the car, I hurried toward his apartment, an oasis of light at the bottom of the alley behind the restaurant. Across the way, Benny's building was dark, as if its real life took place street-side.

I knocked, and after a short wait, Nino waved me in. His color was high, which made him look healthy, not like a man is his cups who smelled of anisette. "Thought you were coming tomorrow."

"I can't stay. I brought you two beautiful Maine lobsters."

We walked back to my car for the box. "I'll make saffron linguine with 'em," he said, shoving down claws that, even banded, intimidated me.

He lugged the lobsters through the service hall to the restaurant, and returned carrying bundles of documents from the wall safe. "Since you're here, look these over. I'll warm up the coffee."

Leftover coffee and drudgery, great. Instead of running for cover, I should have coped with claws on my own. "I'll take a quick look tonight," I said, spreading the papers out on the kitchen table: Tavola's Brookline leases, savings bonds, stock certificates. "Tomorrow, we'll talk."

Nino carried his anisette to the stove, sipping while he lit the gas under a dented percolator. Flames shot out, little blue seething teeth, and soon a cup of burnt coffee materialized at my elbow. "Hey, Susie, I keep meaning to ask. Did you take my pictures after I told you not to?"

"I thought getting them restored would cheer you up. They were supposed to be a surprise, for when you came home from the hospital."

"I don't like surprises."

"Gee, sorry for doing a good deed. Anyway, only one's ready. If I bring it tomorrow...don't be *surprised*." I laughed, but sourpuss Nino banged his coffee pot.

"Which one they give you?"

"A girl about fourteen, long straight hair. From the '80s, looks like." I was wading through canceled checks and correspondence, sorting them by type and date. "She had a cute little puppy."

"My daughter. I took that picture, couple days before my wife walked out."

"First wife?"

"Second." Across from my coffee, which I still hadn't touched, Nino set down a cup for himself. A few drops sloshed on the table, and he sponged them off. "A *troia*, my second wife."

"What's that?"

"A tramp." He dropped the sponge in the sink and came back with a tea cloth trimmed in crochet that he used to buff the table. "Just like my first wife. You could say I got pretty bad judgment when it comes to wives."

"Ya think?" Hardly listening now, I waved a bundle of savings bonds. "These matured eight years ago. Cash 'em in."

The last paper was a ragged sheet that had been crumpled and flattened, an inch or two missing from the top. My eyes passed over the now-familiar lines, and the impossibility of what I saw stunned me. Here was yet another copy of Chaz's forged contract, the wildfire lie I couldn't stamp out. "Nino? Where did you get this?"

He was back at the stove, staring at me over another full glass of anisette. "Ah, you found it. Proof how you sold me out."

"It's a fake."

"I know your signature." He stomped to the table and pawed through the papers until he found his last Tavola lease, which I had witnessed. "There. There it is."

"Lombard must have given Renfrow a copy, so he could use it to forge my name." I lined up the contract and the lease. The signatures were not quite a match, but close. "They were in it together."

"Who else was in it?" Nino slapped the table, and my coffee cup jumped. "You. You were in it."

"Are you out of your mind?"

"Just tell the truth, Susie." His voice softened. "That's all I need from you."

"I told you this morning, Renfrow conned me."

"Renfrow *bought* you. He paid you twenty grand, so he could take over my restaurant, nice and legal. You should admit what you did, so I could forgive you and we could put it behind us."

"There's nothing to admit!"

"Liar! Al Volpe should know how you lie!" He snatched the documents out of my hand and threw them on top of the others. "Get outta my house."

"Not till I've finished talking to you." Not caring if they wrinkled, I jammed his papers together like a deck of scattered cards. "The twenty thousand was my campaign fee. And I returned almost all of it. Did asshole Lombard tell you that?"

"Lombard didn't tell me nothing."

"Then who told you all those fucking lies?" I shoved my cup out of my way, and it tipped, splashing coffee across the table.

"You. Truck driver mouth. Get out!" He tried to drag me off the chair, but I wrenched free. In the sudden quiet, I heard coffee dripping, and too late, I lifted the papers out of the puddle.

"You *do* have bad judgment, Nino. Believe what you want, but Renfrow…he…" I stared at the wet papers in my hand, at the smudged letters. My finger dragged itself through my forged signature, and *Susan Callisto* became a smear of blue/black ink. This wasn't a copy. It was the original. The missing inches were in a police file. And I was holding the rest of the page someone had torn from Chaz Renfrow's dead hand. "Nino?" The catch in my throat made it hard to sound casual. "Did Lombard give you this?"

"You think too much." He clucked his tongue. That dismissive sound. "Your friend gave it to me. And he showed me the canceled check with your signature on the back. Twenty big ones."

"God! Just how hard is your head? The money was my *campaign fee*. Got it?"

He bent close to my chair, his anise breath in my eyes. "When I talked to your friend, I told him I knew it was him kicked the shit out of me. 'Prove it,' he said, and that's what I'm telling you. *Prove* the money was for a campaign."

"You know I can't."

"Because you're a liar, like my daughter and her mother, every woman I ever knew."

"When did you talk to Chaz? Did he come back to Falkman? Or did you go to him?" I knew the answer, but I wanted Nino to deny it. I had been wrong about so many things. I wanted to be wrong about this.

"Day after Benny brought me home from the hospital I called your friend and told him what I knew."

"Chaz Renfrow was not my friend!"

"Okay, your what, your accomplice. Your accomplice drove me in his big fancy car to his big fancy house. Wanted to show me something." Nino reached out, as if to touch my shoulder. "Something about you."

I flinched away from his hand. "Did you do it?" I whispered. "Did you kill Chaz?" I moved to get up but he forced me down.

"I told you, you think too much. Women shouldn't think, it only makes trouble." He moved around the table, his speech starting to thicken and slow down, the second or third glass of anisette kicking in. "So important your friend, sitting at his desk. Didn't bother to look up when the peon…walked behind…his throne…" Short strong fingers that had once patted my hand now grabbed my throat.

I tried to turn. "Nino…"

The fingers let go and a cloth, rough lace, cut into my larynx. "Twenty thousand dollars? That's all my life was worth to you? You shoulda held out for more. Your friend offered me money too, but it was better I killed him."

I tried to drag the cloth away, but it tightened, glitter floating inside my eyes, bright specks of silver and blood. My hands found Nino's hands, clawed his skin. From far away, his voice slurred inside my head. "Don't fight. You can't win. You could've been my daughter. Granddaughter."

My fingers scrabbled, no stronger than Chaz's had been. "Your daughter," I mumbled through the soot in my mouth, and the cloth loosened a fraction of a twist. *Make him talk…* "Where is she?"

"She left me, too." He twisted the cloth again, tighter, tighter. "My beautiful daughter went away."

I was drifting, dreaming, stretching out a long languid arm. My hand found a cup, smashed it on the table, flailed behind me with the jagged edge.

"Bitch!" A fist came down on my ear, knocking me out of the chair. The cloth ripped away. I leaped up and ran for the door, which opened, at my touch. Fresh air streamed like mercy across my face.

"Benny! Help me!" I screamed at the dark windows across the alley. My voice was hoarse, and the words burned coming out. "Benny!"

I made it a few feet from the stoop before Nino dragged me back inside. My broken fingernails tore at his eyes, and when he lost his grip I ran through his apartment for the service hall. Breathing hard, slowed by anisette, he stumbled after me, and as I swept into the restaurant, I heard him trip. "Don't fight!" he shouted. "Just tell the truth."

In Tavola's dimly lit kitchen, I kept the prep table between us, my eyes flitting from Nino to the dining room and, far off, to the Boylston Street door. I feinted left, and he lurched after my shadow. I threw myself on top of the counter, but he pulled me down and pushed me against the stove. His hands found my throat again.

Use your body. Elbows, knees, fists, I lashed out at him, a man in his seventies with the strength of a grizzly, who seemed to be tiring. He let go, and we stood facing each other, gasping for air.

"You can't win. My wife…daughter…" He was talking to himself, to ghosts. "Betrayed me like you." He lifted his hands to his face. A broken line of blood tracked down his cheek. "I wanted to kill the both of them."

"You're crazy. *You* tore up the pictures. You trashed your own apartment."

He stared at his palms, nodded. "Lombard's threats…I wanted to make sure you'd sue him. Couldn't let him win."

I shoved him, and he stumbled, reaching out for me as he fell. Before he could grab me, I boosted myself up and clattered over the burners to the ledge around the firewall. Benny's bucket stood five feet away filled with greasy water.

Nino leaned across the knobs. "Come down, Susie. *Mi dispiace.* I'm not mad at you, I promise." The old Nino, the one I thought I knew, was speaking to me now like a man in his cups, full of regret…but all I could hear was the bully, the liar, sweet talking me to death.

I edged toward the bucket.

"Get down here!" He reached for my ankle, but he was weaker now. "You traitor!"

I took another sideways step. "Nino," I said. "Why are you so full of hate?"

He answered me in fire. One by one, the four back burners exploded at my feet. I grabbed Benny's bucket and flung it over the flames. For an iridescent second they flared, then went out.

Fumes wafted from the doused pilots, and I waited, lightheaded, but ready to fight if he tried to pull me down again.

He looked past me, through me, his body shriveling inside his clothes. His sighs came like bleak winds across an ocean of misery. "Not you. I don't hate you." He turned on the front burners, four new rings of fire, and thrust in his hands.

"No!" I stood paralyzed. The smell of burning flesh clogged my throat. "Don't, Nino!" I climbed down and led him away from the stove. He tried to resist, but I took his elbow and steered him to the sink. While he stood there, still as a fevered child, I ran cold water over his raw red hands. Then I dialed for an ambulance.

"We've already had a call," the dispatcher said.

Benny. He hadn't turned away from my screams.

I left Nino at a table and went outside. Under the arc lights, I saw that my palms were bloody, my shirt torn, and the warm pavement under my feet told me I had lost my sandals. There was no survivor's euphoria to make me giddy tonight; only a kind of calm, as if I'd died and been reborn in this deserted Brookline neighborhood.

A cruiser stopped in front of the restaurant and two uniformed cops got out.

Officer Jowls stared at me. "You again?"

Chapter Twenty-six

Women Mourn

Ten degrees steeper and you'd call it a cliff, not that it stopped the beach brats. They climbed to the top and plunged down, rolling over and over until they hit the surf, then splashed their way back to a distant umbrella. I remembered how it felt. How, for the best spin, you crossed your arms and grabbed your shoulders and screamed all the way. How the sky and your head got mixed up. Sand in your mouth. The cold smack of the ocean.

I hugged my knees. How come, I asked myself, I'm always on time, and everybody else isn't? Michael was driving to Truro from Boston and should have been here an hour ago. At my borrowed cottage, the tuneless casserole I'd brought from home sat thawing on a counter, tonight's dinner, almost ready to go. All it needed, Michael had advised, was a slug of sherry and a lobster garnish, a couple of two-pounders, fresh off the boat.

By late afternoon the tide had turned, and I picked my way down the path, thinking about Deirdre who'd left me a message from a rehabilitation center in New York. She was doing well and would call when she got back. Nothing else. Don't complain, don't explain. Deirdre. At the shoreline, sand rippled away from my feet in wavy braids studded with sea glass and broken shells. One of these days I'd meet Deirdre, bring her here. I'd call the ocean healing waters. She'd like that.

When I got back to the top Michael was waiting with a Thermos of iced coffee and an armful of peaches that fell into the grass when we hugged. We never did find all of them.

"You smell like the ocean," he said.

"And you smell like dessert."

He gave me a kiss, and I gave him two, then had to wrestle myself out of his arms. "Margaritas at six," I said. "So quick, tell me what you found in New Hampshire."

"Torie's earrings. Her evening bag. A memory card with a video clip of the toxic spill. Enough to make it hard for Glenn to recant."

"What about the microtome blade from Lab 45?"

"Not among Glenn's trophies. My guess is you found the one he used on Torie, and he planted it there to incriminate Bart Bievsky. He'd already hidden his father's watch in Bart's car, for Johanna to find. It would've been easy to tag the blade with a strand of Bart's hair or a drop of his blood."

"And I led Johanna straight to it. She must have figured it implicated Glenn. You'll never find it."

Michael was quiet, and I knew he was thinking about lethal families, fatal friends. Things cops see.

"Torie's blackmail wasn't only about toxic dumping, by the way. Her video is almost an aside. EPA found evidence of small nuclear spills, but as it turned out, the contamination never got past the internal drains."

"So what did else she have up her sleeve?"

"Evidence that Johanna stole research from a colleague at Chestnut Hill College."

"The longevity gene stuff?"

"Yes. There was a vial inside Torie's evening bag, and a film-strip. Johanna's fingerprints are all over both."

"Stolen research and Johanna. Why am I not surprised?" There would be endless lawsuits, fleeing investors, civil and criminal penalties. "Now *that* could bring NGT down."

"Forget NGT," he said, filling two paper cups with iced coffee. "Forget margaritas. Let's just settle down here for awhile."

We sat near the edge of the hill, watching the tide run out. A menagerie of clouds, mostly swans and crocodiles, drifted overhead. "Like Adam and Eve," I said. "Just us, and somewhere in the dunes, the serpent."

"You know Nino's out of the hospital," Michael said. Speaking of serpents, I guess.

"And out on bail." I pressed the cup to my cheek. "He's in good hands. Gordon Brenner's going with self-defense and maybe mental impairment from the blow to his head."

"Self defense, possibly. Renfrow more or less kidnapped him to Telford."

"Chaz didn't figure on Nino's rage. The sight of my name on the contract…" I shook my head. "Hard to believe Nino drove the Lexus home without attracting a statie. He hasn't touched a car in years…which I suppose might work against mental impairment."

"That and the fact that nothing showed up on his hospital scans. Face it, Susan. Nino is going to do time no matter what his defense."

A breeze came up and whipped the long grass; a speck on the horizon became a trawler, a ghost boat gliding on steel water. The sight made me weepy. But I was sitting on a sand dune, the ocean at my feet. Here was no place to cry.

Michael stroked my arm. "I'm sorry about Nino," he said.

I couldn't speak to answer. My feelings for Nino were shifting like the clouds. I'd loved that old man, the gruff-but-kindly grandpa who'd never existed, really, except in my mind. So obsessed with betrayal, Nino had betrayed *me*.

Women mourn…

Michael wrapped an arm around me, and I held him close, closer maybe than I'd ever held Gil. The wind hummed in my ears. Michael's warmth seeped down to my bones.

To receive a free catalog of Poisoned Pen Press titles, please contact us in one of the following ways:

Phone: 1-800-421-3976
Facsimile: 1-480-949-1707
Email: info@poisonedpenpress.com
Website: www.poisonedpenpress.com

Poisoned Pen Press
6962 E. First Ave. Ste. 103
Scottsdale, AZ 85251